'Lyrical, assured and simmering with suspense.'
Victoria Selman

'An electrifying crime thriller.'
Woman's Own

'*The Fall* is a rare beast...
Dark, atmospheric and truly original.'
Kate Simants

'Wonderfully woven... oozes class from every page.'
Robert Scragg

'Emotionally charged, atmospheric.'
Eleanor Ray

'Held me spellbound... hugely satisfying.'
Polly Phillips

'Uncoils like the snapping of a whip, lashing the past into
the present with the revealing of dark family secrets.'
Dominic Nolan

'Unwinds slowly and deliberately
to a heart-pounding conclusion.'
James Delargy

ALSO BY RACHAEL BLOK

Under the Ice
The Scorched Earth
Into the Fire

THE
FALL

RACHAEL BLOK

An Aries Book

First published in the UK in 2022 by Head of Zeus Ltd
This paperback edition first published in 2022 by Head of Zeus Ltd,
part of Bloomsbury Publishing Plc

9 7 5 3 1 2 4 6 8

A catalogue record for this book is available
from the British Library.

ISBN (PB): 9781838931766
ISBN (E): 9781838931773

Typeset by Divaddict Publishing Solutions Ltd

Printed and bound in Great Britain by
CPI Group (UK) Ltd, Croydon CR0 4YY

Head of Zeus Ltd
First Floor East
5–8 Hardwick Street
London EC1R 4RG

WWW.HEADOFZEUS.COM

For Dawnie,
a sister in a million

PROLOGUE

'Help!' he shouts. 'Help!'

The wind is cold this high up; the cathedral roof has caught his fall, but it will not hold him for long. The night is dark, like a cloak. It's such a long way down.

What is it? Why am I here?

He thinks about the evening, about the words spoken.

If he knows, accepting it is hard, and working out how, about who...

He spins his thoughts like plates, trying to keep them all suspended; but one by one, they fall, crack.

The cathedral tower rises high, its viewing platform above him, and he lies flat against the sloping roof. His breath comes quickly. He notices everything: the night air smells sweet; tree blossom, freshly cut grass. Someone must be up late: a fire pit, with its flecks of ash rising from a nearby garden like fireflies. Easter is almost here. Rebirth.

So much to lose.

Short breaths. His chest rises. His foot slips and he scrambles to steady himself. He'd tried inching his way back up, but he'd only slid further. If he can hold on, until someone sees him...

What had been said?

His thoughts are fog. The words they'd spoken earlier are tumbling.

Life spins backwards.

He'd come because of the phone call, and stepping out, holding the parapet, he'd felt safe. He's always felt safe.

But now he's here alone. And there's no way back. If he could just inch up...

The heel of his palm pushes against the tiles, and he rises a fraction, towards the security of the rail. Can he? His foot slides and he feels a tile tick out from under him, the rattle of tiny stones fall, scattering below. He slides further, crying out.

His fingernails scratch at the roof, sharp; and he screams as his body slows. His breath now a pant, and he lies against the slate. The dark of the empty park as familiar as the lines on his palm. His fingers grip the tiles on the cathedral roof; one slips beneath his hand, which carries blush knuckles, arthritis swollen.

Dry to his touch, the stone feels secure, like all its stories will stay silent – it will hold his secrets forever.

So he tells them again. He whispers them into the cold air, hoping for an answer. Redemption.

Gusts blow around him, rising to the heavens.

Please, he thinks. *Take my prayers. May God forgive me.*

All his life, the moments that add up to this.

The park opens up like a blanket of night. Speckles of light dot the perimeter of black from homes edging the park.

Remember me. Do not go gentle. Lines of half-remembered

poetry run through his head. He searches for an answer, those words from earlier. *What had been said?*

He still doesn't know. Isn't sure.

But like a chain of events already set in motion, his fingers begin unpeeling. There's no way down. Not now. His fingers are slippery. He closes his eyes.

It had taken so long to get up this high.

Is he sure he can't get back? Is there no way?

'Help!' he shouts again. 'Hello? Help!'

The slip into nothingness, into freefall, happens quickly; his other foot stepping out behind. *Let perpetual light shine upon me.*

If only he hadn't answered the phone.

He clings to the very edge. His feet skim air.

If only he'd already been asleep. Gone to bed early. *Are our paths always set?*

'Behold me then, me for him.'

Of course. That's it. That's what's behind this.

It began more than fifty years ago.

PART ONE

1

WILLOW

Willow cries out. There's a rush of wind. A crack, like a tile shattering from the roof, sounds from somewhere nearby on the cathedral. The shock leaves her trembling.

A whistle? A scream?

She stops, dead. The tiny car park is creepy at night. Again, a rushing sound – *just the wind*.

The April night feels empty.

'Where do we put 'em?'

She jumps at the voice of the van driver. They've spent the last seven hours stuck on the motorway, waiting for an accident to be cleared. She'd only met him that morning. No one's in a good mood. He wheels the boxes of manuscripts along the flagstones.

'There's a door to the side, I think,' she says, her hands still shaking at the suddenness of his question. Feeling stupid, she lights up her mobile phone torch, finds the key.

'Here,' she says. 'Go ahead. I'll just call the verger.'

The phone line dials and she hears an older voice, with a hint of an accent. 'Hello?'

'Hi, this is Willow Eliot, with the Milton exhibition? The roads were bad...' She winces as she says the last part. It's so late, and she wonders how long this man has had to stay up for her. She checks the verger's name on her list, as it flies from her head.

'Sorry for the trouble, Gabriel,' she says.

'I'll be up in a minute.'

The line goes dark, and there's that sound again. She looks up. A whistle. A whizz. A shower of pebbles falls from somewhere high up on the roof. She lifts the torch upwards. Shadows collect in the circles and grooves on the thick stone walls.

Her grandma's voice comes to her, head bent. Nonie has always valued prayer above most things: *Dear God, pray for these girls...* Cathedrals make her think of penance, guilt. They terrify her. Lines from the scripts she'd packed away echo: '*from the bottom stir / The Hell within him*'.

The words are swallowed up in the night, and she moves quickly, following the driver with the boxes.

Thinking of Nonie, she checks her phone again. Willow hopes the doctor has made a decision about Nonie travelling. Her mum is unlikely to want to leave her. Nonie's medication has been off, and she's been dizzy. Mum was going to let her know.

Nothing yet. Thinking of her mum, Willow closes her eyes briefly, hoping that the stress of Nonie being ill hasn't sent her mum spiralling. *Please, not this week. There's so much to do.* Thank God Dad is with her. Her mum has been doing so well.

Willow's phone rings again. 'Hello?' She assumes it's Gabriel and hopes it's her mum, but her sister's voice flies down the line.

'Where *are* you? It's been ages! The party is almost done! I wanted you to meet everyone!'

'Fliss, I texted you – there'd been an accident on the M25. We were stuck for hours. I'm only just…'

'Well, it's too late now to see everyone. But look, I'm not going to bed yet. Come round for a drink? We can stay up.'

'Fliss, I'm exhausted! I need to go to bed when I've finished. I'll head to the B&B. I'll see you tomorrow, when Mum, Dad and Nonie arrive? Honestly, today has been—'

'I still don't understand why you need to do this job now! When I'm getting married. Couldn't you have just taken the week off?'

Willow walks swiftly towards the side door; another shower of pebbles lands behind her. She doesn't hear the end of what Fliss is saying, but she doesn't quite want to hang up. The dark is thick.

Looking up, she thinks of ghosts on the roof, searching for answers.

Is someone up there? Was that a shout?

'Are you even listening to me?'

'Yes. I'm sorry. Look, how about lunch tomorrow, or I probably mean today as it's so late? The wedding is Saturday. It's only Tuesday, or very early on Wednesday. I'm done by Thursday night, then I'm ready for partying. Ready for your hen.' Willow tries to inject some enthusiasm into her voice as she thinks of sour cocktails, pink chocolates in the shape of body parts. The hen invites had come with

9

glitter and a promise of a headache. She'd already been on the one in Paris, at the bargain price of over £600 all in. Someone kept ordering Moët but was happy to share the cost with the group. Fliss's friends seemed to roll in money; none of them worked in a museum.

'This bloody job. I curse Otis. He should at least have had the courtesy to dump you with better timing!'

Willow winces at Fliss's words. She's not wrong, but it's still raw.

'Hello? Where are you going? This isn't the right entrance.'

Someone is walking behind her and he sounds cross. It must be the verger, Gabriel.

'I'll have to go. Call you tomorrow.' Willow hangs up on Fliss, knowing she hadn't spent enough time apologising. She'll need to dedicate more air space to that at lunch tomorrow. She offers apologies as often as her sister offers excuses, and it's a balance no one wants to upset. Sisterhood is a see-saw. If you weight one side too much, there can be hell to pay.

Catching up to the driver at the same time as the verger, tiredness scratches away the niceties in all of them. The driver struggles with the key in the lock – she'd given them to him to open the door. The cathedral had couriered a set, in case of any problems.

'That fits the door to the other side. Oh, for God's sake, give it to me.' The verger's tone is sharp.

The older man pushes past her, pulling the keys from the hand of the driver.

'Alright, mate!' the driver says, ratty and prickly.

Wincing, Willow watches the tussle of authority in

silence and follows Gabriel towards a door further up on the building.

'Sorry for breathing,' the driver mutters.

Checking her watch, Willow sees it's gone 1 a.m.; they should all be in bed now. It's going to be a nightmare finding the B&B. She doesn't have the energy to negotiate between the egos of the men, so she leaves them to it.

The cathedral is haunting at night. Gabriel lights their way in through the newly built visitors' centre; the shadows in the unlit corners catch Willow's eye. It's quiet in here and she thinks of the noises outside. She thinks of all the buried bodies, the stone tombs. Her senses are keen, layers of stupor from the journey stripped away.

Gabriel leads them downstairs to a large cupboard. The aroma of paint and plaster hangs in the air.

'We've had some water damage down here. One of the pipes leaked a while ago. Don't worry – it's all fixed. This room was replastered first, so the exhibits will be safe. My office is still being done.'

Willow looks at the exhibits.

'The damp's gone – they've aired it out,' he says, seeing Willow's face. 'And the room has a lock. You want this kind of stuff locked down overnight,' he says, and Willow nods, thinking of the value of the exhibits and the security guard who was booked to sit with them once they were on display.

The driver doesn't listen, simply starts heaving box after box from the trolley.

Gabriel joins him, and Willow stands back. The room is narrow. Even if she wanted to help, she couldn't.

The driver picks up one of the last few boxes, but the final shelf is out of reach. The end is almost in sight.

'How do I get up here?' asks the driver, his voice still brusque.

Gabriel's arms are full as he pushes a box to the back of one of the shelves. 'Can you get the footstool?' he asks Willow. 'My office is next door. It's in there, at the back. It's still being replastered.

Gabriel's office is small, but deep. Flicking on the light, Willow sees a desk facing the door, and then the narrow room runs deep into the dark where the light doesn't quite reach. It's much like she imagined a verger's office to look. Wooden shelves run the length of the room, one wall of which has the plaster peeled away, and dust sheets are down.

She sees the footstool near the sheets and crosses behind the desk, bending to pick up the steps.

The light in Gabriel's office is yellow from the hanging bulb. Dust drifts in the air, and Willow thinks of the hundreds or even thousands of people who must have stood in this place. She'd read up on the history before she came here. This cathedral was built in 1077, which makes it almost 950 years old.

It will outlive all of them. She shivers. Cathedrals preside over our mortality, she thinks. They stand looking at us now, they'll stand looking at generations to follow. We get a brief window of time. Against the ages, it's just a blink.

Bending to collect the footstool, she sees one of the stones loose in the wall. She touches it, feels its coolness, its timelessness. There're etches in the stone. Initials and a date.

She leans closer. *1960? 1969?* She can't make it out. The initials are faded too. Her finger traces the first letter. An *L*, she wonders? Time has dusted over the scratches, eaten into the edges of the carving.

Nothing lasts for ever.

Finally, everything is in place. Gabriel locks the cathedral door, and Willow shakes the hand of the driver, over-tipping him to compensate for the brusqueness of the older man.

The van pulls away, and she turns to thank Gabriel for his help, but he is already walking in the opposite direction.

'I'll be in early in the morning to help,' he says. 'Do you know where you're going?'

It's clearly rhetorical; he doesn't wait for an answer.

Alone, outside the cathedral, now 2 a.m., she begins to sweat in the cold air. The sound of the wind is back. A scream? It does sound like a scream. She looks up at the roof. Is something going on? Is it more than wind? She squints, trying to make out if someone is up there. Is that a cry?

As Gabriel's torch bobs further away, blackness descends, pressing hard, and she backs up against the stone walls: cold and hard.

The instructions had said the house was only a few minutes' walk from the cathedral doors. But panic is setting in; her teeth grind and her head rears back, with breath coming in short, sharp supply. She has no idea in which direction to walk.

Then she hears footsteps again and it's Gabriel returning.

'I'm sorry,' he says. 'I'm tired and it's always me who has

to stay late. But it's not safe to be out now, on your own. Come on, it's just down here.'

Grateful he returned, she's close to tears as she follows him, her legs wobbly as she steps down into a curving park, sweeping under dark trees and following a path, swinging right; moving out of the circle of amber light from the cathedral, into the blackness.

There's another whistle, and a loud bang behind them.

'What's that?' She spins. 'Do you think someone's up there? There have been some noises.'

Gabriel shrugs; she can only see his outline in the dark. 'Probably a bin falling over.'

Unsettled, Willow slips the keys between her fingers. She splays them wide. She knows she steps on to grass, as it softens underfoot, but she can't see a thing.

Then she stops. Another scream. It's definitely a scream. 'No, I've got to look. That was something else.' She turns and runs, hearing the padding of Gabriel's footsteps behind her.

She runs round the west end this time and into the graveyard. The noises had carried on the wind. Curving up towards the flagstones, looking up, she stands and screams.

A figure dangles, swinging from the edge of the roof, high up above them. It looks as though part of his clothing is caught, and he is screaming. His words are unintelligible, but his terror is palpable.

She freezes for a second, looking up behind him. He must have fallen. The cathedral tower is high above him. He must have come off the tower, and slid, or bounced. How long he's been up there she has no idea – how much of the earlier sounds were wind, or screams?

'Hang on!' she shouts, running forward, with no idea what she's going to do.

'Stay there! I'll call for help!' Gabriel's shout reaches from behind her.

But all of this happens too slowly, because whatever is bridging these last few moments between life and death finally lays itself to rest.

The figure falls, as Willow runs.

She's close enough to turn away and cry out as the body meets the ground, close enough to know that it is a body now, and no longer a person.

She is thankful for the dark. She sees enough, but turns from the brutal truth of the death before her.

Gabriel stutters into the phone behind. His voice shakes, as she sobs.

'Police. There's been a fall from the cathedral tower. St Albans Cathedral. There's been a death.'

2

MAARTEN

The call had come when he'd been asleep. 'Looks like a suicide, the crime scene is being set up now. Can you come in?'

He'd looked at the clock with squinting eyes, sleep already catching in the corners, and Liv had stirred beside him: 2.40 a.m.

'Work?' she'd said, without fully waking.

'Got to go. Not sure when I'll be back.' He'd kissed her. The room had been cold as he'd stood up. He took a breath of the warmth and the homeliness with him, to arm himself against the cold and death. It didn't get easier.

'Possible suicide,' he'd said on the phone to Adrika, his DI. 'No, you're not needed. I'll go tonight, I'll catch up with you and Sunny in the morning. There were only two witnesses, and SOCO will be busy. The officer first on the scene spoke to the witnesses, then sent them home. It's so late. We'll speak to them in more detail later.'

The night air is crisp as he slams the car door. Lights have been set up, and the crime scene manager approaches him, her long legs carrying her quickly and with purpose. He's always thought she must be about his age, but he's never asked. Her humour is dry and she's usually upbeat, but even she looks drawn in the cold light, her fair hair pulled off her face and her skin lit by the shadows. She carries an empty coffee cup and a notepad. 'Morning, Maarten. Or is it still night? I try never to count a new day until dawn.'

'Niamh.' He nods a hello as she raises one eyebrow, checking her notes. 'What have we got?'

'No identification on the body yet. Looks likely he died on impact. The door to the cathedral tower is open inside the building, and the door to the tower viewing platform itself was banging in the wind, which suggests it was used tonight. I can't imagine they leave that open when they lock up.'

'Any idea of timings?'

She shakes her head. 'We know when he fell. There's CCTV I've sent to your team so hopefully we'll know more soon. There's no one around. We were alerted when there was a delivery for an exhibition earlier – it was later than planned due to an RTA. There were two witnesses to the fall, but the female on the scene believes she heard noises when they arrived. It could be the case he was on the roof for a while before he actually fell. You have to climb over the edge of the parapet, through the crenellations, to reach the roof – it's not a sheer drop to the floor. Even if you threw yourself off, you'd hit the roof before you hit the ground.'

Maarten looks up. The sky is black, and it gleams. It's wide open, with the bright feel of a spring night sky – the air is fresh and the clouds have vanished. It's a night where you could see up into the heavens, if you believed in them. He hopes, for the sake of the man on the ground, the heavens have their gates open tonight.

'Anything else?'

'A few tiles dislodged, which suggests impact on the roof. There's also a rail up there – some steps too. We're sweeping for fingerprints to see where he went, and to see if he went alone. As far as I know, the tower isn't open to the public the whole time. If it's not been used recently, then we might stand a good chance of prints.'

Maarten nods, looking upwards. There's a breeze tonight, and it's definitely warmer than it has been. He doesn't know why someone might take their life on a night that anticipates the coming summer, heavy with the scent of a waking park. He hopes that any spirits split open will find their peace.

The walk to the body. Robyn has arrived; the beads in her braids catch the glimmer of the floodlights, which turn the scene yellow in this sea of black.

'Hey, Maarten.' Her voice soft in the cathedral grounds, but her American accent as clear as ever.

'Robyn.' Maarten bends to look at the body, wishing he didn't have to.

'The fall killed him, I'd say. Fingernails suggest he was fighting it. But he could have jumped and then changed his mind. No obvious wound from a gun or knife, or signs of a struggle – on first glance, it all seems in line with the trauma of a fall.' She rises straight up from a crouch, her core lifting her like steel.

Liv had said she'd seen Robyn at yoga before, hair streaked with grey, bending more easily than many of the

18

twenty-year-olds. Maarten likes long bike rides, but his knees crack if he stands too quickly. He's recently crossed the line of being closer to fifty than forty.

'Nothing else?' he asks, scanning the ground for any telltale signs.

'Not yet,' she says. 'I'd say suicide, if you asked me now. But it's a lot of effort to go to, so late at night. That tower is a long way up. I can think of easier ways to die.'

He nods, looking upwards at the roof. Such a location – there must be some significance. Had the victim been religious?

He yawns. The day will be long.

3

WILLOW

With a rush of relief, Willow sees a house before them. She still trembles. Gabriel too.

They are quiet as he walks her to the door.

'We'll contact you tomorrow. It's so late. You've given us enough information tonight,' the officer had said. Leaving had felt like a desertion.

The house is pale, tall and white, in the light of the moon. An iron gate leads through a short patio garden to the front door, where flowers climb the walls, and pots of plants scent the night air. It's a big, old house. Smaller terraced cottages are only just visible further down the tiny lane, under a yellow street lamp. A fire must be lit as a chimney releases smoke.

'Thank you,' she says to Gabriel, who nods his head, already stepping back.

'Aye, see you tomorrow.' He stands for a second, looking up at the house with her. 'Will you be OK?' he asks, still looking forward.

'I think so,' she says, and with this, he disappears into the black.

A quiet settles. Willow knocks quickly on the door, hoping whoever answers isn't angry it's so late. She'd left a voicemail a few hours ago to say the traffic was bad. But this is even later. Tiredness pinches tight.

'You must be exhausted!' The face behind the opening door is smiling: a lady, must be in her late sixties, with soft white hair and blue eyes; and the electric warmth of heating and lightbulbs pulls Willow in. 'I've been dozing on the sofa – don't worry, you haven't kept me up.'

'Thank you! I'm so sorry it's so late, the traffic—'

'Come in and don't you worry. I'm Martha. Here, I've left out some food.'

Willow lifts her case over the doorstep. The hallway is large, with wooden floors, and a vase of yellow flowers stands on a side table, near an umbrella stand and iron coat pegs, over a faded rug. It smells fresh and clean, and the décor is stripped back. A wooden staircase twists out of sight to the right, and the walls are bare of pictures, save one, a pencil drawing of the cathedral. It catches Willow's eye, and she shivers again.

'You must be freezing.' Martha herds her in, banishing the night air and smoothing her into the warm. 'Are the ghosts flying tonight?'

'Ghosts?' Willow asks, dropping her bag. 'For real?' She wonders if Martha has heard about what's happened. But no, she's busy ushering Willow into a large kitchen. Putting on the kettle.

'You don't get a cathedral that old without ghosts. I chat to them when I go up, keep them happy. They get lonely.' Martha busies in her kitchen, with its huge square tiles covering the floor, edges cracked, age-coloured, and the heating kettle rattles on a wide range.

Willow sits at a big wooden table at the centre of the room. The warmth of the kitchen softens the tension of the dark. It's cosy and comfortable, and a little yesteryear. No coffee machine in sight.

Martha is pouring her a cup of tea, taking her coat, pulling out a chair. 'You remind me of…' She pauses, as though she can't quite place it. She smiles.

'My mum must be about your age,' Willow says, thinking suddenly of her mum, packing for Nonie, preparing for the train journey. She wishes she was with her now. Or Nonie – if only she hadn't been unwell and looking after her falls to Willow's mum. Their granddad has been dead for years. *Whisky took him*, her mum had always said, frowning, as she usually did when his name came up.

Eyelids drooping, Willow drinks the tea Martha puts down. 'We should have been here hours ago. We left in good time; but the accident was bad. We just had to sit in the traffic.'

'And I bet you'll be up early. Here,' Martha says, pushing cake towards her. She is pale, make-up free, and looks ready for bed, in a faded pink dressing gown. She sits opposite, looking at Willow as though she's studying a painting.

Willow wonders if she has left her glasses upstairs; Martha's squinting now, rubbing at her eyes. 'Anyway, I'll be off to bed, now you're here. I'm pleased you made it. I do worry.' Martha's eyes now look red, watering, and Willow feels guilt she's had to stay up so late for her.

'I'll head up in a couple of minutes. Which room is

mine?' Taking a bite of cake, Willow's relieved to have a few minutes on her own. Martha seems nice enough, but it's too late for talking, and her mind drifts back to the flagstones, the bang of the body.

'Well, your family have hired all the rooms for the weekend, so it's up to you. But there's a roomy one with a queen bed to the right at the top of the stairs. It has a lovely view of the cathedral.'

Martha pauses, clutching at her chest quickly.

'Are you OK?' Willow rises, the chair legs screeching on the tiles.

'Yes, yes it's just late. I get heartburn if I stay up.' Martha pushes away Willow's offer of an arm to lean on. 'I'll head up now. I'll leave breakfast out on the table and there'll be milk in the fridge. A woman calls Lizzie helps out when I have guests. I think she's in tomorrow, but I can't remember…' Martha's face creases into a frown, and she suddenly looks older.

'I'll be fine, please, go to bed.' Willow smiles, opening the door for her, and to try to lighten the mood, almost as an afterthought, as Martha is through the door, she says, 'Are there really ghosts in the cathedral?'

As she asks the question, the sound of the wind in the empty night, squealing like a cry, the body landing hard, echoes in her head.

'Don't let anyone tell you different. The dead will talk, once they have something to say. They always do.'

4

ALICE

The morning is bright. Alice climbs out of bed, teddy bear in her left hand; Mr Jenkins has lost one glass eye, but she can't sleep without him. She had heard Daddy say they would get something new for her seventh birthday, but he is her favourite. He would be lonely without her.

She looks at the sky as she pulls back the curtains. The park is fairly empty; some people are out with dogs. The light is bright. Daffodils spill down the borders of the lane.

Her feet are bare on the floorboards, and the sun hasn't broken into the house yet.

The park stretches as though it was made for running, and her feet are jiggling before she realises, her fingers tapping on the glass. She feels it. Like she *needs* to run down the hill, not just wants to. And her hands flatten against the pane, palms pressed, her fingers stretched. She knows she can't ask yet. Daddy always says she has to eat breakfast first. Always. But waiting is hard. What if she pops?

She looks again, and the sea of daffodils is waving. She

counts them. Counting helps. In her head. She knows not to do it aloud.

'What are you looking at?' Her twin is just waking, her voice filled with sleep.

'The park. Shall we ask Mummy if we can go to the lake?'

'Yes, let's. But I'm still asleep, Alice.'

Alice smiles at her, then pulls the curtains shut. 'I'll go downstairs. Shall I make breakfast? I can make toast now!' She puffs with pride. They've got a big Aga in the kitchen, which has been warm all winter. Alice has been learning how to cook.

'Alice!' Betty sits bolt upright in bed. 'Remember how much trouble you got in last time! They were so cross about the mess!'

'But I know what I'm doing now. I won't make a mess. We can take breakfast up on a tray, then they're bound to get up and take us down to the lake.'

Betty frowns, her brow furrowing, and her eyebrows rise up and down.

'Betty, don't tell! I see your eyebrows thinking.'

'I won't tell, silly,' Betty says. But she sounds unsure. 'They were *so* cross.'

'I can do it! And they will be pleased. How can they not like breakfast in bed?'

'I'll help,' Betty says, as though deciding. 'Let's go. Let's make breakfast.'

She climbs out of bed and shivers. She pulls her gown over her nightie, tying it tight. 'But as a surprise, before they get up. They'll say no if we ask. So we have to do it right.'

They creep down the stairs, wooden floorboards creaking at the bottom, and they giggle.

One, two, three, four steps. Five, six, seven, eight.

'Come on,' Betty says, pushing the kitchen door open. The tiles in here are even colder, but the heat from the Aga is gentle, and she steps closer.

Alice claps her hands, her mind ballooning with ideas. 'We can do toast?'

'Yes, and eggs. I think I know how to crack eggs.'

'Shall I put a pan on the stove?'

The Aga burns warm, and between them, because it takes both their hands to slide the cover from the hot surface, they push hard and place a saucepan down carefully.

'Ow!' Betty says, sucking her finger, as it proves hot.

'Here, I'll do it,' Alice says, taking over. Eggs spill into the pan, and on to the hot surface of the stove. The smell of egg reaches all corners of the kitchen.

'If I put on the toast, can you get some butter?' Alice says, watching the eggs intently. *One egg, two.*

'Yes. Is there anything else?' Betty asks, bringing a knife, pouring cold milk into a glass.

'I think this is it. Is that the toast?'

A smell of more than eggs colours up the kitchen, and Betty sniffs.

'Ooh, that smells like burning!'

Not wanting the bread to burn, Alice takes her time looking at the toast on the grill, but when she pulls it out, there are flames catching.

'Ow!' she screams, as the hot edges burn her fingers, and she throws it across the room. It lands on yesterday's newspaper, and the edges curl. *One flame, two. Three flickers.*

'I'll go!' Betty shouts loudly, and runs, the stairs thudding as she hits the treads.

Alice stares at the smoking paper, and thinks hard. *Water.*

There is a jug of water on the table, one jug, and she grabs it, throwing the water all over the floor. Some of it catches the newspaper. But she has forgotten about the eggs, and she realises late, as the smell of cooking eggs turns. She starts to cry, as smoke rises from two areas of the kitchen, and her nightgown is drenched. Her fingers are black with the carbon from the toast, and she is sobbing, angry at herself for failing. She stamps her feet as her parents arrive in a flurry of shouts.

Frustration, shame, and burnt breakfast. She *can* do it. She *can*.

5

WILLOW

The alarm is shrill, like a siren, and Willow knocks it off. By the time she wakes again, sun spills in like split lemons, sharp and clarifying. She checks her phone:

Scan clear. They've adjusted her dose. I'll see what the doctors say. Fingers crossed we'll be on the train later today. Can't wait to see you. Mum xxx

Carrying her bag, Willow runs into the cathedral. Despite her dread of facing it after last night, she only has today to set up the exhibition. It's a big deal – the first exhibition she's arranged out of the museum. Her find.

She must phone her mum soon, check she's coping. Her mum has always said how lucky Willow is to have a twin. She copes with Nonie's illness on her own: Nonie forgets things, forgets to take her meds, occasionally forgets names.

You'll depend on Fliss, Mum always says, wheeling out the standing family joke about the imaginary childhood

28

friend she called Naughty Liss: *I had to make up my sister – at least you've got one.*

It's all very well to imagine that Fliss will be a help when their parents are older, but Fliss has always been best at looking after herself. Always apologising for being the first-born, Willow is tired of watching Fliss spend her life making sure she gets everything Willow gets, plus a little bit more. Fliss is never one to be upstaged. Never one to be pushed to the sidelines.

And yet Willow loves her – she's her twin, she's part of her. Her mum firmly believes you can feel your family from a distance. Willow has felt it. Even Fliss had once screamed the house down with stomach ache, only for Willow to be found vomiting upstairs with a rumbling appendix. Toothache from either twin always meant a check-up for both. She can hear her mum: *Blood can spill wider than flesh, senses can leak from the womb as much as from the skin.*

Entering through the welcome centre doors, it's quiet, and Willow's footsteps sound too loud in the shadowy stone light. The mood in here is different. Ethereal.

Slowing, she's stilled by a stained-glass window – huge, circular, and filled with a kaleidoscopic pattern of reds and blues; the light soft. Inhaling, she'd forgotten how cathedrals make her weepy. Tiredness is heavy and the peace of the air is like an infusion.

A follow-up text from her mum pings through:

How's Fliss coping with the pressure?

Willow stares at the phone, irritation stirring. Fliss, as

usual, mustn't have called Mum for a few days. When it's about Fliss, it's all about Fliss.

Willow carries the balance of the family with her like her own religion. The one of God for her is distinctly lapsed: a guilt hangover. Nonie had taken them to church every Sunday when she was young: mints and handkerchiefs, scented with lavender; leather gloves, in which she'd clasped her contribution to the collection. Once, Willow had tucked it under her palm and spent it on sweets. She'd robbed from God, and the childish guilt has stayed with her. She's sure she'll be punished at some point. There's a balance to everything.

Checking her phone again for Otis: nothing. She's not expecting to hear from him. But facing the wedding without him will be hard. Theo will be there, and she closes her eyes for a second, thinking of the first time Theo had walked into halls during freshers' week.

And then how quickly she had lost him to Fliss. At the wedding, Otis was to be her coat to wear, her thicker skin. Theo will arrive with whomever he is with, and Willow will be without armour. Without amour.

The last time she saw Theo... She's never spoken to Fliss about it. It was only one night, out in Brussels. A few drinks. They'd stayed out until almost dawn. They'd sat in the square – it had been hot, and she had drunk beer with strawberries, as sweet as it was strong. When she's lonely, she breathes that night in. It had, she thinks, changed everything. He'd always felt so... out of reach. But surely the girl code, the sister code, all the unwritten codes mean he's out of reach forever.

Sitting on a wooden slatted chair, she takes a minute to look up at the huge effigies ready for the Easter pilgrimage. There's no one to ask where the office is, or the exhibition area. It's empty. Surely it shouldn't be this empty at this time of morning, the week before Holy Week begins?

Maybe the police are still here? Maybe it's not over? She checks her phone for a message.

From above, an old iron chandelier hangs in chains down from the stone arch. Gilt candlesticks and a pattern-tiled floor – it's ornate. This place is beautiful. The terror of last night feels unreal: the shower of stones, the blackness.

Thinking again of Nonie, she briefly mouths a prayer learned in her youth on dry lips for her mum to get her here safely. Dad's back from his work trip; they'll all come together.

With a quick, fevered intensity, the language of prayer returns to her mouth in its half-formed lines, like forgotten song lyrics: *Our Father, who art in heav'n...*

'Hello?' A man approaches, dressed in long black robes, hair black-and-grey peppered. His face is red, his eyes blotchy. He comes down from the right, where a wall of stone figures stand cathedral-tall behind a high altar, beneath an ornate ceiling painted with animals and leaves.

Following is a very tall man, in a long dark coat and glasses with thick black frames: stylish, slightly apart from the setting. He walks with a much shorter, younger woman with a brown bob, and they're both formally dressed; there's something in their expression...

Police, she thinks. And the blackness from the night

before whispers in her ear, the emptiness of the grounds. She had used her key to let herself in – maybe it was too soon?

She rises as they approach. *Dead* is the only word she catches.

'I'm sorry, what are you doing here?' the tall man asks. He must be well over six foot. He has a hint of an accent she can't place.

'I…' She shakes her head.

'The cathedral is closed this morning. It's a crime scene. Not open to the public.' His voice is stern. Already repentant, she feels it heap on her, heavier still.

'I'm… I work in… I'm with the exhibition,' she manages. 'I came in at the side door. I have a key. They sent one in case we were late.' She lifts it, wanting to prove her story, feeling caught out. 'I arrived last night. We *were* late. I was here. I spoke to your officer last night.' She speaks the last part quietly.

The man looks at her carefully. 'You were one of the witnesses?'

She nods.

The man talks to the woman with the brown bob now, nodding to her, saying, 'Yes, good plan.' He still hasn't looked back to Willow.

'Would you like to talk to me now?' she asks, uncertain.

'DCI Jansen,' the man offers, finally turning back. 'Yes, we will need to speak to you. I'm so sorry. It must have been terrible. Thank you for staying and speaking to our officer last night.' His voice is softer now.

'I…' She thinks of the shower of pebbles, scattering from above. She feels faint. 'I felt some stones, from the roof, before. I'm sorry, I just assumed it was the wind. I wasn't fast enough to raise the alarm.'

The man in the black robes is kind when he speaks, but to the point, and his voice is tight. 'Stones don't just fall from the roof,' he says. 'We'd be in all sorts of trouble if that happened all the time.' He looks at Jansen. 'I guess that means he was up there for a while.' He shakes his head. His skin is grey, but he doesn't look very old, maybe in his forties? But he looks exhausted, sleep sore. His eyes crease, tight and dry, as he says, 'Why, though? It just makes no sense! I...'

'Mr Braxton,' the officer with the brown bob says, her voice gentle, 'you must go home.'

Willow wants to ask how he's connected; this man wears grief like a thin skin.

Jansen and the clergyman are walking away as Willow says, to the female officer, 'Who was it? Do they know who died?'

The officer checks her watch, then says, 'It seems it was an older man, eighty years old. I can't really say anything else. I'm DI Adrika Verma. Come with me? You won't be allowed in here until SOCO finish up. I'd love to talk to you, and I've got an hour. Come on, I'll buy you a coffee – might even run to croissants if you're hungry.'

6

WILLOW

The coffee shop in town is small, with white metro tiles and low-hanging brass light fittings. It feels modern and fresh after the cathedral with its ancient stone. It is empty, which Willow sees Adrika check; she won't want to be overheard. 'Eighty years old?' she asks, as Adrika sits with two flat whites and a plate full of croissants and questions.

She nods. 'Yes, the identity was confirmed earlier. It will be in the press later.' She pushes the coffee towards Willow. 'How are you today?'

Willow takes a sip, hot and bitter. She has no idea how she is. It had been cold last night; he had been so high up, so alone.

She separates her jaw, forcing it to relax. The grinding happens before she realises.

Adrika eats, giving her a moment, and then asks, 'What time were you there? We have you down as arriving at 1 a.m.?'

Willow struggles to think of the details. She's only had about three hours' sleep, and the night had wormed its way into her dreams – dead faces, whispering their secrets, had woken her more than once, and chased her back under the covers. She'd looked for a book to read, the floorboards creaking; she'd been nervous she'd wake Martha.

She nods. 'We arrived at 1 a.m. We were there for as long as it took to unload the boxes. We saw him fall later, after we'd finished. That's when we called the police.'

'And how long do you think he'd been up there?' Adrika prompts.

Willow thinks of last night, of the two men and their power tussle over the key, and how exhausted she'd been. 'I have no idea. The idea that he was on the roof the whole time, and maybe we could have helped…' She shakes her head. 'I heard a sound – I thought it was the wind, but… Well, it sounded like a cry at one point.' She shakes her head again. Tears slide into her throat. 'I wonder if I had listened harder…'

Adrika drinks her coffee. 'You can't blame yourself – at that time of night there really wasn't anything you could have done. It's hard though, processing death, as a witness. If you feel you're struggling with it, then there are people who you can talk to?'

'Thank you,' Willow says. 'It was so late. It's just so sad.' But these are words for Adrika's benefit; she hears herself say them as she thinks, *Could I have saved him?*

'And other than the driver and the verger, was there anyone else around?' Adrika asks.

Willow thinks, shaking her head. 'No, the driver arrived with me and left before… And Gabriel – the verger. I was supposed to call him when I arrived. He'd said he would be in the local pub waiting, but I worried it was so late he'd just gone to bed. I was in two minds about calling; but he came. No one else.'

'Do you travel with the exhibition?'

Willow appreciates Adrika's change of direction. She nods. 'I'm bringing the exhibits here. And now I'm also here for a wedding.' Willow thinks of Fliss's impeccable timing. Willow announces the first exhibition she's curated outside of the museum, and then Fliss announces a wedding at the same cathedral, the same week.

'My sister – it's her wedding.' Willow lifts the coffee.

Adrika is biting her lip, on the brink of a question. 'You're not related to Fliss, are you? That's one of the reasons I suggested a coffee.'

'My twin.' Willow smiles.

'Oh, how brilliant! Twins run in the family, don't they? I always wanted a twin.'

'Not in ours,' Willow says. 'We're the only ones. You know her?'

'She's marrying my colleague. Sunny? You must have met him.'

Willow shakes her head. 'Not enough – very briefly at the engagement party, and a few times on Zoom, but I've heard a lot about him! I was in Rome for a while, on placement with the museum.' *Giving Otis a chance to look around*, she thinks. 'I was supposed to go to their party last night, but it was so late. It's been quite quick?'

'Yep – a proper whirlwind,' Adrika says. 'I wouldn't have expected it of Sunny. But goes to show, you never know! There's a party at the cathedral tonight, isn't there? With the exhibition?' Adrika asks. 'My boss is going. We've been invited. The mayor too – the exhibition has had a fair bit of press.'

'Yes. The owner's family are coming. They're allowing this short exhibition, then donating the exhibits to our museum. The original owner was Sir Rupert Scott, who died recently; he's from St Albans. He was also in a mental health hospital here for a long time,' Willow says. 'The manuscripts were in a loft with some diaries from his time in the institution. They seemed to tie so well together, both passions of Sir Rupert – Satan cast out of heaven by God, trying to find his way back to Paradise, stuck in Hell. And the years Sir Rupert spent campaigning for more enlightened mental health treatment – after his time in hospital. His diaries are full of references to the books and poems he read when he was in there.'

Adrika nods as Willow talks. Sir Rupert was well known.

'He tracked down the early notes on *Paradise Lost* later when he was a successful lawyer and campaigner for mental health, before his knighthood. When he died, his family found all the diaries. It seemed only fair to put on an exhibition first, here.' Willow thinks for a second of Nonie, reading her the poem when she was young. If times had been different, Nonie would have studied literature or theology. Nonie left school at sixteen.

'Which hospital?' Adrika asks.

'Hill Barnes – closed down now. Mental health treatment is so very different today.' Willow thinks of her mum, of the pills she takes, and has taken for years. She'll be seemingly fine, for long stretches of time, then sometimes even tiny tasks overwhelm her; she struggles to make decisions, to get out of bed, as if there was some part of herself she couldn't reconcile.

Willow had read case histories of wives sent to hospitals for depression, for disagreeing with their husbands, for not wanting children, or worse, for being a woman and becoming pregnant without being married. Mental health care is a different country now.

'I know nothing about *Paradise Lost*. More a fan of comics,' Adrika says. 'Is Satan not the evil one?'

'In a sense, yes. But he's also the compelling one. He gets all the good lines – his poetry draws you in, makes you think he's the hero, because Milton wanted to show how seductive evil can be. But then again, he's privately riddled with pain and loss, while publicly claiming he's happy being king of Hell. So is he really evil, or has he just realised nothing has quite gone according to plan, and although he would swap anything to undo it, instead he'll pretend he's OK with his choices?' She smiles wryly, picking up the coffee.

Adrika laughs. She finishes her coffee, her cup landing with a bang as she pulls out her notebook. 'Thanks for talking to me. I'd better get back to work. Jansen is a good boss, but his work ethic is in overdrive.' She smiles, pulling out a business card, handing it to Willow. 'Here's my number. I mean it, just give me a call if you fancy another coffee, or want to talk about what you saw.'

Willow lifts a hand in a half wave as Adrika leaves. Really, she could go back to bed for an hour as the police are still busy with the cathedral. She'd been planning on borrowing a dress from Fliss for the cocktails. She has nothing to wear tonight. But now Fliss is angry because she missed the drinks last night, and asking for a dress won't improve her mood.

Looking at the street out of the window, the market and old shops with their sloping roofs are much more appealing than Martha's starchy bed sheets. She should take advantage of the sun, let it burn away the echoes of the night.

7

MAARTEN

Maarten's fingers are cold despite the bright April sun. The park lies before him, green and new in the spring.

Michael Braxton, the clergyman, had finally gone home. Arriving for work earlier, he had recognised his father's car outside; then he'd been able to identify his watch. Luckily it hadn't been him who had found his father's body.

Maarten will question him at home once he's finished here; he hadn't wanted to probe earlier.

Kak, he curses. Michael had been very quiet, apologetic. Almost sorry for taking up police time. It had made it worse. And the family had no idea what he was doing up there. *As far as we knew*, Michael had said, *he was asleep. Something must have happened, for him to leave the house after they had all gone to bed. Not suicide, no way. Surely not?*

Michael's face is stark in Maarten's mind, white and blank. He'd stared at him, bewildered. *Why? Why? I don't understand. We all had dinner. The kids showed him their Easter drawings...*

His hand had flown to his mouth to catch a cry, but it had bled out through the fingers anyway.

Sunny arrives at his elbow, hands him another coffee. 'Looks like we're all done here, sir. There's CCTV in the building, but not over the tower door, and no sign of anyone on the other tapes, other than a cleaner and Joel Braxton. The CCTV near the tower is broken – apparently, it's been out of action all week. Shall I start heading back to the station?'

Maarten nods. 'I'll speak to the family again, Sunny. Can you make sure you finish up with the witness statements? Particularly the cleaner.' So far, the evidence indicated the man had been alone.

'Yes, I spoke to her briefly. She'd left her purse at work and went back to get it. She didn't speak to him. She did wonder why he was here so late, but she knew his son worked at the cathedral, so it hadn't seemed so strange. Her husband was waiting in a car outside, so she was only in there a few minutes. There were no other witnesses inside.'

Maarten nods. 'Well, hopefully the woman, Willow Eliot, might have seen something. And the verger – they'd both been on the grounds when he fell.'

Sunny scans the edge of the park that rolls down from the three main doors of the huge cathedral. Tall, wooden, all hidden under their own alcove. 'At least the sun has come out,' he says.

Maarten still can't feel the sun, not yet. The face of the man had stared up at him. Unrecognisable. He won't forget that in a while.

'What's the story on the family?' Maarten asks, looking

down across the park. What could have driven a man to such an act?

'Local family, as far as I know. I don't know them, but my mum does. She called earlier, asking if it was Michael Braxton's dad.' Sunny shrugs. 'My mum knows everyone, sir.'

Maarten smiles. 'And what, according to your mum, is the story of the family?'

'He used to be a verger here at the cathedral, years ago. They all moved north when he retired, but Michael, Joel's son, came back when there was an opening for clergy. I think they've lived here for about four years. He's married with two kids. Everyone is shocked. No suggestion why his father might have killed himself.' He shrugs. 'She mentioned another death here years ago, in the early 60s. Another tower death. Joel Braxton would have worked here then. A woman, I think. Mum said that rocked the community back then, but before my time. She was sure Joel Braxton had a connection to that.'

Maarten nods, thinking. 'Was the earlier death a suicide?'

'Not sure. Mum said it was a woman – a mother. Nothing very clear. Only thirty-six years old. She left a daughter behind, who went into care. Really sad.'

Maarten glances at his watch. He'll have to visit Joel Braxton's family soon. 'If Michael Braxton has kids, maybe the children saw something. I'll ask when I go.'

'I'll chase his phone records,' Sunny says, as his phone beeps.

Wedding, Maarten thinks.

With only a few days until the wedding, Sunny has been

half in the job and half down the aisle. The wedding is to be in the cathedral, which Maarten had assumed was only for the elite. It will be one of the fanciest weddings he's attended.

Sunny's phone rings, and he answers. 'Look, Fliss, I'll call you soon. I'm still at work...'

The April sun is gaining strength. Maarten wonders just how much time Sunny has spent working, and how much he's been standing outside, warming up, in communication with his mum and his girlfriend.

Deciding to give him a break, Maarten remembers the bluster of wedding planning. It had almost been a military operation. Sunny had proposed three months ago. They'd only been together five months when he popped the question. Maarten wonders at the rush. Sunny never does anything in a hurry.

'How are the preparations going?' he asks. 'Any last-minute hitches?'

Looking sheepish, Sunny half smiles, sounds apologetic. 'Good, sir. Fliss is doing most of it. I had to try three different types of cake the other week.' He grins. 'They were all fine. All tasted of cake. I picked the one in the middle.'

Maarten laughs. He looks up at the cathedral tower. 'All done here? Dig around. See if we can get the full story on the 1960s tower death. As for Joel Braxton, can you do the friends, wider family members?'

The Dean is heading towards them. She will want her cathedral back.

8

ALICE

'Alice, you'll get in trouble!' Betty stands with her mouth wide open. 'You can't stick those on Hector!'

The hamster is curled in a ball, in his cage. He sits there all day sometimes. *He's a house pet*, Mummy says. *He won't like it outside.*

All day. Alice's tummy feels funny sometimes when she thinks of Hector, all day inside. Never running in the park, as fast as he can. Never feeling free. He sits in his cage, old, and she worries he minds.

He likes being inside, running on his wheel, Mummy has said. But Alice still worries. What if one day someone said you couldn't leave the house anymore?

The glue in her fingers is sticky; she holds two cardboard wings.

'I think he'll like it,' she says, 'flying. I think he'll love it!'

'But will it work?' Betty doesn't sound sure, and it makes Alice doubt herself. Doubt the logic of it.

'But aeroplanes can fly with wings?' she says.

44

The glue starts to clump in her hands, and she can roll it in balls between her fingers. She doesn't want it to dry and then not stick to him. Pushing gently, into his fur, she holds the gluey clumps against his body. The cardboard wings are large: big ones will be better. She cut the edges of the feathers carefully. She'd drawn them first, exactly like she'd seen on the swans in the park.

Doubt creeps at the edges. Even though she'd tried so hard with the scissors, they're still not as smooth as she thought they would be.

Would Daddy be angry? Should she ask Mummy first?

But he will say no. And Daddy has shouted a lot recently. And he will be so *pleased* when they see what she has managed to do!

She had counted the feathers on the swan's wing the other day. She closes her eyes and counts them again.

'Shall I ask Mummy?' Betty says. She looks over her shoulder. 'Daddy was cross last time, when we tried to wash the goldfish. Remember?' Her hand is in her mouth, chewing on the end of her fingers.

Alice pauses; the rush of feelings slow. She thinks of how the goldfish had flopped a bit, and then stopped. But they had dried it very gently in the towel. As gently as she liked to be dried after a bath. When Daddy had shouted at her that it was *dead!*, she had felt cold. And his voice had got louder and louder. She had counted all the breaths he had taken between noises, counted the ticks on the clock.

The goldfish had lain on the towel. She had felt sick, felt

tears coming, but Daddy's voice just got louder, and she had looked down at the floor and counted tiles.

But this was not the goldfish. 'He *was* angry,' she agrees. 'We wouldn't do *that* again! This is different.'

She wonders if this will make him proud of her. Finally, for something.

'I'll go and ask.' Betty starts walking to the door. Then she stops. 'Do you really think it will work?'

'Do you?' Alice sees Betty's eyebrows working again, and she waits for an answer. Betty never gets into trouble. If she says not to, then they won't do it. Alice holds her breath, one second, two seconds, three seconds, four seconds, five seconds, six seconds…

Finally, Betty's eyebrows slow, and she nods. 'I think it might be alright?'

Alice feels warm, the sun coming in through the window. The park looks green outside. 'Oh, Betty! Hector can fly now!' Alice can feel stirrings in her tummy, a bubble rising. She feels like all the thoughts she has might make her pop. Sometimes all the thoughts are so big. 'We've always wanted to fly. But we're too heavy. But Hector can fly! Shall we try it?'

Betty still looks unsure.

'This will get Hector out of the house.' Alice looks at him in his metal cage. 'Imagine having to just sit inside all the time, on one cushion. All your life.'

She picks up the furry animal, its eyes like big black glass beads.

'You can fly, Hector. I know it, you can fly!' she whispers, thinking of air, of speed, so high up. She thinks of soaring over the park.

'Anyway, Mummy and Daddy are downstairs. They won't know. We can tell them afterwards, we can tell them that Hector flew! Can you open the window? Let's try now.'

9

WILLOW

'Willow!'

Fliss's voice carries across the restaurant, its wooden floors and distressed tables bouncing the sound.

'Hey, sis,' Willow says, stepping into the outstretched arms.

'Now, I don't have long. There's a problem with the flowers.' Fliss rolls her eyes and is already scanning the menu. 'I'll probably have the eggs. Or the soup. I'm not eating too much.' She taps her stomach, almost concave, and swings her hair over her shoulder.

Willow catches their reflection in the mirror. Clearly sisters, twins even, but Fliss is the shinier of the two: highlights, slimmer, better clothes. Theo had picked the glossier version. The waiter comes over, and they order.

'Theo's coming,' Fliss says, as though reading Willow's mind. But Willow has long since worked out that while their thoughts frequently run in parallel, Fliss is far less attuned to any crossover: too much effort.

'He is?' Willow feels a kick in her stomach.

Theo's dad ran a French clothing label. This is the other reason Willow sometimes wonders if Fliss picked him out of the crowd. For her, it had been his smile. He had laughed at a joke she had made when terrified, and he'd been wearing a crumpled T-shirt with the name of a band with which she was obsessed. It had taken two and a half minutes for her to lose her heart to him. Whole.

If Theo had felt the same, he had made no sign. She'd been talking to Fliss that night about the people in their halls – Fliss was already popular. She hadn't noticed Theo. Willow mentioned his name – it must have been written on her face. And the next day someone told them all who his dad was. And by the end of the second day, Fliss was draped over him, laughing at whatever he said.

'I've no doubt you'll spend most of the time gossiping with him rather than finding someone new. I could kill Otis!' Fliss jabs two fingers into Otis's imaginary eyeballs, and Willow laughs.

'Have you heard from him?'

Willow shakes her head. 'No. He asked me to clear out my stuff, and that was that.'

'Someone else?' Fliss cocks her head sympathetically and Willow's skin crawls. It's happened to her twice, but never to Fliss. This show of understanding grates. Fliss has never been dumped.

'Who cares! Now, tell me about the dress. I still haven't seen it.' On safer ground, the food arrives and Willow nods along, listening to the plans.

The waiter pauses for a second longer than necessary, speaking to Fliss. A few heads turn. Fliss's job as a fashion advisor on a morning show makes her a well-known face. As children, they had both visited the studios where their dad worked as a TV doctor, and Fliss had set her sights on a slot there at a young age.

'So, you'll come to drinks tonight?' Fliss says, signalling for the bill. 'I've got to run – flowers then nails!' She nods to a neat manicure. 'They're in a terrible state.'

'Oh, there's this cocktail thing at the cathedral, I think I said… I'm free from tomorrow evening?' Willow hears herself already beginning to apologise.

'Well, I kind of assumed that as you didn't manage to make it last night, you might try a bit harder tonight to *finally* spend time with Sunny?'

Closing her eyes briefly, Willow says, 'I did travel all the way to London a month ago for the dinner. But neither of you could make it last minute.'

'Well, I explained all that. We'd had a row. I was hardly in the mood to go out!'

'Yes, but…' Willow trails off, hating the plaintive catch in her tone. 'Fliss, I have to go. I'm setting up the exhibition. It opens tomorrow, then I'm all yours.'

Fliss's lips are pursed. Tight. 'Well, why you have to work this week…'

'Oh, sis. Don't you remember, I was doing this first? I get that it's your wedding—'

'You *get* that it's my wedding? Come on, Wills. Even you must see a wedding is a bit higher up the scale than a few poems by a dead man and an old hospital!'

Willow's teeth clamp as she refuses to answer.

It's her wedding week, calm down, Willow thinks, as

she forces herself to smile. She tries a different tack. 'You could come to the drinks? Bring Sunny? His boss is going, I think. And the mayor...' Willow knows how much Fliss likes a line-up. 'Did you get anywhere with Mum's birthday present?'

'Oh, yes, I said I'd do a family tree – it's so the thing now! Maybe you could take over for me? I can check it when we're back from honeymoon?'

Willow stares at her sister.

'Look, I'm late for this appointment. Call me later, if you change your mind about drinks at ours – if not, we can try to come to this thing.' Fliss offers her a kiss from her fingers, waves across the table and vanishes quickly, with a chair scrape. Willow realises she's been left with the bill.

The see-saw of sisterhood. She will need to apologise a little more. Mind a little less.

10

MAARTEN

Maarten knocks on the door of the house, gravel crunching underfoot as he looks up the road with its wide-spaced houses and broad pavements. Liv has always wanted to live on this street, but it's way out of their price range.

'Maarten,' Michael says as he opens the door. 'Thanks for coming.'

'Who is it?' calls a female voice.

'DCI Jansen,' Michael answers, then smiles at Maarten. 'Your DI is already here. The girls are climbing all over her.'

'Lovely home,' Maarten says, as he takes his coat off.

'All the clergy live in houses owned by the cathedral. We're lucky ours is so nice. They don't often have money to update them though, so we dig deep for that.'

Maarten enters the large lounge to see Adrika covered with two small children, windmills of arms and legs.

'Girls, off the officer!' Michael says, then to Adrika, 'I'm so sorry.'

'They're lovely,' Adrika says, but Maarten can see a hint

of panic in her eyes as one of them climbs up behind her and starts to fasten clips in her hair.

'Your hair is so shiny,' the blonder of the two girls says.

'Here, let me do it now!' The other one, hair with glints of autumn, climbs up and grabs the clip and a handful of Adrika's bob.

'Down, now!' A woman enters, carrying a tray loaded with coffee, biscuits and milk.

The two girls immediately climb down and look sheepish.

'If you go to the playroom, you can have the TV.' The woman places the tray down on the coffee table and lifts two biscuits from a plate, bending and lowering her voice, as though imparting secrets. 'Here, one for each of you. Say thank you to the officer for playing with you.' The girls stare wide-eyed at the gingerbread biscuits, hands outstretched, Adrika's shiny hair immediately forgotten.

'Thank you,' they chorus, looking at the treats, and Maarten smiles, thinking of his own daughters, Nic and Sanne, when they were small enough to be pacified with sugar.

'We haven't told them yet,' the woman says, as she watches them leave and closes the door. Her face falls, the smile slipping away. 'We thought we'd wait, until it's sunk in. We've been baking. A few kitchen disasters this morning already, general domestic disorder.' She takes Michael's hand, and they sit on the sofa. 'Please.' She gestures to the tray. 'Please, take a coffee. I'm Heather.'

Sinking into the other sofa, grey with mustard cushions, Maarten reaches for a drink, and Adrika sits up straighter in the armchair at the other side of the room.

'I'm sorry, there's no further news. We just wondered if we could ask a few questions.' Maarten thinks of the morning's blood on flagstones. 'When was the last time you saw your father?'

Michael looks to his wife. 'We went to bed about 11 p.m.?'

Heather nods. She has black hair, dried straight and long, and her eyes are blue – they're red-rimmed, as though she's already been crying. 'One of the girls was up not too long after I fell asleep. I took her to the loo, then put her back to bed. I was thinking' – her hand tightens on Michael's, the skin of her grip white – 'that maybe it was him leaving that woke her. If I had checked on him too, realised he was missing, we could have raised the alarm.' Her voice catches; she looks at the floor. 'He was an old man, and a bit disorientated I think, after the journey here. He didn't settle. He was up and down all evening.'

'He only arrived yesterday?' Adrika asks.

Michael nods. 'He's here for the Easter week. He was going to stay for a couple of weeks. He loves Easter week – the procession from the clock tower to the nave, the foot washing, the Easter Vigil. And the girls have been so excited about seeing him.' He looks at his wife. 'They're going to be devastated.'

Heather nods. Her eyes fill with tears. 'They've made him a cake. We hadn't even given it to him.'

Maarten glances at Adrika to give Heather a moment, but Michael speaks, and he sounds almost angry.

'All we got to do yesterday was head to the cathedral. He wanted to see it. We all went once the girls were back from school. Had a coffee in the café, and he gave us all a tour. All he got to do...' He shakes his head. 'You know he was verger there, for years. But going back so late – why? What could have made him want to return?'

Maarten gives him time. 'And when you visited the cathedral yesterday afternoon, how was that?'

'Good.' Heather speaks now, taking Michael's hand. 'The tour was detailed – he even showed the kids a piece of horse hair sticking out of a wall that's been there for years. They'd never seen it before!' She smiles. 'He was always so good with the children.'

Michael's fists are balled. His knuckles are white. The anger that comes with grief can be overwhelming.

'Did he speak to anyone when he was there?'

Michael looks at Heather. 'We saw Lizzie and we went to the café. Did he speak to anyone else?'

Heather shakes her head. 'No. He sat with the kids while I went to get drinks. You went to the office to get something. Lizzie came back with you. Then we finished the tour? We saw Gabriel there – the verger.'

Michael nods. 'Yes. Noah and Jaz were in the office.'

'Who's Lizzie and the others?' Adrika asks, making notes.

'Lizzie's the cleaner. She's been there years. I think Dad knew her when he worked there. And he knows Noah from previous visits. Jaz is Dad's grandson – he's my nephew. Noah and Jaz work in the office.'

'Nothing unusual?' Maarten asks. 'Nothing you think he was upset about? Nothing health-related, or money-related?'

Michael rubs his eyes with his fists. 'I haven't been paying enough attention. We're so busy, with family and work, I took my eye off him. It's not your fault, Heather. If it's anyone's fault... For what it's worth, he's my father. It's my fault.'

11

MAARTEN

'All finished?' The super sticks her head round Maarten's door.

'Yes,' he nods. 'We're not expecting anyone else to be involved with the death. The door to the tower must have been left unlocked that afternoon. They'd opened it for him so he could give a tour to his family. The cleaner who saw Joel Braxton enter the cathedral didn't see anyone else, and she left a while before the fall. It must have been deliberate. It's too hard to fall from the tower – you'd have to climb the wall.'

'Good work. Why would someone in their eighties take their own life? Have you checked medical records? Maybe he's been diagnosed with something he can't face. That name rings a bell for some reason.' She pauses for a second. 'No, not coming to me. Keep me updated.'

Maarten nods.

'Now, how's this speech coming along?'

'Speech?'

'Sunny's bachelor send-off drinks, in the office. On Friday. Surely you're coming?'

'Yes, but…'

'Oh, Maarten. You can't imagine you won't have to say a few words? You're his boss! You better get writing. And the whip-round?'

Maarten shakes his head. 'There's a whip-round?'

'Of course there is! Adrika must have organised it. Out of your comfort zone, Maarten. Get ready for a party send-off!'

12

WILLOW

'Mum?'

'Willow, I missed you earlier. We're on the train, finally!'

'How's Nonie? How are *you*?' Willow pauses outside the cathedral.

'All's fine. The medication will take a day or so. Your dad's going to keep a firm eye on her.' She lowers her voice. 'He's enjoying his celebrity in the carriage – found a table of fans. They're all telling him their ailments.'

Willow smiles, imagining her father, filling every inch of the carriage, larger than life. He always seemed to sense when her mum was in retreat. He made himself bigger, spoke so she didn't have to.

'Nothing to Fliss – let's tell her about Nonie after the honeymoon. She doesn't need to be worrying about her grandmother on top of everything else. How is she coping with the wedding planning?'

Willow thinks of the panic over the perfect nails. 'She's being very Fliss about it all. I think she'll come to the cocktail party tonight.'

'Great. I can't wait, Willow. I better go. We'll be celebrating soon.' There's a determined note of positivity in her tone, and it almost breaks Willow. With Nonie and Fliss, she prays she doesn't have to handle her mum crashing. It's selfish, but she is exhausted. The image of the man falling will not leave her brain.

'Love you,' she says.

'And Otis?'

'Nothing.'

'Good. He was a rat.'

Willow opens the door to the tiny office attached to the welcome centre in the cathedral. She carries with her a large coffee and it spills as she enters.

'Shit,' she says, wiping her hand on her trousers.

'Hello.' A man with coffee-coloured hair, tight in curls like wrapping paper ribbon, raises his eyebrows expectantly. He's older than Willow, but not by much. He carries a pile of files and there's half a smile on his face.

Willow's face flushes, aware she's just sworn in the house of God. Nonie would be ashamed of her. 'Sorry,' she says. 'I'm Willow, with the exhibition? I came earlier, but…'

'No bother,' he says. 'I'm Noah. I'm the entire exhibition department.'

He whispers, glancing to the back of the room, 'It's been crazy. A death this morning. The exhibition, and a wedding at the weekend.'

'I can hear you, you know.' The voice comes from the corner, where a very pale face sits beneath black hair.

'Are you related to the bride? You look like her. I'm Jaz,' he says, staring at Willow. His ivory-white face is devoid of expression. His eyes are green, like gems. His long thin frame looks squashed behind his desk and he looks very young, early twenties maybe.

'Hello,' she says, trying her warmest tone. 'Yes. I'm her twin. Sorry,' she says, before she can stop herself. 'Is it all causing a lot of extra work?'

'It was Jaz's grandfather who died,' Noah says quietly. 'He's not going home. Says he wants to stay at work today.'

'I'm so sorry,' Willow says.

She doesn't know if his pale face is a result of grief. 'I met your dad earlier. I'm so sorry for you all.'

'You must have met Uncle Michael. My dad lives in Devon. I live here.'

'Uncle Michael got him the job,' Noah mutters, and Jaz frowns.

Willow, shocked at the insensitivity of Noah, compensates. 'How lovely to work with your uncle – you must both be torn up.'

'So-so,' Jaz shrugs, and quickly looks down.

Is he crying? Willow wonders, and she tries to look elsewhere in the room. 'What a lovely office!'

'This?' Noah raises his eyebrows again. Then he frowns. 'Jaz is right, you do look like the bride for this weekend. She's not from round here.'

Willow nods, starts over-explaining. 'Not local, no. She's Fliss, I'm her twin; we're from Edinburgh. Her fiancé is local.' Willow feels coffee drip down her arm and looks for a tissue.

'Here.' Jaz stares at her, a box of tissues on his desk, but he doesn't move.

'Jaz is responsible for marketing,' Noah says, rolling his eyes skyward. 'Which means he doesn't do much.'

Jaz redirects his gaze to Noah. 'Moving boxes from one room to the next this morning, Noah?' he says, his tone as pale as his face.

Noah speaks to Willow, turning his back on Jaz. 'Come on. Bit late getting started today, what with the police. Want to get set up now?'

Willow's hands are sticky and she puts the coffee down, the base of the cup still wet on the desk. She realises she has the new clothes she'd bought for the party in a paper bag over her arm. She must look heartless: a man died, and she'd gone shopping.

'Come on, it's this way.' Noah doesn't wait for a response.

With a last smile to Jaz, who is still staring, Willow hurries after Noah, dumping her bag under a desk nearby.

'I don't know if you're familiar with the cathedral layout, but it's built in the shape of a cross. The temporary exhibition area is in the north transept. The north and south transepts are the arms of the cross.' He talks quickly, stepping ahead of her.

They walk towards the huge rose window, beneath which an exhibition space is marked out with display boards. The mental-health exhibits from Hill Barnes and other hospitals are mostly pinned up: black-and-white photos of the Hill Barnes wards, a nurses' staffroom, a Christmas party, the original farm belonging to the hospital, a large aerial photo. There are also a number of handwritten diary entries – some belonging to Sir Rupert, but entries from other hospitals as well.

'This is the exhibition space,' Noah says. 'I made a start with some of the exhibits. Got to be ready for these drinks tonight.' He rolls his eyes. 'Champagne, I heard. Out to impress, I guess, what with the "Sir"; normally it's warm white wine. Feel free to change anything you like,' he says, peering at a photo. 'The last standing building from the hospital is due to be demolished next week, so there's already been some local interest. It's quite timely.'

'Really?'

'Yep – most of the original land is residential. There's a park now; a school has been built on part of the land. I think the last building was bought for development but never came to anything. Some kids were found playing in there and started a small fire. So, they're demolishing it. More houses to be built. So many houses.' Noah shrugs. 'I've read some of the diary entries you've collected. Some of those entries are pretty rough. And treatments in the 60s: the ECT, insulin coma therapy, narcotherapy, leucotomy...' He shakes his head. 'I've never heard of most of them.'

Willow crosses to the boards and scans the writings she'd collected, with help from a retired doctor from the hospital and some local history pages and Facebook sites. She reads an account from a boy in a hospital south of London from the 1960s:

Woke up early and worked on the farm for an hour. I had 100 mg of Largactil three times today, and also paraldehyde orally and by injection. Heard they're closing all the farms soon? It's now 4.45 p.m. and feeling sleepy from paraldehyde I think. A new patient arrived – Joe Kettering. He pulled my towel from me when we were queuing for the bathrooms. Then he kicked me over. The nurses took him away. My head hurts from where he pulled my hair. Mother said she'll be in soon to visit. She said they've suggested ECT but she will wait for me to decide. Hope I can go home soon. I think Wolfie misses me. Mother said he didn't eat his food when I first left, and wouldn't go on walks or chase his ball. My sixteenth birthday is now only 45 days away. I hope I'll be home for that.

She can't reread some of the entries. One was of a mother who had lost a child and then been committed to a hospital east of London for what seemed like depression – she'd been cutting herself too. Her agitation had increased in hospital, and then she'd received a lobotomy. The thought twists Willow's stomach. Some of the reports had mentioned violence on the wards, but also the dedication of many overstretched staff and doctors.

She scans an entry from a nurse: *I was moved to the children's wing today and had to introduce a seven-year-old girl. She was shaking – they all do at the start. But where else do they go?*

And that was the problem – last century, there didn't seem to be anywhere acceptable for patients to go. The hospitals were the only option. Now, thank God, there are treatments in the community.

'Gabriel. These all the boxes for the Milton and hospital exhibition? No more anywhere else?' Noah calls.

Looking up, Willow recognises the verger from last night. He looks tired; moving slowly this morning. He must have slept as badly as she did.

'Morning,' she says, unsure what to say. The horrors of last night don't seem real today, with all this light.

'Alright,' he says quietly to her, by way of a greeting. Neither of them mentions the previous night, then Noah coughs deliberately, and Gabriel replies to his earlier question, saying, 'Where else would I put them?' His tone like a tack. The same as with the van driver. He stands, slowly pulling his back upright, and nods at Noah. 'Can you lift that on your own?'

Willow presses her lips tight. She's starting to like Gabriel.

Noah flushes pink and heaves a box up on to a stool. 'I would think so,' he replies, his curls bobbing, as Gabriel winks at Willow, shuffling off.

'We should be fine, thanks! We'll give you a shout if we need your help. No need to hang around!' Noah calls after Gabriel's retreating back.

'Some people,' mutters Noah. 'Honestly, between Gabriel and Jaz, I think I'm the only sane one here. I do practically everything!'

They work quietly and say little. Every now and again, Noah makes a suggestion and Willow agrees or disagrees, but after a few hours all the exhibits are on display. The tiredness of the night drags her limbs and her head spins a little as she stands to look at their work.

'He had a rough time of it, didn't he?' Noah says.

'Who?'

'Satan. Argues with the boss and ends up in Hell for all eternity. Tricky.'

Willow looks at a couple of pages of very early drafts of Milton's *Paradise Lost*, full of anguish and glory. 'Yes,' she says. 'You know he gave birth to Sin, too? Came out of the side of his head. That's quite a hangover. Women don't do so well in the poem. One is called Sin and the other commits the original sin.' She rolls her eyes.

Noah laughs. 'Amazing the museum managed to get hold of these.'

'Yes. There's a much bigger collection that did the rounds a few years ago in galleries, with some of Blake's drawings. Sir Rupert managed to find these six early pieces of drafts of the text. I love them.' She wipes the glass framing one. 'I do feel sorry for the poor old Devil. And Eve. No leeway for negotiation after one mistake. Absolute rule or nothing.'

'You're a Satan sympathiser.'

'Might be. My gran, Nonie, used to read me the text and somehow I really connected with it.'

'All that burning ambition and fiery struggle?' Noah raises his eyebrows.

Willow laughs. She looks at Noah again. He's not unattractive.

'Coffee?' he says. 'Come on, we'll go and let the security guard know he's on and steal his table in the café.'

'I'll follow. I better stay until he gets here.'

As Noah heads off, she stands back and takes a photo of the display to send to the boss. She lifts an empty box that's been left out.

'It's looking excellent,' says a quiet voice. It belongs to

an older lady, with auburn hair loose in a French plait. She smiles. 'I'm Lizzie, I'm the cleaner here.'

'Thank you. All done. Ready for the party later.'

'I suppose it will go ahead, even with Joel dying.' She speaks half to herself, then smiles. 'As it should. All your hard work.'

Willow hesitates. 'Oh, I hadn't thought... We could always postpone?' *Why hadn't it occurred to her?* It seems glaringly crass now. Champagne so soon after a death.

'No, it's the right thing to do. There's a vigil planned for tomorrow. He wouldn't want to disrupt everything.'

'Did you know him?' Willow asks.

'I did. I just can't believe...' Lizzie says. 'They're saying in town they're going to declare suicide. He was the verger here when I started cleaning in '74. I've been here over forty years. Apart from yesterday, I haven't seen him for...' She shakes her head, closes her eyes. 'I just can't believe it's over!' Tears fall quickly and she wipes them away. 'I'm sorry. I just wish I'd spoken to him now. I saw him come in...'

'I saw him fall,' Willow says, 'at the very end.'

They stand quietly.

Lizzie breaks the silence. 'After all these years... he'd changed, gotten older, but I knew it was him. And I thought about speaking to him, but I wasn't sure what I'd say. And now I'll never...' Another tear falls, and she is silent once more.

Willow thinks of Martha's ghosts and of pebbles falling from the roof in the dead of night. Her teeth clamp hard and her jaw clenches with a familiar ache.

Lizzie wipes the back of her face with her hand. 'I'm sorry. I've worked myself up. Good luck with the party tonight.'

Willow watches Lizzie as she walks away. She looks up at the huge red-and-blue window. She can't imagine blood spilling anywhere so peaceful.

13

MAARTEN

Maarten is sitting with coffee as Adrika enters, carrying the latest notes.

'How's it going?' he asks. 'Anything new?'

She sits down and shuffles the papers, crossing her legs. 'Not too much, to be honest. He was a verger most of his life. Also, he was a witness to the 1960s tower death that was mentioned. He was doing some work at the top of the cathedral on one of the walkways, and he saw a woman fall. It was an accident, not suicide. I haven't got all of the details, but there's quite a lot of press. Sunny is pulling it together now.' She glances down at a notepad. 'It happened so long ago.' She shrugs. 'Nothing else. His medical records are clean – no last-minute terminal diagnosis. No money problems – the opposite. I know suicide isn't so easily explained away, but no real tells.' She smiles. 'We could do with Sunny's mum. A bit of local background gossip might help throw some light on to something!'

'When exactly was this, the 60s tower death?' Maarten

asks. A few people have mentioned the fall. It seems to have shaken St Albans.

'Nineteen sixty-two,' Adrika says. 'Can't have been easy to watch. I wonder if maybe he's suffered from some kind of survivor's guilt? Maybe he wondered if he could have done something, saved the woman? Also...' She looks at Maarten.

'Yes?'

'Well, it seems the court ruled that it was an accident, but it seems a child was involved. I'll have to have a proper look into it.'

'A child?' He shakes his head and glances at the board. Last night's fall so far looks like a suicide, but they weren't finished with the investigation yet.

'You know what I thought was a bit funny?' she says.

Maarten looks at her.

'Michael Braxton, right at the end this morning. He said, "*For what it's worth, he's my father.*" Bit funny?'

'Is it?' he wonders. With English his second language, he doesn't always get the shades of colloquialisms. 'I assumed that's just something people say.'

She nods. 'They do, but it's more derogatory. He said it almost without thinking, but it's quite revealing. Maybe they're not all as happy families as they seemed.'

'They never are,' Maarten says. He checks his watch. 'Is Sunny around?' Maarten realises he hasn't seen him for a while, possibly since the cathedral.

'He's interviewing, I think. Background.'

Maarten can hear it in Adrika's voice.

'Is he dealing with some wedding crisis?' He raises an eyebrow.

Adrika looks uncomfortable.

'I get it. It's quite overwhelming.' Maarten is annoyed but when he thinks of his own wedding, he understands. They'd got married in Liv's home village. He'd left Rotterdam a few years before, and both his parents were dead. Large groups of Liv's family and friends attended, and if he could have run away and hidden in a hotel for a couple of nights, he would have.

Maarten sighs, shakes his head. 'I do not envy Sunny the next few days,' he says. 'The last-minute crises, the family arguments, writing the speeches—'

'Have you written Sunny's send-off speech yet?' Adrika asks innocently.

'Thank you, DI Verma. I think that's all.'

Adrika laughs as she stands, gathering the papers. 'Good luck, sir.'

14

WILLOW

Willow swings her arms as she enters the office. The light from the nearby stained-glass window tints the white walls a pale green. No Jaz, and Noah had headed off to a meeting. The office is quiet and she checks some paperwork that's been left out for her – a list of attendees for the party tonight; a few items to mention in the speech later when introducing the mayor.

Noah had bought her cake, and when she'd asked if he was going to the party tonight, he'd suggested he come and get her: 'I could collect you? Nice if we walk in together?' He'd reddened quickly, and she'd realised it was prompted by more than mutual convenience.

Her mum would tell her to go on her own and just live it. But then Mum had had an imaginary best friend when she was small, where she always got to be the visible one. Willow had got Fliss, and Fliss had got everything.

Willow had grown in the shadow of her shinier self. She remembers a friend of her mum's leaning down. *I bet you're the brainy one*, she'd said. Even small, Willow had understood.

Stuffing the ballet flats she runs around in at work in a bag, leaving them for tomorrow, Willow pulls out her trainers for the walk back to Martha's. She touches her dress, new and crisp in tissue paper. She'd bought two in the end, planning to take one back. She still can't decide. Blue or green. New shoes.

She still can't believe she's pulled this together. The promise of the evening ahead is part exhilarating, part terrifying. She can only pray that nothing will go badly wrong.

The taxi pulls up outside the house, in full view of the front of the cathedral. The sun is bright and Willow feels a load lift.

'Willow!' Her mum steps out of the car with her arms outstretched. Her hair was once light brown like Willow's, but when her natural colour left her, she embraced blonde. She now resembles Fliss, with all her golden highlights, more than Willow. She wears her huge sunglasses, which she is rarely without outside.

Willow knows the sunglasses work as a shield: a way to look pulled together, even if she doesn't feel it. Her mum wears contacts, good clothes... The days when she doesn't get out of bed, she is transformed. Willow is always taken aback by the vulnerable, older woman she sees beneath the bed sheets.

Arms wrapped around Willow, her mum whispers, 'Your dad's already had two glasses of champagne. You know what he'll be like now.'

Willow grins, and sure enough, her dad is red-faced and over-jolly. 'Willow!' he cries, arms outstretched. After two glasses, he usually embraces life then falls asleep. 'What a beautiful cottage!'

Her mum frowns slightly. 'Jack, it's more than a cottage, it's huge!' She looks at it and blinks. Five tall windows span the uppermost floor, promising a number of spacious bedrooms. Wisteria climbs one half of the house, and three chimneys rise from the roof. The door is dark green, sitting behind flower beds of reds, pinks and yellows. 'So pretty – it's like something out of an English film. And with this view!' She looks back to the cathedral. She shakes her head. 'I feel like someone just walked over my grave.' She stares out at tall doors, the park. 'Sweetheart, is that the tower where you saw someone fall? That must have been awful!' She looks up, her hand shading her eyes.

Willow leans in to the rear car seat and kisses her grandmother. Her cheek is warm, and she clasps Willow's hand, the veins standing thin and blue on the back of her paper skin.

'She fainted on the train when we told her you'd witnessed a death,' Willow's mum says.

Nonie rolls her eyes. 'Elspeth, stop your fussing. I'm fine. It was a shock, that's all.'

'Oh, Nonie! Should we take her to hospital, to get her checked?' Willow looks to her dad.

'It could just be the medication adjusting,' he says. 'Any more incidents and I'll take her.'

'Do no such thing.' Nonie's voice wavers a little. She looks at them all, then back to the house. 'I haven't drunk enough water. That's all it is. These blood pressure pills say I should drink all this water, but I never want to use the train loo.'

Nonie looks up at the house as Willow winds her fingers into Nonie's and kisses her again on the cheek. Nonie's hands are cold, her thin fingers tremble.

She tries to help, saying, 'I'll take your bags. Come in, there's cake, lots of cake.'

Nonie's breath is short. It blows on Willow's cheek, getting shorter and shorter.

Willow climbs out and holds out her hand to Nonie, moving slowly.

'Oh, my goodness,' Nonie says as she rises. Her face pales to grey.

'You've stood up too quickly – Nonie, here, hold on to me.'

'I'll take the bags in,' her dad is saying.

Willow holds out her arm, but Nonie pushes it away. 'I can manage, dear. Please, check your mum. Check your mum is OK?'

Willow looks at her mum, still staring up at the cathedral. 'Mum?' she calls.

Her dad is whistling, finishing with the bags, as Willow reaches her mum and puts her hand on her arm. 'Mum?' she says again.

A cry sounds out, not heavy, but light in the warm air, and they all turn, looking back to the taxi.

And as though in slow motion, Nonie, looking at the house, leans to rest on the car, and then carries on past it. She floats down to the floor, curling in a heap, like a scarf folding lightly on the ground. Willow reaches her just before her head touches down.

'Mum!' Willow shouts. 'Mum!'

Her mother doesn't turn immediately. Her body turns first, her eyes still fixed on the cathedral. She seems caught, like a bird catching a flash of something bright.

'Nonie!' she cries, finally seeing, as Willow holds her tight. Nonie is slight, but she is still heavy enough to mean Willow can't easily lift her alone.

And her eyes are tight closed. Nonie has fainted again and this time she is out cold.

15

ALICE

'What do we do about her?'

'Do? What do you mean, do?'

'She threw the hamster out of the window! She set the kitchen alight! It's getting out of control!'

Her father's voice is angry, and Alice bites her lip. Her stomach feels tight, and in her fists her nails dig into her skin. Opening them, she looks at the deep red grooves, counts the seconds until the fingernail impression vanishes back into smooth skin.

'I don't think there's anything to worry about. She's just enthusiastic!' Mummy now.

'Betty's not like that. It was Betty who came to tell us about the kitchen, and thank God she did! Betty didn't throw the hamster out of the window!'

'She was there, too. It's both of them, just playing. Alice means well.'

'I'm not joking. This has to stop.'

Her father's tone is angry. Frustration prickles under her skin. She'd been trying to help, trying to…

Alice cries, and Betty puts her arms around her. 'It will be OK,' she says.

'If it doesn't stop, then we need to talk to someone. It's not normal. What will people say?' He shakes his head. 'What will they say at the cathedral? It's ungodly!'

'She's our daughter!'

'Exactly. That means it's up to us to stop her. What else is she capable of? What will she do next?'

16

WILLOW

Willow checks herself in the mottled mirror of her room. Martha's house is faded in its glory, with white chalky walls crumbling slightly at the edges where the stone has grown old and been forgotten.

She looks fine. No, she looks *great*.

She spins again.

Fine.

She gazes at the short green swingy dress on the bed. Is it better than this blue one? Scrunching her eyes up tight, she tries to see herself afresh.

Her mum has gone to the hospital to help bring Nonie home. *Just low blood pressure*, they said: rest, water, and to wait for the medication to adjust.

'Willow, I feel terrible, I really wanted to come!'

'Don't worry,' Willow had replied. 'It will be a bit like a wedding – I won't get to speak to you at all. What have you told Fliss?'

'That we're all tired. I managed a coffee with her. I've said we'll help her write the place cards tomorrow afternoon.

When I say help, I'd imagine she'll be overseeing us.' Her mum had grinned. 'She had an appointment with the florist so we've arranged a brunch tomorrow and I said you'll come.'

Willow had nodded, pleased her mum was coping. She's exhausted. There hadn't even been time for food.

Willow's phone buzzes; Noah is downstairs. *Fine* will have to do.

Like Bambi in the new heels, Willow clings to the banister, which gives a little against the wall. The stairs have no carpet and the click-clacks on the treads rattle round the house like mice.

If she is honest with herself, going with Noah makes her uncomfortable. But he'd been so eager. When she'd said yes, he'd perked up like a puppy seeing a ball.

'You look amazing!' Noah says, then blushes. The dark rose hue of his colour visible in the fading April light.

'Thanks for coming to get me,' she says, thinking of seeing Theo and hit with guilt by Noah's expectant face.

Stepping into the dusk, Willow sees the cathedral tower rising above the park, illuminated in pale amber. Willow's teeth clamp tight. Last night sails back to her. She fights with her jaw to relax, but Joel Braxton falling is vivid in her mind.

Had she written off his cries as the wind?

Her teeth grind before she realises.

She shivers, and Noah puts his arm around her, tentatively. 'You OK?' he says.

His touch is kind, but she recoils, bending to adjust her shoe, allowing his arm to fall naturally.

'Yes,' she says. 'Just nervous about the party.' But she thinks of blood seeping between the flagstones, and of what Joel Braxton might have been thinking, standing above the site of his death.

Noah is talking. 'I did some research,' he is saying, 'after what you were saying, about your sister getting married in the cathedral. What's interesting...'

'Willow!' a voice calls behind her.

'Martha!' she says, surprised. 'Is everything alright?'

'You left your phone. Here. It was on the doormat. It must have fallen out of your bag.' She smiles. Her white hair is tied off her face and she wears a pale yellow dress. She's less drawn than last night, and must have added a touch of make-up. Her glasses reflect the fading sun; it's hard to see her eyes, and Willow searches for them. She looks younger today, she looks...

'Hello, Noah. It is Noah, isn't it? I've seen you at the cathedral. I volunteer there,' Martha says.

He nods.

'Thanks, Martha. Are you coming tonight?' Willow decides she likes Martha. There's something reassuring about her. Motherly.

'Oh, I did get an invite. I hadn't been planning on going. But now, maybe.' She smiles, and a shout of 'Willow!' is loud from the direction of the cathedral.

'My sister,' Willow says, gesturing. 'The one in the sparkles.'

The three of them look up.

Fliss, true to form, has dressed with flair. Willow immediately realises the green dress on the bed was the better of the two.

'I better head up,' she says to Martha. 'Hope to see you later.'

'It's 945 years old,' Noah says, as they enter through the centre door, tall and wide.

Willow thinks of cracking a joke about how old she feels so low on sleep, but Noah is staring at the high ceiling as though he's never seen it before.

'The Romans built the first abbey here,' Noah is saying, 'and St Albans was a key site in the Wars of the Roses. That's why they're painted into part of the roof. Not many people know that.'

Willow imagines Noah enjoys imparting knowledge rather than receiving it. She nods at him, offering appreciation in exchange for his efforts.

'Willow! There you are. Come and say hello to Sunny!' Fliss calls from halfway down the nave aisle, which is flanked either side with rows of wooden chairs, the ceiling tall and arched, the smell of stone walls calming.

The party is taking place mainly in the crossing, the space beneath the cathedral tower, at the heart of the cross. The exhibition is in the north transept, and drinks arrive from the café through the south transept. Here, in the nave, a hushed tone presides, and Fliss's voice carries clearly.

Organ music is soft, and Willow catches her breath, thinks of Nonie's hand, warm on hers. Closing her eyes, she sends a prayer to the hospital, *Grant, O Lord, thy protection*. The older man dying has rung a bell loudly on the fragility of life.

Noah tuts as Fliss calls again, her voice clear, jarring with the reverence of the high vaulted space, the colours of stained glass.

Then, frowning, he realises who it is. 'Your twin!' he says. 'Getting married.' He smiles, pleased with himself, and Willow nods, moving towards Fliss quickly, to pre-empt another shout.

'Sunny,' Fliss says, pushing towards Willow a blond man who is smiling, charming, but has what Mum would call an honest face.

'Lovely to see you again,' he says, looking shy.

'Such a big week,' Willow says, hugging him, and Sunny smiles again, his blond hair flopping forward, brown eyes warm.

'You're so alike!' he says.

Willow laughs, knowing that Fliss will not like this. 'Well, thank you. We are twins. I'm the older, so therefore the wiser.'

'Yes, well, you work in a museum and you're involved in this exhibition, so, you must be clever,' Sunny grins.

Willow's surprised – and relived – at liking Sunny. Fliss has dated some complete arseholes in her time. The better looking, the richer, often the more arrogant; some had looked Willow up and down, dismissing her quickly; or had fawned over her, to elicit praise from Fliss, buying good will, using Willow as romance currency.

Sunny does neither. He begins asking her about the exhibition, but Fliss says quickly, 'Sunny, could you go and get us some champagne? I'm so thirsty!'

Willow remembers Noah. She links her arm through his, pulling him forward. 'This is Noah.'

'Hello,' Fliss says, smiling quickly, then gesturing back to Willow, waving her hands in her face. 'Nails are appalling! I'll have to go again tomorrow. Honestly!'

They walk down the aisle, and Noah tries again to impart knowledge, offering a fact about this being a place of pilgrimage, that St Alban, Britain's first Christian martyr, was executed here; he points out the original Norman paint on the arches down half of the aisle, but Fliss overrides him with an account of how it had gone with the florist: '…and I had said I wanted yellow ribbons, but they've used gold, so I'm making them switch. You know Mum loves yellow, and I can't have…'

Noise builds: the chatter from the crowd lifts and echoes round the stone walls. It's a warm evening and people are dressed to celebrate, here early and in full flow.

The ceiling rises at the centre, below the tower, with a painted grid of crests of shields, and Willow sees Noah's white and red roses. The north aisle leads down the ancient pilgrim route to the shrine of St Alban, and Willow sees signs for Abbot Ramryge's little chapel and another saying she is standing in the longest nave in England. The noise of the cocktail party seems flippant against the reverence of the ages.

'Here we go,' Sunny says, managing three glasses, which fizz and sparkle, and Willow takes one, seeing DCI Jansen is over by the exhibition. He leans over a manuscript.

'Your boss,' she nods.

'Yep,' Sunny says. 'He's not one for much chatting, but he does like his poetry.'

'What's he like?'

'Clever. He's from Holland, Rotterdam, I think. He's a good boss. Can be a bit short. Keeps us on our toes. Fair though. His wife is really nice.'

As though on cue, a slim, smiling blonde woman, probably in her forties, squeezes Sunny's arm and says, 'There you are!' She offers both cheeks to Fliss, and says, 'Now, there're only a few days left. What can I do to help?'

'Liv, this is my sister, Willow,' Fliss says, and Liv smiles.

'Oh, you're the one responsible for this brilliant exhibition! My husband is loving it. I doubt I would have got him here otherwise – hates big social events. And I read that you collected the diaries of the patients? Fascinating – mental health back then was a different world!'

'Is Maarten still busy? With the death from last night?' Willow asks.

'A little. Am I right in thinking you were here? That must have been horrible for you.'

Willow nods. 'I do wonder…' But she can't finish.

'There isn't anything you could have done,' Liv says quickly. 'Nothing at all.'

'I could show you the tower if you like?' Noah says, eager. 'I could take everyone?'

Liv grimaces. 'No thank you, though you're kind for offering. Oh, Adrika!' She waves.

Willow takes a step back and says to Noah quietly, 'I'd like to. See the tower.'

Noah lights up, his eyes bright, and he blinks a few times,

his coffee-coloured curls bouncing. 'You would? Fantastic! Shall we go now?'

'In a minute,' Willow says. She'll need a few drinks first. Confronting the tower from which Joel Braxton fell might be one way to shift this unease, the chill she feels.

'Well, I can't wait! Look, your glass is empty. Shall I get some more?' Without waiting for a reply, Noah dashes off into the throng of perfumed people, and Willow closes her eyes for a second, pleased to have a moment on her own. She sees Sir Rupert's family in the south transept where the welcome centre begins, and they wave a hello. Someone from a TV magazine show is talking to them, and a photographer is taking photos of the crowds.

It's a success. Her first exhibition, her first find – it's a success.

'There you are.' A whisper in her ear; breath, fresh and as familiar as her own.

She knows the voice. She'd know it anywhere, but still a half-cry escapes. She trembles from head to toe. It's Theo. Of course it's Theo.

'Sorry! I didn't mean to scare you.' He looks abashed, but Willow is relieved. Her hands would have trembled anyway, and at least now she has an excuse.

'You're shaking. I'm sorry, I shocked you. Here, sit down?' He gestures back towards the altar, but Willow can't stop the trembling. The suddenness of Theo, the nearness of him. She shakes her head.

'Outside,' he says.

Carrying two glasses, he pushes open a door and steps

into the fading light. He sits on the grass, which overlooks the park. 'It's not damp.' He prods it, smiles.

The night carries the warmth of the sun, traces of gold, flickers of summer. Willow pulls out the cardigan in her bag, the thin cotton soft in her fingers, and as she lays it down, she thinks of her eighteen-year-old self, and what she would have given to sit in a dimming park with Theo Durand, drinking champagne.

'Better?' he says.

She nods. He hands her a glass, and tips his towards hers. 'Cheers.' He smiles. 'To seeing *you* again.'

The clink of the glasses is soft and the chime fades away, leaving the roar of a distant car, a dog barking, and music floating from the cathedral like candles, lighting the air, lightening the atmosphere.

For a second, she appraises him anew. She does this every time. Does she still feel it? He wears a T-shirt, and his forearms are lightly tanned. His fingers are long; he looks forward with a clean profile, relaxed. He's her height. When he hugs her hello, goodbye, she just has to step into him. *They fit*, she thinks. They've always felt as though they fit.

'So, how are you? It's been ages,' she says, not mentioning the last time they'd met.

'No,' he shakes his head. 'You first. Fliss told me you and Otis have split up?'

Willow curses Fliss.

'Yes,' she says, apologetic; it feels like a failure.

'Never liked him,' Theo says, shrugging. 'You know at park picnics when we all used to meet, he'd chuck his beer cans in the hedge when he was pissed. I used to nip back and get them, throw them in the recycling.'

Willow smiles, looking at her shoes. 'You didn't like him?'

Theo says, 'My father would call him a *conard*. Dad loves a good native swear.'

Willow laughs.

Theo looks at her, sideways on. 'Are you sad?'

Mulling this question, not sure she's been asked it yet, Willow can't decide. 'I don't know.'

'It was two years, wasn't it?' Theo asks.

'Yes. But it didn't feel that long. I think we fell into it. He chased. Then I was the one pushing. At some point we stalled. Something had to change – a change of girlfriend, as it turns out. He's now dating a nineteen-year-old influencer who drives a Porsche and never looks at a carb without crossing herself first.' She tells it for laughs, but the cringe is real.

Theo laughs this time. He nods back towards the cathedral. 'Love the exhibition. Very you. Hats off, Eliot. You breathe life into the dusty poetry and bring alive the forgotten voices of the past. Excellent move.'

'It is, isn't it? Fashion journalism for you, I heard?'

'Nah, still on the politics, but I did some sub-editing recently for a weekly, to top up funds. Go on, test me on something. I can tell you what an AHA is: Alpha Hydroxy Acids...'

'Make it stop!' She lifts her hands to her ears, pleased to be off the subject of Otis. 'Have you met Sunny?'

'Yes, good bloke. I was at their flat for drinks last night. He's funny, likes his beer. He can take the piss out of Fliss too – loves her. Adores her. But he's no pushover – good-looking, better looking than me.'

'Well, Fliss needs someone handsome. You're kind of good-looking, but, you know…' She pulls a face.

He pulls a face too, screwing his eyes up. 'Cathedral gargoyle?'

Last night begins to feel much further away, but tonight is work. Theo hasn't mentioned Brussels and she can't be the first.

'I've got to get back.' She stands. 'I'm going on a tour of the tower later, with one of the exhibition organisers. Want to come?' She thinks of how crushed Noah will be if she brings Theo. But she would take Theo anywhere.

'Sure, find me, before you go? I heard you were here, last night?'

She nods.

'Shit timing, Eliot. You OK?'

Draining the last of the champagne from her glass, she smiles. 'Yes, will be. Come on. We've been long enough.'

17

MAARTEN

'Oi!'

A chair falls backwards and knocks a pot of pens. There is clattering and a crash.

'Ow!'

'What's going on?' Maarten says. He'd stepped away from the crowds to look around the welcome centre near the offices and had heard the commotion.

The fight is quick with fists, but they flail like windmills; a lot of movement, but the blows are glancing. It's a flurry of arms and words.

'Get off, Jaz!' the man with coffee-coloured curls shouts. 'Get away!'

'It's my bag, Noah!'

'What's going on?' Maarten says again. 'What are you doing?'

'Jaz...' shouts Noah, but doesn't finish as he ducks from a jab. 'He has something, my—'

'It's mine! Give it back now!' Jaz shouts. He turns to Maarten. 'Noah, give it back—'

Noah muscles in, his face red as he speaks. 'On his desk, he has something – well, I could tell, and I was reading...'

Jaz flies at him. 'Give it back!' He grabs Noah's arms from the side, trying to clamp them. They both unbalance, falling to the floor.

'Stop!' Maarten shouts.

Noah is puce. Jaz's ivory skin has turned pink at the cheeks.

Both scramble to their feet quickly, staring at each other. Anger and a desire to justify leak from both.

'He was taking something from my...'

'He's hiding something! I saw him... He's got some letters, I think...' Noah waves his arms.

'Noah, this is my bag and these are my letters! You've got no right to—'

'I was just looking for a pen, when I saw them! And I *do* have a right, because those letters are about the cathedral, I'm sure of it!'

'You've no right to go through my bag!' Jaz is indignant.

Maarten looks from one to the other. Since he entered the room, the argument seems to have run its course. They both fall silent.

'They're your letters?' Maarten asks, stepping forward to Jaz.

Jaz nods.

'Please.' He holds out his hand to Noah, who hands them over, shame-faced.

'I'll take you in if I see this again tonight,' Maarten says. 'There's no excuse for stealing, or for violence.'

Dismissing them, he stares back at the desk.

The fight over the bag makes no sense. It's annoying. Why did Noah think he had the right to go through someone else's property?

Where else has he pushed his nose? It's characters like him who end up in trouble. Nobody likes a busybody. Hoping this is the only incident he has to deal with tonight, Maarten glances back at the office uneasily, before returning to the party.

18

WILLOW

The noise in the cathedral is loud, chatter echoing high up and rebounding off the gilt statues, the tombs, the coloured glass. Starving, Willow swallows some kind of vol-au-vent, fairly certain she hasn't seen one since the late 90s, and Fliss glides over, head held up, wearing a megawatt smile like jewellery.

'Willow!' she says, a good few strides away.

Willow's head reels. She's about three vol-au-vents away from whole. She's barely eaten today and the champagne has made her light-headed.

The chill of last night and Martha's ghosts sit with her – she hopes the tower will blast away this miasma.

'I've barely seen you! Come on over and talk to Sunny. It's like you're ignoring us!' says Fliss, clearly insulted she isn't the first port of call for Willow. Again. Always again.

Anger – be it hunger, tiredness, or genuine rage – fires in Willow's veins. She knows it's the wrong time to start, but the words are out of her mouth before she can bite them back.

'This evening isn't about you, Fliss. The wedding is a few days away, you know. Have you not read your own ornate invites?'

'Willow!' Fliss's eyes widen, and her hand flies to her mouth. She shakes her hair, literal shock waves. 'I'm here to support you. I didn't even want to come! I came because you clearly weren't going to celebrate with my fiancé!'

Her voice is loud; eyes swivel their way. Fliss is always able to command attention.

Willow tastes bile. She loves her sister, but the stress of pulling tonight together, and then witnessing Joel Braxton's fall... What must it have been like to face mortality at the top of a cold tower, with only the empty night and flagstones to hear your final words?

And Nonie, not telling Fliss she's been unwell to save her the worry. Willow is carrying it all. Again. The pressure is crushing.

'I've said a million times that last night was because of traffic, and tonight I have to work. This is my first exhibition! It was *my* idea to unite the texts, to gather some stories on the old hospital – this is *my* big moment. So far, I've spent a small fortune on your hen do, and last night, a man fell to his death in front of me, and you haven't asked about it once!'

'Willow, I'm getting married on Saturday!' Fliss's eyes narrow. Her chin lifts. 'I'm sorry if it's inconvenient for your work schedule, and I'm sorry about a man who threw himself off a tower, but all that doesn't change the fact this is my wedding. And I only get one. And if wanting my twin to share it with me makes me a monster, then so be it! I'm sorry—'

'Inconvenient for my work schedule? I told you about this exhibition first – weeks before you announced the wedding. What did you do – talk Sunny into proposing quickly so that you could trump me?'

From the look on Fliss's face, Willow can tell she's crossed the line. And maybe hit the nail on the head. People are now openly staring.

She's committed. There's no back-pedalling. And the resentment rises, arranging sentences into her head, like bullets.

'How dare you!' Fliss shrieks.

'I'm right, aren't I? What kind of person arranges a wedding date in the same week as their sister's first exhibition? What kind of—'

'It's my fucking *wedding*, you absolute bitch! How can you do this to me? You think you're so clever, waving your MA around at family events like you're the glory twin. Always creaming off the praise. Little old Fliss pushed to the side so that everyone can admire her clever sister—'

'Little old Fliss! My God, do you even know yourself? You take everything I have! You take everything I have and you trump it! Everything! Just because I came first, you want everything I want! Any toy I was playing with when we were young; every birthday party was your choice; you cry louder than me; you scream louder than me; and you take the man I—'

'What? What man? Oh, hang on... You're not talking about my ex, are you?' Fliss speaks slowly, narrowing her eyes. 'Are you wishing you could run off and find *Theo* again?'

Willow holds her breath. She's really gone too far now. Not just to Fliss, but she's exposing herself. She scans the area for Theo, desperately hoping he isn't nearby.

Fliss's eyebrows lift. 'I saw you two heading outside. For a *chat*. Waiting for my marriage before you move in on my sloppy seconds?' She tosses her head. 'Sometimes, sis, it's like you've decided you want to *hurt* me! Could you actually care any fucking less?'

'It's always you. Always. Never me. We're all dancing around you. Did you know that Nonie's in hospital right now, and no one's telling you? Just for once, can you drag your selfish, self-centred head out of your pampered, narcissistic arse!' Willow speaks quietly, delivering the lines with precision, and they slice her sister, their edges sharp.

Fliss spins on her heel and a few more heads turn her way. As she disappears into the mass of people, the crowd follow her with their eyes. Willow included. The sequins on Fliss's dress light her exit like an emergency landing strip. All flare and flash.

Shit, Willow thinks. She grabs another vol-au-vent from a passing tray, nodding a thanks to the waiter. Her blood rages and partly it's shame, but mainly adrenaline. Dumping years of pent-up frustration... She swallows the vol-au-vent fast.

Refusing to allow Fliss to ruin the night, Willow heads back towards the exhibition, trying to slow her breathing.

Martha stands nearby, talking to Gabriel. Jansen stands out above the crowd, his head the highest there.

She looks for Theo, but Noah appears on her left. He carries a glass of champagne, which he holds out. 'Want that tower trip now?' Noah sounds so hopeful, Willow could back out. But the pull from last night. The idea that Joel Braxton could see her – she wants to know what it's like to stand up there. Had the shouts been for her? And she needs air.

'OK, but I don't have long,' she says, looking at her watch: 9.20 p.m. Not long until the speeches.

Noah smiles. 'Come on then, this way.'

Heading towards the door for the tower, Willow is surprised to see Michael Braxton. He is standing next to a woman, who Willow assumes must be his wife. 'I can't believe he came tonight,' she says. 'He must be so upset.'

Noah looks in the direction she speaks. 'That's Heather, his wife.'

Michael Braxton looks exhausted. Willow thinks of her own father, how she'd feel if he'd been found dead this morning.

He stands at the side of the quire, what look to be organ pipes rising high up above where the choir would usually sit, and his head is close to his wife's. Her hair is tied up and the black looks blue under the lights. As a group step aside, Willow sees Jaz talking to them. He's leaning in, his shoulders hunched.

As Willow watches, Jaz gesticulates and Heather's head rears back.

Noah takes a step forward, in their direction.

'Noah, are we going up? I don't have long.'

'I'll just speak to Jaz,' Noah says. His hands ball into fists and his colour rises.

'Why?' Willow says. She likes Noah less and less. It would be wrong to disturb them. The family are drenched in grief, they reek of it.

But he's off, and Willow leans back against a stone wall, thick like an aged tree trunk, and watches. It feels as though a car crash is coming and she can't bear witness. Noah's voice travels across the chatter, rising up into the rafters on breath fuelled with alcohol and machismo.

'Still here, Jaz?' Noah's voice is louder.

Jaz sees him and looks surprised. He glances back to Michael and Heather, and shakes his head at them, only slightly, a warning.

What are they talking about? Willow wonders. *Why have they come?*

Jaz takes a deliberate sidestep, and so when Noah stops to talk to him, his back is to Michael and Heather. Michael takes Heather's arm, tugging; they walk quickly from the quire, towards the south transept and the car park. Heather looks back over her shoulder, reluctant.

They approach Willow.

'Michael, this is stupid! We should say something!' Heather is saying as they pass. Her voice isn't loud but it carries, staccato and tense. 'They might find out anyway, and then it will be worse.'

'No,' Michael says, or Willow thinks he says – she watches his mouth. He looks left and right as he speaks, looks over his shoulder. 'I think…' But Willow can't make out anymore. His mouth moves too fast, too furious.

Whatever he thinks is lost in the crowd as they pass by.

They head towards an exit as Noah arrives at her elbow with a puff of bravado.

'All sorted,' he says, and Willow detects an actual swagger.

'What? What did you say to him?' she says.

'Enough.' Noah takes the glass from her hand. 'Come on.'

19

WILLOW

'Over here. There're a lot of steps.' Noah looks dubiously at her heels. 'You could leave your shoes behind the door?'

Willow can't see Theo as they weave through the crowd. The mayor stands chatting nearby; her dark blonde hair bounces in curls as she laughs. Her general demeanour of relaxation has the reverse effect on Willow, remembering she has to catch her before the speeches. It's her job to do the introductions. It's 9.30 p.m. now – the speeches are at 10.30.

The heavy wooden door closes behind them after Noah unlocks it, and the noise of the crowd muffles. 'We'll take this route. The other door is too near the crowd.'

They pass through another door, and Willow looks upwards from the bottom of the stone steps, which wind in a spiral. She's already got the beginnings of a blister.

'Ready?' Noah smiles; his hands fly towards each other almost in a clap, but he stops himself just before skin strikes skin. His eagerness is repellent.

If she was younger, she'd be worried he would be

expecting something – some assignation at the top of the tower. But surely she does not need to worry – she tells herself this. Men are not entitled to affection, even if they do put themselves out.

She wishes she'd tried harder to find Theo; she can feel the warmth of seeing him again like a heat patch. It sticks to her, hot, makes her skin tingle. It sits beneath her clothes, present in her thoughts. She knows he will be hard to shift for weeks after she has said goodbye.

Some things, she thinks, pausing before the steps level out above them to a platform…

'…only remaining original tower in Britain,' Noah is saying.

… *some things just are out of reach.*

Is life about coming to terms with ungranted wishes?

Noah is breathing heavily as he reaches the higher steps. They climb up to a walkway that runs above the exhibition like an indoor balcony; the crowd is laid out beneath them. The steps have led them close up to the huge rose window, and looking at it, Willow breathes for a moment, dizzy from twisting. They stand silent, air coming in gasps.

Leaning over the thin wooden rail, she looks for Theo; she looks for Fliss. She can see neither.

And no one looks up. The whole of the cocktail party is spread before them, and she feels like an observer, a private viewing. She could do anything up here and no one would see. They're all so focused on the party. Heads bob, colours flash, laughter rises.

'We have to follow this walkway to the next set of steps,' Noah says. 'The belfry's up here. There's a floor where the bell-ringers stand, then another platform where the bell chamber is – we can see the actual bells hanging, all twenty-one of them. Then the roof.'

How did Joel Braxton manage these steps? Why would he choose to do this climb, if he was planning to throw himself from the top? Surely there are easier ways to die?

'The vergers come up here most days, to raise the flag or for other reasons,' Noah says, as though answering a question. 'I think they're the fittest of us all.'

Upwards they step, the smell of the cold stone steps and musty air intensifying as the walls narrow. They arrive at a platform, where huge bells hang still and silent.

'Imagine being here when they ring!' Noah says. 'These tower walls are seven feet thick, but the tower actually shakes ever so slightly when the bells ring – they do full peals for special occasions. It's the only cathedral tower in the UK made of Roman brick.'

Willow wishes she had more time. She'd like to touch these bells: their cold smoothness is seductive. Is this where Martha's ghosts sleep at night? She gazes round at the thick stone, the wooden beams, the rope. They are so high up. Alone.

'Here.' Noah offers a hand to Willow after the next climb, as he pushes the door to the top of the tower. Tucked under his arm is a small collapsed stool that he'd picked up from a ledge near the door.

She takes his hand, feeling it rude to refuse. His fingers are warm, soft – sweaty.

Pulling her hand away, she hates herself for taking it in the first place. Her teeth clamp hard.

He reads her retraction with disappointment.

Reaching for the stone wall of the doorway, she fakes a wobble, as though she'd needed the support to steady herself, and she tries not to apologise as she pushes past him, walking out onto the viewing platform.

The night air is chilled. It's dropped in temperature since she was sitting in the park with Theo.

'Beautiful, isn't it?' Noah says, close to her ear.

'Yes,' she says, taking a step forward. The centre of the tower rises up like a squat pyramid, and the viewing platform follows the perimeter, bordered by the crenelated walls.

Noah unfolds the stool and places it on the ground for her. 'To see over the crenellations more easily,' he says.

Willow looks out over the parapet and breathes in the park at night. She can see the cathedral laid out below like an aerial photo, illuminated in the amber lights. And the dark of the park is vast, like a new county. She thinks of the texts pinned up below: *this new World; at whose sight all the stars / Hide their diminished heads*, and she imagines the words falling to the roof below.

To her relief, she can barely make out figures on the ground. The angle just isn't right. The cathedral slopes downwards from here. If you wanted to climb up on the edges of the tower, you could slide most of the way down. Fall, then slide. Fall, then crash. Jump…

He wouldn't have been able to see her. If he was calling, it wasn't to her.

'Willow. I don't know what's going on between us.'

Fuck. Noah is taking control of the moment. And she

sees it. There are stars above. She's barefoot up here, in a short blue dress. She's come up with him alone.

'I don't know if you feel the same, but since I met you this morning, I've felt something. You're so beautiful.' His voice has taken on a wistful tone.

Willow looks determinedly ahead, looking out at the black sky, dotted with the silver of stars. The day has been too tiring for this. She has barely slept. She has rowed with Fliss, and somewhere below, there is Theo. Briefly, she allows herself to imagine it is Theo behind her.

'Willow.' He touches her shoulder.

She can't help it; she flinches.

'Willow. You must feel something. You wouldn't have come all this way, up here with me, on your own, if you…' He pauses, lets the unspoken speak for him.

Her jaw clamps tight.

Her thoughts crowd with Joel Braxton.

'Do you think he did it? Do you think he jumped?'

'What?' Noah's voice is full of surprise. Taken aback. 'You mean last night?'

'Yes. Do you think he jumped, or was it something else?'

'Erm… I suppose I think he jumped? That's what the police have said? He must have climbed up, then leant over. Or you could sit up on the parapet and just tip.'

He gestures round. 'I would guess he'd maybe still have a set of keys.'

'*This horror will grow mild, this darkness light,*' Willow mutters, the exhibits fresh in her mind. She thinks of a man standing here, pressed with some kind of hell, some horrors he could not face – did he try to reason his way forward? What had Nonie always said? *This too shall pass*. There are moments in life when everyone needs someone. Had Joel Braxton felt he had no one? Had he felt entirely alone?

'Willow.' Noah takes a step closer.

It's time to go down. 'The speeches,' she says. 'I have to go.'

'Not just yet, surely.' Noah's voice is soft.

Willow's hands flatten against the wall. Light-headed, blood sugar low. His words land at a distance. Looking at him, it's like she's catching up with him, a fraction out of time.

He takes a step closer.

She can't move.

'How was the private tour?' he asks.

His conspiratorial air is nauseating. A man died here. How does he think this might be a turn-on? She's here because guilt lies on her, refuses to shift.

Taking a step to the side, she reaches further along the wall. She turns, and gestures to the night, the park. 'But this – surely this is too much? If a man, an older man, wanted to die, this is too complicated? Maybe something else happened?'

'Willow, I don't know. What I do know is that we're here now.' He takes a final step towards her, and she can feel his breath on her cheek.

He's going for it. He's going to move in. For a second, Willow wonders if she should feel afraid. But no. She can just say no. She winds her fingers around the edge of the brick that runs the perimeter of the tower.

'Noah—'

Too late, his lips land on hers, and his fingers twist in her hair.

She pulls back quickly, stumbling up against the edge, and he falls forward, banging his head on the stone.

She yelps and he cries out.

Blinking, she leans back, wondering if the tower is shifting beneath her feet as her head spins. Her heart races and she trembles, trying to find her footing.

It happens so quickly. They clash, her head stings, as his fingers, caught in her hair, follow him in his fall – strands of hair twist in his hand, and he swears. Standing up straight, he wipes blood from his cheek.

Her heart thuds. For a second, she had panicked he'd fall from the tower they are so high up. Follow Joel Braxton.

'Noah! Are you OK?' Willow leans in to look at him, touches his cheek. 'God, you landed hard!'

'Why did you pull away?' He is cross now, and he lifts his fingers from his cheek, looking at the blood. 'I thought that's why you came up here? Why else would you come?'

'To see the tower and the view, Noah. Like you said. To see the tower. You can't just plant your mouth on women and expect them not to pull away, unless they're really into you. It's not politeness, to kiss someone back. I have to want to.' She keeps her tone reasonable, but her head prickles. She shakes it back, shakes off the needles on her scalp.

Concern for his bleeding cheek is tempered with irritation. Unsure which is winning, his pride makes the decision easy for her.

'Well, you could have at least hinted! Or let me know! I wish you'd made this clearer, sooner!' Noah has pulled himself up to his full height, and just as he opens his mouth to deliver what Willow can only imagine will be a speech about her refusal of his advances as some kind of slight, the bells ring.

Up so high, so close, they both grab the wall in surprise, and Willow wants to laugh. She looks at Noah, hoping it has broken the mood, but no. His pride is too wounded. He will need to get licking his cuts and scrapes.

Waiting for the ringing to calm, he steps to the door, pulling it open for her. Willow remembers the speeches, and her adrenaline, already running, races.

'Look, that's time ticking. I've got to go and start these speeches. Come down with me?' she asks, knowing what the answer will be.

'I'll be down in a minute,' he says, his voice pained and high. 'I'll just check my cheek first.' He touches the blood, almost black against his skin in this light.

'Well, I'll see you down there. I'll get you a drink?' She offers the last bit as an appeasement, biting down on the apology. She's had enough of apologising.

The stairs are easier on the way down for climbing, but their narrow confines are claustrophobic on her own.

Reaching the last few steps, the sounds of the cocktail party swirl up against the wooden door, and Willow's teeth clamp hard. She hasn't got long, and she hasn't practised what she's going to say. She thinks of Noah up on the tower, his cheek and his lunge.

Shit, she can't see her shoes. Looking again, all round the base of the steps, she can't see them anywhere.

Shit. They were brand new, good shoes – anywhere else

she'd never have left them, but who in this crowd would steal them?

Nowhere.

Cursing, Willow thinks quickly. Did she leave them here? Maybe she'd carried them to the top of the tower? She remembers taking them off. Noah had said to leave them…

She'd been so focused on the climb, on Joel Braxton, the speech, seeing Theo, the argument with Fliss – she can't for the life of her remember what she ended up doing with them.

She needs shoes. She has to go on stage and introduce the mayor. She doesn't have time to climb the whole lot of steps again. *The office* – she'd left a pair of flats in there, in her bag, stuffed under the desk. Her ballet pumps for running around at work. They aren't cocktail-ready but they'll do.

Skirting round the back of the crowd, her bare feet cold on the stone floor, she finds them. It's 10.25 p.m. She has to run.

The black ballet pumps are light on her feet, and she bumps into Sunny, skidding to a halt at the edge of the crowd.

'Have you seen Fliss?' he says.

She doesn't want to think about Fliss right now. Shaking her head, she scans for the mayor. 'No. Have you seen the mayor? I need to start the speeches.'

'Over there,' he gestures. 'I think I've really upset Fliss. I think she's stormed off. We had a silly row about nothing. She wanted to leave and I wanted to stay to hear the speeches.'

Willow looks at his face, brow creased, eyes searching

the crowd. She knows it's her row that has upset Fliss, and now she has caused problems for Sunny. He wasn't to know what had happened. Guilt prickles. 'Look, give me half an hour, and then I'm done. But don't worry, Fliss loves a drama.' Although this is true, Willow knows this time she went too far. 'I'll find you here?'

His blond hair flops forward as he nods. Willow smiles. 'Don't worry – Fliss won't have gone far. Really.' She crosses her fingers, and hopes it's true.

20

MAARTEN

Maarten flinches at the whine of feedback and the crowd begins to quieten. They turn their collective face towards a pulpit, ornate with gold and gilt, where the mayor stands alongside Willow. The mayor is pink and relaxed. Willow is smiling broadly, but she's blinking a little, and while her voice is clear, it catches as she begins speaking over the final whisperings of the chatter. Someone drops a glass, the shattering loud.

'Good evening, and thank you for coming,' she begins. She outlines thanks to the owners of the exhibition, what a privilege it is to work with the manuscripts. 'Without Sir Rupert's love of *Paradise Lost*, we wouldn't be here tonight. And personally, they mean a great deal to me. My grandmother read the poem to me when I was small, and they inspired my MA thesis.'

'She speaks so well,' Liv says, leaning in to Maarten as Willow continues with her speech, and he can smell her perfume. He slides his arm around her waist, enjoying being with her without talking to others.

Liv is still speaking quietly. 'I like her. She's a lot more confident than Fliss.'

Maarten raises his eyebrows. 'Fliss not confident? Have you got the right sister? She rules Sunny with an iron fist!'

'No, she doesn't. He lets her do that – he gives her the confidence to be her most unfettered self.'

'I bet she's always been like that. I don't get the impression Sunny impacts her much at all.'

'Oh, Maart, you always write him off. He loves her unconditionally – that gives anyone a boost. They're perfect together.'

Maarten considers Sunny's position as perfect for anyone. He makes a note to include that in his speech on Friday.

Willow is finishing up. 'And without any further ado, may I please introduce to you Mayor Nicola O'Connell.' Standing back, applauding, Willow smiles out at the crowd.

'She's changed her shoes,' Maarten says.

'Oh yes!' Liv says. 'Bet she'd had enough of heels. Mine are killing me.'

'And she's got something on her arm. Is it blood?'

'She does? Are you sure you're not working overtime?'

Maarten studies Willow carefully. She looks unsettled. 'I wonder if something's happened?' he says, frowning.

The mayor is closing her speech. 'And I would just like to say a huge thank you to Willow Eliot. She personally tracked down doctors and nurses who worked so diligently in their field of mental health at Hill Barnes Hospital, and some of the past patients. The amazing work they did there may look different with our contemporary hindsight, but time itself was different. In celebrating Sir Rupert's love of poetry, and in bringing to light the diaries of his stay in the hospital, Willow has given us an invaluable peek into the past and illuminated the need to further commit to understanding our mental health, and the importance of supporting those in need.'

The applause is resounding, and Willow smiles, blushing. Cameras flash in her direction, and she and the mayor stand together for a second, all eyes pointed their way.

Waiting until Willow climbs down the steps as the applause from the mayor's speech is ending, Maarten approaches. She's talking to Sunny now, their heads bent together. Sunny looks miserable.

'Honestly, this is Fliss we're talking about,' Willow is saying. 'You can't have upset her that much. She bounces back very quickly.'

Maarten hears her words, but she looks tense. Her shoulders are high; her tone…

Something's off.

'Everything OK?' he asks, smiling at them both.

Sunny nods, but he can't manage a smile. 'I had a row, with Fliss.'

Willow tries again. 'Look, I had one earlier as well. And I would imagine I've upset her much more than you.'

'What's that on your arm?' Maarten asks, looking more closely. It looks even more like blood.

Willow glances at her arm, then flushes pink. 'Oh God, was this here when I did the speech? Shit!' She rubs at it with the sleeve of her other arm.

'Are you OK?'

'Yes. I went up the cathedral tower, with Noah. He tried…

Well, he slipped, and cut his cheek. It's his blood – or at least I think it is. I knocked into him.'

'Willow, did something happen?'

'No.' She shakes her head, still rubbing at the arm. 'Is it all off? No, he sort of... well, he went for a lunge, but I kind of sidestepped, and he tripped. It was embarrassing, but nothing... untoward.'

Nodding, Maarten thinks that lunging at a woman when alone in the dark is at the very least clumsy and intimidating; possibly threatening. Probably all three.

'Where is he now?' he asks.

'Down here, I'd think, somewhere. He said he'd follow me down. I had to do the speeches.' She looks around, searching.

'Look, I'm sorry, I have to find Fliss. I haven't seen her for ages. I'm really worried,' Sunny says. 'I'll catch up—'

'Eliot!' A man walks over, sliding in with a hip bump. Willow visibly relaxes, Maarten thinks. This affection is not unwelcome. 'Well done!'

'Theo, you know Sunny. This is Maarten Jansen, Sunny's boss.'

'Hi.' Theo smiles a hello, turning back to Willow. 'I saw you head up for the tower visit – sorry I missed it. Can I get you a drink? We need to celebrate.'

Liv and Adrika arrive, talking, more champagne in hand. The lights in the cathedral are dimmer now, candles flicker. The noise swells again, now the speeches are over.

Liv hands Sunny a glass. 'Sunny, has Fliss gone home? Did you call her?'

He nods. 'Nothing.'

'She won't answer if she's angry,' Willow says. 'Wait a sec, is that her?' Willow heads off into the crowd.

Theo makes a start to go after her, as Maarten says, 'Have you and Willow been friends long?'

Theo's eyes follow Willow. 'Since university. We were all in halls together.'

Adrika joins them, and the chatter softens.

'You know Fliss,' Theo is saying to Sunny. 'She'll come round. Her moods never—'

His sentence is cut off by a scream, and Maarten's first thought is that someone has stood on the broken glass from earlier. He glances around, looking for hopping, for cursing.

But there's another scream, loud and bold, and it slices through the air like wildfire – catching. The temperature rises, the crowd jostles.

'What's going on?' Sunny pales. 'It is Fliss? Has something happened?'

Standing taller than most, Maarten searches the guests. There's a shift – a movement towards the centre of the cathedral. The guests are gathering.

'What is it?' someone shouts.

Then another scream.

'Maart,' Liv says. 'What's going on?'

Adrika is by his arm quickly. 'I'll go round the side. They're all moving. It's a crush.'

And they are. At first slowly, then fast. And then feet run.

'Is it a bomb?' someone screams.

'Up there! Someone's hanging from up there!'

Shouts and cries pile in from all directions. Running feet pound the stone.

'Stay here,' Maarten shouts to Liv, and he speeds through the crowd, skirting the edges, looking up.

Above one of the windows, a balcony runs above them. He hadn't noticed it before now, but it's high, too high for a fall.

And the reason for the screams, for the movement of the crowds, is that from one of the pillars legs dangle, kicking the air. The body is swinging, feet almost landing on the top of the stone rail.

Another fall?

Maarten shouts to Sunny, 'We need to get to him. Try over there! I'll try here!'

'I'm on it!' Sunny runs.

Adrika is shouting, 'Police,' as she heads into the crowd.

Men are now throwing themselves at the door in the transept wall, and they step back as Maarten runs up.

'It's locked!' one shouts. 'Have you a key?'

Grabbing the handle to the door leading to the walkway from which the man hangs, Maarten pulls, but it won't turn. Searching the crowd, he sees the verger, who is standing stock still, staring up with everyone else. 'Gabriel, do you have keys?'

The older man looks over at Maarten. His eyes don't seem to see him. Maarten shouts again. 'The keys, Gabriel! Do you have the keys?'

Shaking his head quickly, coming back to life, Gabriel nods, and steps forward. His hands shake as he pulls out a bunch of keys. His fingers tremble as he finds one, pushing it into Maarten's hand.

'I don't know... It's Noah. It's Noah up there! What's happening?'

Two men run over. 'We'll help!'

Maarten unlocks the door, and they run up the steps, taking two at a time.

Arriving at the balcony, Maarten sees the crowd below. People bottleneck; some are crying.

'Noah!' he shouts. 'Hang on!'

The air is colder up here; he runs to the pillar, which stands roof high.

Candles flicker below. There are people with phones out, and they light the crowd, throwing the shadowy surrounds into even darker shade.

The crowd is loud, fingers point. People scream.

'Noah!' He's almost there. Noah's arms are hanging round the stone pillar, kicking his feet to try to reach the safety of the balcony.

As Maarten approaches, Noah's hands slide, and he screams. He manages to stop his fall, by grabbing one of the arches below. He now swings over the cathedral floor, and the crowd immediately beneath scatter.

Noah is crying. His sobs are loud, and as Maarten reaches for his hands, the two men are so close behind he sees their fingers in his periphery.

Noah cries out, '…pushed me!'

Maarten climbs over the edge of the walkway balcony, and leans down. He manages to get hold of one of Noah's wrists; he holds it tight, reaching his long arms down.

One of the men behind him grab hold of Maarten's other arm. It is a long way down.

But Noah is trembling; Maarten can feel his fingers shake. 'Hold on!' Maarten shouts, leaning further forward.

As one of the men reaches from the other side of the pillar, almost within reach of Noah, Maarten feels Noah's hand, sweaty and cold, begin to slip.

'Hold on!' Maarten shouts.

But instead, there is a scream. And it comes from Noah, whose fingers slide through Maarten's reach, and his eyes light in terror as he falls, flailing, into the crowd below.

PART TWO

21

MAARTEN

The ambulance drives away slowly, lights flashing against the black of the sky, and Maarten watches it, steady over the flagstones. It turns the corner to skirt round the cathedral, heading down towards Holywell Hill.

Outside the cathedral, crowds are clustered and quiet. Some murmuring creates a gentle hum against the silence of the night. Officers stand at the perimeter of tape where the guests are gathered, and Maarten goes inside to find the super, who had been at the party; she's on the phone.

'Let's do it now,' she says, lowering the phone. 'Maarten, where are we?'

'We've got invite lists, but we'll need fingerprints for all guests. We're letting them out slowly now, but we need to take names and addresses as they leave. We're going to make a start on fingerprints for some. SOCO are heading inside now. We need to keep the inside clear. Keep the crime scene separate. The older guests are sitting in the pews in the nave outside of the scene itself.'

The woman who saw Noah fall stands crying, an officer

with her. The low-level buzz of the crowd elevates her words, lets them sail through the fractured air: 'He was screaming! Hanging on the edge!'

Maarten hears the officer try to pacify her, but she's caught up with telling. She gestures to the roof of the cathedral. 'I watched him! It was like he bounced. Oh my God! He swung round half of the pillar, then seemed to find his footing on a ledge. I thought he could climb back up, that he'd be OK...' She cries loudly, her voice full of tremor; her pitch elevates. 'I tried to run to catch him! He fell hard, like stone... He landed, his arms banged – they twisted, his legs...'

Her words, her voice, taints the air with unease. People point to the high platform up in the roof. Many are crying.

'What's happening?' The woman is loud, her voice shaking. 'Someone fell last night, too! Tonight, he said he was pushed. Someone's pushing people from the roof! They're being murdered!'

This last bit sears the edge of the crowd. The heat of the word bites, and Maarten hears 'Murder!' echo and ripple, all the way up round the edge of the cathedral, up to the roof, the balcony.

'Murder!' Maarten hears again, and he nods to Sunny, who immediately begins calming the crowd, speaking to the PCs, and Adrika waves at Maarten, gestures to outside. Something has been found.

'Ma'am, I'd better get going,' he says to the super, who is already back on the phone. 'I'll let you know once we hear back about fibres. I'm assuming if he was pushed, we'll find something.'

'Maarten, with all this press, we'll need answers quickly. The mayor is already speaking to the local paper. There were a lot of people here tonight.'

'Yes, ma'am. I'll get Robyn and Niamh here, to check the scene. If Noah doesn't pull through, then we're looking at a murder charge.'

Phone cameras are flashing, and some are filming. He wants to roar at them, but there is too much unrest already. He leaves the crowd control to his officers.

'Look,' Adrika says, pointing to something lying on the ground. The lights in the area are still going up, but an object lies clear in the yellow circle from the nearby spotlight. He and Adrika stand back from it, as the crime scene officers do their work.

'A shoe?' he says, thinking it feels significant – it fits somewhere. He'd been talking about shoes only recently.

'A high-heeled shoe,' Adrika says. 'And it's covered in blood. I'll bag it. Keeping this scene clean is almost impossible.'

Maarten thinks back. He'd mentioned shoes to Liv. 'Willow Eliot changed her shoes, before her speech. But if that's Noah Lewis's blood, what is the shoe doing outside?'

'She was on the roof earlier, with Noah,' Adrika says. 'Could she have come outside to try to dispose of it? If she used it on him?'

He nods. 'She said he was alive when she came down. I was worried – it sounded as though he'd tried something on up there. She was upset, but it could have been the bang on his head that had unnerved her. This is worth checking. Get a description of the shoes she was wearing earlier.'

What else? Something else bothers him.

'She had blood on her. She said he had fallen, but she was marked with his blood.'

Adrika scans the dispersing crowd. 'Where is she now?'

'Sunny's looking for her. Then he's going to take the staff from the cathedral to the station for questioning. We need to know who has keys to the balcony and tower. Whoever pushed Noah needs access but also the knowledge that he was up there. So who knew Noah was on the roof? We need to find out.'

Adrika is making notes. He thinks of a name, and it comes back to him slowly.

'Theo. Sunny said he'd heard Willow mention he was going to go up the tower with her. Did he follow her up? It seems unlikely – I can't imagine Noah making a move if there had been someone else there. However, ensure he's taken to the station. We should try to get the statements tonight, make some headway.'

He looks over to where the super stands. She's talking to the mayor.

'We've had so much press here. This is already high-profile. We'll need to move fast.'

22

WILLOW

Willow comes round. Her head aches and her back hurts. Muffled noise comes from the cathedral and she puts her hand out – a wall. She opens her eyes and looks round. She's at the top of the steps which lead down to the toilets in the welcome centre. The table of glasses and bottles of champagne sit unattended nearby. She's only a few steps from the south transept but she doubts anyone has spotted her on the floor.

What had happened? She remembers running footsteps. Had they come from behind her? Then nothing else.

'Miss, are you OK?' A man runs towards her, holding out his hand to help her up. She notices the uniform. *Are there police here?*

'Yes, I...' What was she going to say? Her head swims. She must have passed out. What had she been doing? The last thing she remembers is saying she'd look for Fliss. But it's a blank after that. She touches the side of her head. There's fresh blood. Did she hit her head when she passed out?

'Did someone attack you?' The officer helps her up and looks over her shoulder. 'Come on, you need to be checked over.' He offers his arm for her to take.

'Why are the police here? Attack? I'm fine – I think I must have fallen. I—'

'You know there's been an attempted murder?' He looks serious. 'Maybe they got you on their way out?'

'What?' Willow has no idea what's happening. She's dizzy. She still hadn't eaten enough. She'd drunk more champagne. Her mouth is stale.

'Someone else has been attacked!' the officer shouts as they enter the main exhibition. Police are everywhere. Someone screams from behind a taped area.

'No, I…' But events are taking over. Officers approach.

'We need medical assistance!' one of them shouts.

Someone in a paramedic's uniform approaches. It's all so fast. So quick.

'Willow!' It's Theo, he runs towards her.

'Oh my God! Theo! What's happening?'

'Theo, I don't…'

'Ms Eliot? This way, please.' An officer smiles, but Willow grips Theo's arm. She's been sitting in the station for about half an hour. All she's heard are whispers. Someone else had fallen from the tower: but it's all just whispers.

She'd been checked by a medic, had a CT scan quickly at a hospital, then had insisted on going to the station with Theo. She has to watch for vomiting, dizziness over the next couple of hours. Her head wounds are superficial.

She has tape holding them closed. They had offered to take her straight home, but Theo had said he was going to the station to make a statement, and she's unnerved.

Maarten had said she was free to go – they could speak to her tomorrow. He'd been kind at the cathedral, but there had been an air of urgency, which she couldn't ignore.

Cold, like a knife, had sliced straight through when she heard someone else had fallen from so high up. There's no point going home. She won't be able to sleep.

'Willow, are you OK?' Theo places his hand over hers.

Her fingers hold the cloth of his T-shirt like she's clutching her consciousness. Both aren't far from slipping away from her.

'Shall we take your statement now, Ms Eliot? Then you can head home?' An officer speaks kindly to her.

'I can come in with you?' Theo offers.

'I'm sorry, sir.' The officer is polite but firm. 'We were wondering if you wouldn't mind coming with us to another room, so we can take your statement?'

'But…' She starts but can't finish. There's a ripple in the room. The whispers have reached her. She knows. She knows but surely it can't be. Surely…

'Noah?' she asks. 'It can't be!'

The officer says little. 'I'm sorry. If you could just come with me?'

'No – please, can he come too?' Theo feels real. He is solid. She can't let him go. Not until there is something else she recognises. She searches desperately for Sunny or for Fliss.

The back of her mouth dries slowly, scratchy. Her head swims.

She is frightened. She'd been with Noah; she'd probably been the last person to see him and she has no idea why this scares her so much, but it does.

'Adrika!' she says, the name landing quickly. 'I'd like to speak to Adrika Verma. Is she here? Can she be the officer who talks to me?'

The officer exchanges glances with another PC. 'I'm afraid DI Verma hasn't returned from the scene of the incident yet.'

'Then I'd like to wait. I'd like to wait for her. Please.' Willow remembers to smile, not to be tricky.

'I'll wait with you,' Theo says. 'Here. Let's sit here.'

The two officers exchange looks again. One picks up the phone and dials a number, turning his head slightly away. The other says, 'Can I bring you coffee?'

Sinking to her seat, Willow's teeth chatter, her jaw aches. The dull pain radiates up into her head. She almost misses Theo's words, just catches the last part.

'...from the balcony.'

'What?' she asks.

'I was just saying, I can't believe he survived, after he fell from the balcony.'

She shakes her head in confusion. 'He survived?'

'Yes, looks like Noah survived,' Theo says. 'Surely you know? I just thought... Well, with everyone talking about it. I just assumed you'd heard. Noah fell from the balcony, but he's still alive.'

Willow leans her head back against the brick wall of the station. Posters are stuck around the room: *Wash your Hands. Think Bike...*

She had thought he must be dead. The night had been empty when they'd led her from the cathedral earlier. Theo had gone in a different car, and Sunny had been somewhere else. She hasn't seen Fliss since the row. Willow has felt so light-headed, dream-like.

'Is Noah OK?' she says. Her hand is still on Theo's arm as coffee appears. Its sterile styrofoam cup hot to touch. The warmth of his skin radiates through the pale cotton. And she finds all her sentences begin with Noah.

'Noah... He's alive? Oh, thank God. Noah and I were up there, and I don't see how he could have fallen – there's a railing...' Like dust, the rest of the words fall gently to her tongue. Disintegrating. Is it her fault? He had hit his head, and she'd left him up there – on his own. All those steps to come down, the platform with the bells. All it would take was a misstep, on the walkway, to feel dizzy. Her fault for leaving him. Again. Another fall.

'I'm sorry, Willow, I don't know any more. I heard someone say he was alive. I didn't see him. The ambulance took him. Hopefully they'll be able to tell us more soon. I know he came with you tonight. Were you and he close?' Theo's voice is gentle.

'No, no, we only met today. He was working with me on the exhibition. But I need you to understand. He... He couldn't have fallen. Oh my God, I left him up there. Bleeding, on his own! Theo, I...' She can't bear to say it. 'He might die! He might die and I would be the last one to see him alive... I can't believe I left him!' A cry sounds in the room, and Willow knows it's come from her because of the tightness in her throat. She thinks of last night, Joel

Braxton falling, the cry, the wind. 'Both of them. I could have stopped both of them.'

'It's not your fault,' Theo says, sincerity as solid as rock. 'It really isn't.'

Willow's hand rises to her mouth. Tears are wet on her cheeks.

23

MAARTEN

Maarten enters the station, blinking at the flashing lights of the press. The migration from the exhibition opening at the cathedral to the station has brought with it a change in tone. The relaxed interviews and smiling faces of earlier are taut and grey; the press are sharper. The second fall has spun the evening on its head.

'Have the statements all been taken?' he asks.

A PC stands quickly. 'All except Willow Eliot. She asked if she could wait for DI Verma.'

The clock on the wall reads past 1 a.m. Maarten runs through a list in his head: Willow Eliot's statement; SOCO were pretty much done; the stairs to the tower have been swept for fingerprints; the tower itself is finished. He will need to deliver a press statement. Noah's family had been contacted and were on their way to the hospital.

'Any word on Noah Lewis?' he asks.

'I'll find out. Last report wasn't looking good. He's going into surgery for a bleed. He hasn't regained consciousness,' Adrika says, following him in. 'I need to take Willow's statement. Want to come? I've sent Sunny home.'

Maarten nods. He'd been worried about Willow. Had she been attacked? What exactly happened between her and Noah up on the tower? The blood on her arm: now that Noah is in hospital, the blood is important for so many reasons.

He thinks of Noah's words: *pushed me*. Who could have pushed him?

Maarten had been with Willow after the speeches. They'd all been talking and Sunny had been worried about Fliss. But then Willow had stepped away.

How long had she been gone? Could she have got up to that level quickly, to push Noah? She'd left to chase after Fliss in the crowd, but how long had she been gone before he fell? Long enough to go to find Noah?

Had she lied about coming round on the stairwell?

His instinct is saying no, that he trusts her – but she could be lying.

Noah had been clinging on to the pillar before he slid to the arch. If he'd been hanging on for a while, then it's possible that he'd been pushed a little while before he fell. Whoever pushed him could have got clean away.

'Noah said he was pushed. We're going to have to assume his fall was attempted murder – someone who knew he was up the tower, and had access.'

'And Willow? If she was the last person to see Noah before the fall?'

'She's a suspect. But I checked and there are a few keys to the tower. Jaz has a key; Gabriel, the verger; and the clergy.

Maybe there was more to the fight between the two men than I thought?' He curses his earlier decisions. The clarity of hindsight can sting.

Adrika frowns. 'We need to ask about the shoes, and what happened on the tower.'

Maarten nods. 'Yes. Let's information-gather. It's late. We need all the pieces of the puzzle, then we'll start early tomorrow. Who was where, when, with whom. There were a few hundred people at the party tonight, but only a handful knew that the door to the tower Noah and Willow used had been unlocked – or had keys to open it. The other door was locked. They are our list.'

24

WILLOW

Willow forces her eyes wide, stretches her mouth, tilts her head from side to side. Her eyelids have started closing on their own. She'd asked for Adrika so she needs to be able to stay awake for her return. The PC had said it would only be a few more minutes.

She'd called her mum in the end. Fliss still wasn't answering her phone, and Theo wasn't allowed to accompany her into the room. She'd called her mum to let her know how late she'd be, and she'd insisted on coming up. Now Willow is heavy with concern that it will be too much for her mum to bear.

'No, please don't! It's so late!' Willow had tried to insist, but Mum had been clear.

'I'll take a taxi. I'll leave your dad in the house with Nonie. I'll put something in the oven. It will stay warm.'

For all of Willow's protestations, the idea of hot food and a warm house is everything. Her mind splits between Joel Braxton and Noah. If only she had paid more attention, not run off. If only she had kicked up a fuss – sent someone up to speak to him.

Finding herself praying again, after years of a withering faith, she adds Noah to her list: Joel Braxton, *may he rest in peace*; Nonie, *please keep her well*; Noah, *please may he pull through*. Whether she just needs to say it aloud, or whether she believes it will help, she doesn't know. But she'll take anything right now.

The sheer scale of the helplessness she feels, here in this room, is overwhelming.

'Willow? How are you holding up?' Adrika enters, smiling, sympathetic. Maarten Jansen enters with her.

Willow nods, touching the tape on the side of her head. It's still sore.

'I know it's late. Thanks for waiting.' Adrika smiles, and runs through the opening admin.

The room hums as Adrika asks the first few questions, eases her in.

Maarten says, 'When you went up with Noah, to the tower, whose idea was that?'

Willow drinks water, thinking back. 'He offered. He offered to Liv, as well.' Willow remembers Liv's shudder, and Maarten nods.

'And it was just the two of you?'

'Yes. No one else wanted to go. Well, Theo did,' Willow corrects herself, 'but I couldn't see him anywhere. And I didn't look for long. I had to introduce the mayor, start the speeches.'

'And was there any particular reason you wanted to see it tonight? You didn't think about waiting until the next day?' Adrika asks.

Surprised, Willow thinks carefully. It would have made a lot of sense to wait. Why hadn't it occurred to her? 'I think it was being there, the night before. Knowing that someone had been up there. Knowing that I was below.' She tries to articulate the guilt she feels. 'I was worried I could have helped. But I should have waited. It would have made sense.' She looks at Maarten Jansen. He watches her carefully. 'I wonder if I could have stopped whatever happened to Noah from happening, if I'd stayed up there with him. After he... Well, after he tried to kiss me, and I pulled away – after he had banged his head. I left him. I didn't want to hang around up there with him, on my own. But if I had stayed... I'm worried I'm to blame. I should have made sure he got down. Tried harder. Done more.'

'If someone makes you feel uncomfortable, on your own, then it's always important to leave,' Maarten says. 'How disorientated was he? Was he speaking clearly?'

Willow nods, relieved. 'Yes, he was perfectly clear. I didn't think it was too bad. He caught my hair, as he fell. I think he'd had his hand near...' She thinks of his fingers twisting in her hair.

Maarten's phone beeps, and he looks down. His face alters – it straightens, devoid of expression, and he looks directly at Adrika.

'I think we'll leave it there for today,' Adrika says, smiling at Willow, the smile too bright. It is clear there has been a change.

Willow feels cold. She grips the edge of the table with her fingers.

'Thanks for staying so late, Willow. Are you feeling OK?

Do you have someone to drive you home? I can have an officer take you.' Maarten's phone rings now, and he glances at it.

'No, my mum's here. I called her.' *It's Noah*, Willow thinks. *Has Noah died?* The look on their faces...

Adrika smiles, but it looks forced and they stand quickly. Willow panics. 'Is Noah...' she starts, but she can't finish.

Maarten Jansen's phone is still ringing. 'So sorry.' And he leaves the room.

'I'll call you tomorrow,' Adrika says, opening the door, and walking Willow down the corridor. 'Go and get some sleep.'

Her mum waits for her by the entrance. 'Oh, Willow!' Her arms are tight. 'Come on. It's not far. Only a minute in the car. Theo's with me. He's going to take the taxi on to his hotel.'

In the passenger seat, Willow looks out of the window at the sleepy streets, the low roofs, the cobbles. As they pull up outside Martha's house, she feels like she has been stretched: left part of herself in the station, fretting about Noah; delivered half of herself back to this house for respite. She thinks of Nonie and seeing her. She thinks of Fliss. Why isn't she answering her phone? Guilt is heavy when she remembers the row. She wishes she could turn back the evening. Rewind. If Fliss would just turn her phone back on. The calls still go straight to voicemail.

If ever she needed her twin, it is now.

25

ALICE

The cross on the study wall is large. Brass, with the body of Jesus hanging.

Alice's fingernails curl into her palms. There's a thumping in her ears, like when she puts her head under the water in the bath.

Daddy's study has always scared Alice. And it scares her now. She looks away from the cross and counts the books on the shelf: *one, two, three...* Right to left. Then left to right. *Twenty-three, twenty-two, twenty-one...*

Betty is already kneeling. But Betty finds kneeling and saying the words easy. Alice pushes her body into a kneel but it seems to unbend on its own. She fizzes. Her toes open and close in her socks, and her head rocks back each time she tries to push it forward.

'Be still, Alice! *God* is waiting for you!'

She tries again. Her knees rest on a thin cushion and Daddy begins another prayer.

At school, someone had found out about Hector. They'd made up a song about her, and when she'd gotten angry with

Colin Hegarty and stamped on his foot, the headmistress had called in her parents and said it was *no way for a lady to behave* and now Daddy is making her do extra prayers.

Betty doesn't have to do them, but she said she would. *I'll help*, she'd said, and she holds her hand.

'Just close your eyes,' Betty whispers. 'Don't worry. Just close your eyes and think of when we're being still in hide-and-seek. It's like that. Just be still and then it's over.'

Alice thinks of where she hid last time. She'd hidden behind the bed and Betty and their friends had looked for ages. Betty had known where she was – it is Alice's favourite place – but she'd never tell. Alice is good at finding places to hide.

Playing it out in her head, Alice realises she's been kneeling and now Daddy is saying something. And he must be saying it again as she hears her name, *Alice, Alice.*

Her eyes fly open and the big brass cross is still there. With the body, all kind of turned, and looking sad.

Why is Easter about feeling sad? At school they make it out to be happy, but Daddy always explains that it's about *sacrifice* and *prayer* and *sin*. Which don't sound much like things to celebrate.

She looks at her palms, and there are thin red lines where her nails have dug deep, and one of them has blood on it.

There had been blood on Jesus's palm, she remembers. And she feels her body grow hot. They'd put him in a cave.

What if she ends up in a cave? What if they roll a stone in front of her, and everyone forgets where she is?

She looks at the books again. *One, two, three...*

And she rubs her palm against her skirt, so hard it hurts.

But nothing stops the feeling of the bubble rising in her tummy, and she knows Daddy will be angry. She tries to swallow it down, but it just keeps coming.

Frightened, she feels it behind her tongue, then it bursts from her mouth. A huge cry, something like a scream. She can barely hear it through her ears – she hears it in her head – but she knows she's doing it out loud, because Daddy's face is changing. The colour is changing.

Betty squeezes her fingers tight.

Daddy lifts his hand high in the air, and running feet sound on the floorboards of the house. But Alice doesn't think Mummy will be in time to stop Daddy, and she closes her eyes, as his hand goes as high as it will go, then comes crashing down.

26

WILLOW

The night is sleepless. Faces loom, like cartoons. Willow sails the cathedral steps, looks through eyes that peer over the edge of the tower.

Nonie appears in her car. Her mum drives her to the station, an invisible friend whispers in her ear, flying in like an apparition.

Willow struggles to wake; drowning in sleep, she fights for consciousness.

The words whisper again like a lullaby.

Her mum, Nonie, eyes flying open; she screams.

Fingertips brush stone, fingernails bite. The night opens up in a black void, a pit. Then she falls, back on the tower. Down. The vast abyss.

A scream, piercing, cuts her like a blade.

Fliss!

Willow sits up, sweat so thick the sheets rise with her, a second skin, stuck like plaster. The room is dark.

Checking the clock, she's been asleep for only an hour or so.

There. Again. A scream.

Is it real or in her head? A scream has echoed round her head since she arrived at the cathedral. But this is an old house. Wind whistles.

She listens to the settling silence. A pipe creaks somewhere; a screech in the garden like a cry – but it could be a fox, or a cat fight. The night amplifies sounds, a twig snapping becomes a limb breaking. There is no rest for the fevered brain.

The idea of lying back on the damp cotton makes her stomach turn. Why is she thinking of Fliss?

Willow goes to the cottage window, single pane, sash. She lifts it and leans out. The sky is clear. Stars are vivid. There is a chill to the night; a cloudless sky. She sucks in the fresh air like it's water. It fills her up, calms her down. The park is dark. The low terraced cottages down the street just visible in the pale street light. This could be thirty years ago; three hundred years ago. The present makes no stamp here.

I just need sleep. Her mind is spiralling and her jaw aches.

Willow opens the closet in the room and finds sheets folded. Their crisp fresh cotton is soft on her cheek as she pulls them out, buries her face in them. They smell like her mum's house. Thank God for Martha, a sense of home so far from home.

Making the bed, Willow pulls off the damp bedding, piling it in the corner of the room; she changes her shirt, climbs back into bed.

Again. A cry. She's sure of it. Is she imagining things? Are there spooks in her head?

She pulls the pillow down over her ears, turns her face away from the distortion of the night.

Fliss!

27

MAARTEN

'It's Noah's blood on Willow's shoe,' Adrika says.

It's 7 a.m., Thursday, and Maarten had wanted to start early. Noah's operation had not gone well. He's in critical care, not expected to pull through.

If this fall became a murder investigation, then it was impossible to rule out a connection with Joel Braxton's fall.

'She's identified the shoes?'

'They match her description, and the other one was found on the roof of the tower. She's coming in later to verify but she gave us the make, size and colour yesterday.'

'So what – she kicked them off? She carried them up? Is she saying she definitely left them by the bottom of the stairs?'

'Well, interestingly, she isn't clear. She says she remembers Noah suggesting she leave them at the bottom, but it's possible she carried them up with her. She phoned here about ten minutes ago. Said she couldn't sleep and wanted to know how Noah is.'

'And what did you say?' Maarten asks.

'Nothing. She asked if he was dead – I didn't tell her anything, obviously. But the consultant operating on Noah said his right ear is injured. The consultant thinks it could have come from anything sharp – easily a high heel. They had to stitch it up when they operated – it's part ripped. However, it could have happened when he fell. The consultant is not a pathologist. But forensics worked fast on the shoes – the super is all over them. If Noah's blood is on the shoe heel, it makes sense Willow Eliot's shoe hit him.'

Maarten thinks back to the cocktail party, the swirl of people and seeing Willow after the speech. 'It's possible she hit him with the shoe during an altercation, but didn't intend for him to fall. It's possible he was more injured than she realised. She might have struck out, run away and not looked back. She could be scared – that she wouldn't be believed. If he attacked her, it could be a case of self-defence. Or maybe she threw her shoe at him and left him, and hadn't even realised?'

He thinks about how she had seemed last night. There had been no hint she was hiding something. She had been focused on the speech. 'Maybe the shoe is a separate issue to the fall from the tower. We need to be careful about focusing on it and allowing ourselves to be thrown off. Or someone else entirely could have used it. It doesn't solve anything – but it will be important.'

Adrika glances at her list of notes. 'We need to find out if anyone else was up on that roof. The door we used to get to Noah was locked, but the other tower door that Noah and Willow used earlier was still unlocked, and that leads to the balcony Noah fell from.'

'Did Theo Durand say why he didn't go up the tower with Willow?'

Adrika checks her notes. 'Actually, sir, he did go up. He said he followed Willow up later, looking for her. He didn't see her, but he did see Noah.'

'What?' Maarten thinks this through. 'Ask him to come in this morning. If he saw Noah after Willow came down, then that might clarify the incident on the tower. We're still left with establishing if she had time to reach Noah after the speeches, push him, then arrange to be found on the stairwell.'

Maarten thinks of Noah doing a guided tour of the tower on the night of the party. Then falling – if Maarten hadn't heard him say he was pushed, said it to Maarten, he would believe that a disorientated man could fall, after a bang to the head. But he had been clear: *pushed me*.

'We need as many witness statements as possible from the guests. Make that a priority today. Ideally, everyone on that list is spoken to.'

Adrika nods, makes a note.

Taking a swallow of the watery coffee he'd grabbed from the canteen machine, he winces. He'll need something stronger than this before the briefing. He'll need to be as awake as possible; he'd looked back at himself half dead in the mirror, shaving in the electric light this morning. They'd finished so late last night. Two nights with barely any sleep. For him, his team, and for Willow.

'The question that's coming in a lot, sir, is whether it's connected to what happened to Joel Braxton,' Adrika says.

Looking out of the window, the early morning sun is

bright. Maarten had walked to work, while the city had changed from dark blue to pale gold.

He nods. 'Two falls from the tower in two nights. *Kak*, they must be connected. I just can't see it yet.' He glances at the clock. Two hours. Two hours to beat the press. If they had found any links between the two men that they had overlooked, he'll be crucified.

'After this press conference I'll head back to the Braxton family. I've arranged to speak to the two girls. Come with me? They like you.'

She nods, touching her hair. 'I might wear a hat this time.'

28

WILLOW

'How is she?' Willow asks. 'How's Fliss?'

It ticks past 8 a.m.; she's waited until now to call Fliss. It was never good to try too early. But her phone is still turned off, so Willow had tried Sunny.

'I don't know,' Sunny says. 'She's not here.' His voice is tight. He coughs. 'Look, I'm really worried. I'm hoping she's gone to a hotel. She's been threatening to. She wasn't here when I got in last night, this morning – whenever it was. But I was late, what with everything. She'd mentioned it a few times last week – that it was all getting a bit much, and she could do with twenty-four hours on her own. And after our fight...' His voices trails to silence.

Bloody Fliss. It all happened to her, never to anyone else. She'd missed the end drama of the evening, so focused on her own. Willow's irritation settles on her like a familiar coat. She is so tired.

But underneath the irritation worms guilt. Willow's words come back to her: *selfish, self-centred*. And she'd thrown Nonie's illness at her like a grenade. And the scream in her nightmare, that sense of falling. It couldn't be… She pushes the image of Fliss, twisted and skewed at the bottom of a tower. It was just a nightmare.

Sunny had looked exhausted last night, the last time Willow had seen him. Dealing with the worry about his fiancée and a fight wasn't what he needed. Even Fliss would know that. What if something is really wrong?

Willow thinks of Noah. 'No real update,' Adrika had said when she'd called her earlier. But Willow feels sure she's lying. Their faces last night. Something serious had settled in the room as they'd stood to leave.

The only reason he had been on the top of the tower was to show it to her. And the only reason he hadn't gone down the steps with her was because of wounded pride.

Not my fault, not my fault. I didn't imply anything; didn't promise anything, she recites, but her natural inclination to guilt makes it harder to believe. If she hadn't agreed to see the tower, if she had just kissed him back…

'I feel so *guilty*,' Sunny says. 'If I had handled it differently, she might have not run off.'

Easier to calm Sunny's guilt than her own, Willow is clear. 'Look, don't worry. Fliss has taken herself off before. We were on holiday once, and she booked herself into a spa hotel on her own when the group got too much for her. I think it was mainly down to the fact it was her night to cook.'

Sunny laughs, but he sounds tired, drained. 'I've got this morning off. There's a five-star spa hotel nearby, I'll try that. There's another just down from the cottage you're staying in. It's got a lake – maybe you could try there, if you're not too busy?'

'I'll head there now. I need to speak to her. I shouldn't have argued with her,' Willow says, thinking that she really shouldn't have. She knows Fliss. Head-on confrontation wasn't how to deal with her. She needed to go in at an angle, point out the various issues involved gently – allow Fliss to see things for herself.

Fliss, Willow thinks, *has always resented coming second.* If she had emerged first, blinking and screaming, instead of eight minutes behind Willow, then maybe things would be different. At times, it is as though Fliss defines her whole life by the amount of attention she receives in comparison to Willow. All she had ever wanted, from a very young age, was the thing that Willow was holding. From toys to accolades to friends. As toddlers, Willow couldn't have a snack without Fliss pointing at it and demanding the same, only more. As they became older, the things that were desired became bigger, harder to match. More important to best.

In fact, it sums up their entire sisterly bond: Fliss must have the same, only more.

And does that, Willow thinks, *extend to boyfriends?* She'd never known if Fliss had made a beeline for Theo after seeing how Willow had looked at him. As a couple, they'd never made very much sense. But to take what Willow had set her heart on – well, that made sense.

'Willow, if we haven't found her soon, we need to escalate it.' Sunny sounds serious.

With his words, she finds she can't breathe. The scream from the nightmare is vivid in her brain, and she thinks of how much she loves Fliss. The thought of her, screaming in the dark, alone...

Willow heads down to the kitchen to get coffee before she searches for Fliss. It's been quiet this morning – no sounds of Martha around.

The kitchen is silent. Willow finds a cup to fill. Martha had told her yesterday that Lizzie would be in this morning to do a cooked breakfast, and there is bread for toast and cereal on the side. Willow picks up the bread, but her stomach churns. She feels sick. The thought of last night.

Why had she picked last night to confront Fliss with home truths? When all is said and done, she loves Fliss. Fliss is her other half.

The morning is bright, and she heads out into the fresh air, the winding, narrow road leading down to the lake. Houses bank high on either side, top heavy.

The manor house hotel stands tall and grey, taking in Willow's dishevelled, exhausted frame with an arched eyebrow.

Here I am, chasing you again, Fliss.

It's not the first time. It won't be the last. But what if something really has happened to her?

Willow needs to find her.

Fliss, for all her faults, will need Willow. She's always needed Willow.

As for Willow, if anything were to happen to Fliss, she'd be destroyed.

29

MAARTEN

'And so, Willow Eliot had invited you to see the tower with them?'

Adrika has begun the interview, and Maarten sits down, light with the relief of the press conference behind him. He studies Theo Durand, wondering just how much of an accident it was that only half the story was told last night.

'Yes, but I missed her when they went up. I bumped into Fliss – she was on her way out. I must have caught her after her row with Willow. I didn't know about the argument at the time. She was pretty angry, storming out. I know Fliss quite well, I know when she's storming out. It's one of her specialities.' Theo smiles, to show he's joking, but it's misplaced. Surely, if your friend is upset, you'd ask her what was wrong?

'So, what, did you follow her, make sure she was OK?'

Theo adjusts his expression. 'Sorry, I didn't mean to be flippant. Yes, I followed her out. I offered to walk her home, but she said she'd had enough for one evening. I watched her leave but she stopped to talk to someone on the way out, so I figured maybe she was calming down.'

'And then?'

'Well, then I went to follow Willow up the tower. I'd seen her leave, from across the room, when I was talking to Fliss. I have no idea what time it was. I'd had a few drinks.'

'And you actually went up the tower? To the top?' Adrika asks.

Maarten watches him. Is this the truth?

'Yes, after a bit I went up, saw Noah. Well, not to the top. I saw him locking a door. I asked if Willow was still there, and he said she'd already gone down, so I just turned around and came down. He was a bit off, to be honest. Not very friendly.'

Maarten looks at Theo. 'You're here for the wedding. You're a friend of Willow's?'

'Of Fliss and Willow's. I dated Fliss for a while at university.'

'Oh? For how long?' Adrika asks.

'I suppose about three years?'

Maarten allows his eyebrows to lift. 'That's not dating, that's a relationship. And she invited you to the wedding?'

'She invited our group to the wedding. They're not arriving until tomorrow night. I came early to see Willow's exhibition. Be great to have a reunion.'

'And when you came down the stairs, there was nothing of any interest? Nothing unusual?'

Theo lifts his shoulders, almost in a shrug, like an apology. He looks to the ceiling and back to Maarten. 'You know, there was something funny. He shouted. I hadn't really thought about it.'

'Noah?'

'Yes. As I was walking down the stairs, I thought he shouted something. I waited for a second to see if he called again – I wondered if he was shouting for me. But then why would he? He doesn't know me. I waited for a second, but there wasn't anything else. No sign of Willow, so I headed down.'

'And do you know what he shouted? What the words were?' Maarten watches Theo's face.

'Not exactly. I didn't think it was meant for me, and it made no sense. But he must have been talking to someone. There must have been someone else there.'

Maarten leans back in his chair. His lifts his mug but it is empty, and he holds the cold ceramic against his lips as his mind swims. He lets it all pool together: a locked door, a bloodied high heel, and now this shout. It feels like paint blending. Blue meets yellow to become green. Red waters down to pink. Altogether, when paint is mixed en masse, it ends up black. He needs to let those colours swirl only so far, before it all seems opaque.

30

WILLOW

'How's Nonie?' Willow asks her mum, sitting down at the table at Martha's. Lizzie has arrived. She's out of her cleaner's smock this morning, wearing an apron and currently talking to Willow's dad about a suspicious mole. Once they recognised him as the doctor from the morning show, people often told him their ailments.

'I took her a cup of tea up earlier. She's OK, just tired. I think the journey was too much,' her mum says. 'And speaking of tired, you look exhausted. How did you sleep?'

'OK,' Willow lies.

'And your head, sweetheart? How is it today?' Her mum reaches out and touches the tape holding together the wound Willow got when she fell.

'It's OK. I've got a lovely purple bruise to accessorise with the bridesmaid dress.'

Her mum smiles. 'Come on, have a coffee.' She pulls out a chair.

'Have you spoken to Fliss or Sunny this morning? They might have some news about that poor boy who fell?' her mum asks, pushing jam towards her, and Lizzie places eggs on the table.

Willow mentally crosses her fingers, lying to her mum. 'No, not yet. I'll catch up with them later.' Fliss hadn't been at the hotel by the lake. The sun had been warm as Willow had stood on the stone step, heart sinking, and left a message for Sunny. There had been no check-ins at the hotel yesterday.

Willow takes an egg. 'I haven't heard anything about Noah. I called Adrika earlier so hopefully she'll phone back. Theo's going in to the station this morning.' He had called just as she'd finished leaving Sunny's message.

'I'm heading in to give a statement now,' Theo had said, his voice clear down the phone. 'What is it – 8.30? I can't imagine I'll be long. Meet you 9.30 for a coffee?'

Willow had named the place she'd been to with Adrika.

'Theo, you don't think…'

'What? What is it?'

'You don't think they might think I pushed him? Well, do you think I might be…'

'A suspect? You're not a suspect, Eliot.'

'Are you sure?'

'Why would you want to push someone off a balcony? I'm sure you have to have a motive. If you inherited a million pounds or something, then sure, but why would you want him dead? The police aren't mad. Look, I'm going in now, but I'll call once I'm done. Go and eat something, Eliot. You're spiralling!'

Willow stares at the egg with toast – and hopes that Sunny has found Fliss.

'Is Fliss coming for breakfast?' Her mum looks round the kitchen, as though Fliss may appear from behind a chair.

'I haven't seen her this morning,' Willow says, trying to keep it light. 'I said I'd meet Theo in town, and then I'll try and catch up with her soon.' Willow tells herself this isn't a lie. 'Shall I pop up to see Nonie now?'

'I'd give her some time to get ready. Meet us here for morning tea later? And bring Fliss. I can't wait to see her. She must be so upset about last night – it's only two days until the wedding.' Her mum frowns. 'Something wrong?' She looks over at Lizzie, who is cursing a cupboard door.

'I can't get this open.' Lizzie's pale auburn hair is high up in a bun this morning, and strands escape as she pulls on the handle.

'Here, let me.'

'Elspeth, I'll do it,' Willow's dad says, crossing the kitchen, but her mum leans in and kicks the bottom of the door as she pulls the handle. The old larder cupboard swings open.

'How did you manage that?' Lizzie stands back in surprise. 'It's been like this since I've worked here. Martha usually leaves it open for me, but I haven't seen her this morning.'

'I'm old, you get the hang of things.'

'Impressive!' Lizzie lifts a box of tea from the larder and brings it back into the room. 'Would you like a cup?'

'The fabulous Elspeth.' Willow's dad drops a kiss on her head, then follows her gaze out of the window at the cathedral. 'Quite a view.'

'Yes, but you know cathedrals give me the creeps.' Willow's mum pulls a face. 'I have no idea why people are drawn to the gothic in literature and films. There's nothing appealing about cathedral towers and cobbles.'

'Here, Elspeth, want to try your magic touch on this old biscuit tin? I have no idea why Martha doesn't throw away this old stuff. She's sentimental.' Lizzie hands over the tin.

'Remember I fainted in Paris in the Notre Dame? Poor Jack!' She laughs, leaning against him. 'He was so embarrassed. Marries a woman who can't cope with his favourite piece of architecture.'

'You've done it!'

Looking down, Willow sees the biscuit lid in her mum's hand.

Elspeth laughs. 'Do I get two, for helping?'

31

MAARTEN

Adrika rings the doorbell as Maarten checks a message in from the super – overall, the press were wildly theorising. There was no concrete suspect. Even his attempt to settle a theory about a serial killer from one paper hadn't quite worked. Two falls in two days has caused a media frenzy.

Heather opens the door. 'Come in. The girls are excited to see you, Adrika. They've even painted you a picture.'

Maarten notes how tired Heather looks this morning. Her black hair again tied off her face. A white roll-neck jumper only further washes her out. The death has hit them all hard.

'DI Verma!' the girls shout loudly, racing towards Adrika, whose shoulders brace slightly as two pairs of feet skid to a halt.

'Can we do your hair?' they ask.

'No, girls, remember what we said. DI Verma is here to speak to you, but we said we'd leave her hair alone this time. She's really excited about seeing the picture you've painted. Who can get it?'

Legs flailing, they power into the front room.

'Can you sit in with us?' Maarten asks. 'We won't take long.'

Heather nods, eyes dry but red-rimmed. 'Michael will be back soon. He went in early to speak about the vigil tonight. He's going to lead a prayer. It's at 8 p.m. if you'd like to come along.'

Settling into the deep sofa in the spacious room, Maarten leans back, making sure he looks relaxed when speaking to the girls. He isn't, though. They're sharp as tacks, these two.

Adrika makes a start, and they inch towards Tuesday night.

'I hear you were up, asking for Mummy?' Adrika says, building a Lego tower. She gives a piece to a hand smeared with melted chocolate. They had brought chocolate cookies for the chat.

'Yes, I heard something. At first, I wondered if it was the Easter Bunny coming early. I went on to the landing, but it was dark. I couldn't see anything. So I shouted for Mummy.'

'Oh, I see,' Adrika says, nodding, handing her a blue brick. 'Look, if we put this on top, it might get wobbly – shall we put a few more bricks at the bottom?'

The girl nods, and the other girl, with the blonde hair, narrows her eyes. 'Are you asking if we saw Grandpa leave?' she says.

Maarten waits a second, leans down and picks up a Lego figure. He plays with it for a second, adjusting the arms, the legs. 'Did you?' he asks, as casually as he can manage. 'Did you see him leave?'

'Yes.' She nods importantly. 'I saw him go down the

stairs. I thought maybe he wanted cake. We had made him a cake, and we said he couldn't eat it until the next day, as the chocolate was still setting when we put the topping on after tea. But I thought about it in bed. And if I was a grown-up, I think I would have gone and had some. Grown-ups get to do whatever they want. It's unfair,' she says.

'Did he say anything?' Adrika asks, looking at the Lego, starting another tower.

'No. I think he saw me, because he looked up the stairs, and I heard him say, "Shhh". Like people do when they're asking you to be quiet. Then I think he said, "I love you", like Mummy and Daddy always do at bedtime. So, I knew I may as well go back to bed. I don't think he was going to give me any cake.'

'Ah, I see,' Maarten says, handing her the Lego figure. 'Well, I suppose you might get some cake soon?'

'We will. But we're going to save that one for Grandpa. Daddy said he's forgotten something from his house, so he's gone back home to get it.'

Maarten smiles at her, and sees Heather, sitting on the sofa behind the girls, obscured from their view. Grief awash on her face.

'Will you need to speak to them again?' Michael asks, as they head into the hallway. He is grey, tired.

'I don't think so, but I'll let you know. Thanks. I know it's not easy.'

'Do you really think there was something... untoward about his death?' Michael shakes his head. 'It's not that I think he had any reason to... you know. But it seems crazy that someone would want to hurt an old man?'

'We really don't know at this point,' Maarten says. 'But the truth is important. Your father deserves a full investigation.'

Michael nods. They're almost at the door.

'I realise you'll want an idea of when the body will be released, so you can let the rest of your family know. I know how difficult all the arrangements are around a death,' Adrika says.

Michael looks at her in surprise. 'The rest of the family? I suppose so. There isn't much of a rest of the family though. My mother died years ago. And he only had one sibling, who isn't with us anymore.'

'Jaz is his grandson, isn't he?' Maarten asks. 'We spoke to him yesterday, at the cathedral.'

'Yes.' Michael looks uncomfortable. 'Well, yes. Except...'

Maarten says nothing. Michael doesn't finish.

It's Adrika who prompts. 'Yes?'

'Well, Dad didn't get on so well with my brother. Or Jaz. I don't think they'll be attending the funeral.'

Maarten catches Adrika's eye.

Her tone light, chatty, she says, 'Is that a new thing?'

Michael's colour changes a little. The earlier grey tinges with pink. He scratches the back of his neck. 'They had a falling-out.'

'Really? What about?' Adrika persists, in the same chatty tone.

'I... I don't know, really. I didn't get involved.' Michael pauses over his words, sounds uncomfortable. He looks back to the lounge, as if for Heather.

'When was this exactly?' Maarten asks.

'Years ago,' Michael says. He shrugs, looks to the floor. 'Must be twenty years ago at least. To be honest, I think Jaz has only met his grandfather a handful of times. Even in the cathedral, they barely spoke.'

'And you don't know why?' Maarten presses.

Michael shakes his head. 'They had a huge row, years ago. We still see Ferdie, but we don't talk about it. He's my older brother. About seven years older than me. He left home a few years after Mum died. I was only five. Dad sent him to boarding school when he was eight. I didn't go. When Mum died, he stopped coming home for the holidays. Then he left school as soon as he could.'

'And you have no idea? Why they fell out? No idea at all?' Adrika asks.

'I think you're better off asking him. I'll give you his number.'

'Hello? Ferdie Braxton.'

The voice is clear, forthright. Maarten can hear the rush of wind blowing against the phone. There is engine noise in the background.

'This is DCI Maarten Jansen,' he tries again.

'Sorry! Can you give me a minute? Hang on.'

Maarten is back in the office and calling from his desk landline. It's on speakerphone and the rush of noise fills the room. There's a click, the bang of a door and someone shouts, 'See you in ten!'

'Hi? Much better. Sorry, go again. I heard St Albans.'

'Yes, I'm DCI Maarten Jansen, and I'm investigating the death of your father.'

There's a beat. Maarten can almost hear the nod.

'Go on.'

'Well, firstly, I'd like to pass on my condolences. I'm so sorry for you and your family, for the loss.'

'Thank you.' He's polite, but his tone is short. 'How can I help you?'

'Your brother mentioned you didn't get on well with your father. I wanted to ask you about that.'

'Why? You think I travelled a few hundred miles to kill him?'

'No, Mr Braxton. But we're just trying to ensure your father gets a full investigation. Family relationships are procedure.'

'Call me Ferdie.' He sighs; the sound of the air folds into the room. 'That's fair enough. Is this because I'm excluded from the will? Because Michael gets everything? On paper it would make me angry with him, I see that. Michael gets it all. He'll be rich now Dad's dead. I haven't spoken to my father since I was sixteen. He was a proper shit. A full-on crock of shit. I know you're not supposed to speak ill of the dead, but he won't know, he'll be burning somewhere.'

Maarten gives Ferdie Braxton a minute to compose himself, but his clear tone doesn't waver. He doesn't sound upset. 'Michael said you two had a row, years ago?'

'Oh, he told you, did he? He's usually quiet on the matter. I gave up talking to him about it, years ago. He's younger than me, he didn't live through it in the same way. Some things need to be experienced.'

'What did, Ferdie? What needed to be experienced?'

'The violence. The sheer unadulterated, bloody and vindictive violence. Not to me, not really, but to Mum. Joel Braxton was a wife beater. I was packed off to school when he saw me watching one too many times. He was practically a professional. She didn't die young at his hands, she died to get away from them.'

'The part I don't get,' Adrika says, as Maarten finishes briefing her about the telephone call, 'is why Michael won't engage with it. Does he even know? Surely he'd care – it was his mum?'

'Ferdie said he told him, when he was sixteen. But that makes Michael nine years old. That's no age to even understand what it means. And they've never spoken of it since.

'Ferdie said Michael tried to broker some kind of peace between him and his father when he was about twenty, but Ferdie shut him down. He said he referenced the violence once and Michael just closed down on him; they didn't speak afterwards for months. Ferdie didn't want to rupture their relationship any more. They've managed to become friends, it seems. Michael was the one who helped Jaz get the position at the cathedral. I get the impression it's Jaz who's the angriest. Ferdie said he told him once, when he was old enough. He told him why he never saw his grandfather. He'd been asking, and he said it came to a head.'

'Christ, that's a lot to take on.'

Maarten nods. 'Yep, it sounds like it went badly. Jaz was

upset. He said he regrets it, but he couldn't risk...' Maarten shrugs. 'It's a hard call. If he's right – and I have no reason not to believe him – if he's right then that's something that is difficult to forgive. He's not a suspect. He's an airline pilot and was flying into Manchester when his father fell. He didn't land until Joel Braxton was dead.'

Adrika scribbles on her notepad, underlines something. She looks at Maarten, pen still in hand.

'Should we pay Jaz another visit?' she asks.

Maarten smiles. 'That was going to be my next suggestion.'

32

WILLOW

'Over here!' Theo raises his arm and Willow spots him sitting with coffees. The café is filling up. The sun is bright and people sit with dogs and chat in clusters; a bag of Easter eggs sits at someone's feet. The wooden tables are small, and as she sits down, the nearness of Theo makes her smile. But it disappears quickly.

'Did you find her?'

Willow shakes her head. 'I'm really worried. So close to the wedding. God, I hope nothing's happened to her. I'd rather she'd just changed her mind about getting married than thinking something awful has happened, that she's lying somewhere, hurt, unable to tell us, bleeding. I wouldn't put it past Fliss to just run off for a while for attention, to pay me back. But Mum, Dad and Nonie are here. She'd normally make much more of an effort to see them. Mum is expecting to see her for brunch this morning.' Willow lifts the coffee; it's strong and bitter and exactly what she needs. 'Even Fliss would usually have calmed down now. Her tantrums are over quickly.'

Willow feels a clutch of guilt as she says this. She'd known how stressed Fliss had been, and still she had let rip years of frustration. She should support Fliss, not choose this moment to chuck it all at her.

Her sister, for all her flaws, is her sister. And Willow is not without her own faults. She remembers winding Fliss up when they were small – knowing how to provoke her. It wasn't just about that either, not just petty childish games; Willow had always known that Fliss wanted something from her. Nothing concrete; she had wanted her approval, wanted Willow to allow her to shine a bit brighter. And Willow hadn't. Not always. Fliss had always craved something from Willow, and to be honest, a lot of the time she just had no idea how to give it to her.

There have been moments when Willow knows she could have pulled back. And she hasn't. Something arrives with the firstborn. Even with twins. Something is given to the eldest, that the one coming second can never get hold of – the ephemeral fragment, the halo of the first footsteps.

She wishes for yesterday, when Fliss was here and she had the liberty of criticising her. Now, out of reach, she would claw bricks with her bare hands to get to her.

'Have you any twin inklings?'

Willow shakes her head. She knows Theo is mostly joking but she has reached out for that invisible cord – that meant if Fliss was in pain it touched her too. But there is nothing. And that is the scariest thing of all. Without Fliss, she is only half a person.

The scream she had heard in her dream last night flies

back to her, turning her cold. The feeling of falling. Had it been Fliss's scream?

She can't think that way.

'Willow?' Theo says gently. His brown eyes are kind. 'Willow, what does Sunny think?'

'Sunny?' He had sounded worried about Fliss, rather than worried about her changing her mind. 'He's checking out a few more hotels. He's concerned. She still hasn't come home or turned her phone on.' Willow scans the customers: relaxed, some typing on a laptop, some eating cake. But the chatter reaches her:

Did you hear about last night? Someone fell from the cathedral!

I heard they threw themselves off the tower.

I think that was the night before – there was another one! It's crazy!

I saw cameras down there earlier. The BBC!

Two deaths in the same way—

I think they were different, but both in the cathedral…

I heard it was two murders!

'It's all over the city,' Theo says. 'It's a big deal, Eliot, in a small city. They're reporting that Noah said he was pushed. Someone heard and told the press. I bet the police are livid. The rumours are in overdrive. One report mentioned that a shoe was found too, with blood on it.'

Willow swallows a throatful of tears. 'What's happening? It feels like everything is running out of control.' The last part of the conversation lodges in her brain. *A shoe*. She had lost her shoes, and Adrika had asked for a description that morning when she had phoned to ask about Noah.

Her shoe has Noah's blood on it?

'Don't let your mind go dark – this isn't some horror show. Something sad has happened – it's likely the first was a suicide, and if Noah banged his head, then he will have been disorientated.'

'Theo, I was there the first time. I left Noah the second time… Why do I feel like this is about me?'

'Eliot, you don't even live here!'

'I know – it's ridiculous. But I can't sleep. I could hear crying last night…' She wonders again. It wouldn't be the first time she and Fliss had shared senses.

'You're staying in a really old house. It will be the wind, or maybe your landlady had a bad dream – or was crying about some tragedy you don't know about. It won't be about you. You're tired.'

But the voices drift across the café:

I heard there was loads of blood.

There's a vigil tonight. I'm going.

That verger worked at the cathedral for almost his whole life.

What a way to die.

Indeed, Willow thinks, putting her cup down, the bitter taste of the coffee not as bitter as the thought of Joel Braxton, falling from the tower, and her unable to save him.

What a way to die.

33

WILLOW

Coffee, sweetheart? I haven't heard from Fliss yet. Are
you with her? She's not answering her phone. See you
back at the house soon? All OK? xxx

Reading the text, Willow curses. Still no Fliss. What does
she say to Mum and Dad? She can't tell them. Not yet. Sunny
had called the hospitals. And he said he was meeting Adrika
later, to go over statements to see if anything stood out.

If only she had kept her mouth closed. Had she chased
Fliss outside? To some danger? No, surely not. It was
classic Fliss to storm off in a sulk. Maybe she was probably
punishing Sunny for something. Nevertheless, panic mounts.
The thought of Fliss makes it hard to breathe.

The cathedral office is quiet. Jaz is around somewhere,
and she'd seen his uncle, the clergyman, when she'd come
in. She thinks of their faces last night, pinched and tired.
Grief and some kind of rage. It was all part of the process,
but it was odd they were at the party, when the death had
been so fresh?

On impulse, she walks down to Gabriel's office. The door is ajar, and she knocks.

'Hello?'

Smiling, feeling awkward, Willow enters. Gabriel rises, looking surprised.

'Come in – it's Willow, isn't it?'

Wondering why she's here, she steps closer. 'Horrible couple of nights,' she says, and as he nods, she realises he's the only other person who understands what it had been like, seeing Joel Braxton fall.

'Did you know him?' she asks. 'Joel Braxton?'

Gabriel's face is guarded as he replies. He looks down at the desk. 'I'd met him,' he says.

'Do you think he killed himself? I wonder, with Noah last night…' She trails off.

'There's no accounting for people,' he says. 'You can never know what they'll do, why they'll do it.'

She nods, looking at Gabriel's head as he busies at the desk. 'I'm sorry, I'm disturbing you.' She turns to leave.

'No, you're alright. Come in. Here, I have biscuits.' He smiles, pulling the lid from the top of a tin. 'I've been verger here for twenty years. I've never seen anything like this.'

'You're from France?' she asks – she's heard Theo's dad's accent, but Gabriel's is much milder. No more than a lilt.

'Originally from here. St Albans. But I spent much of my life in France,' he says. 'There wasn't much round here to keep me.'

She nods, unwilling to intrude. Looking past him, she thinks of the carvings on the bricks she'd seen the night she arrived. 'I saw initials on the bricks,' she says. 'When I came to get the stool from your office on the night I arrived. They looked like they had initials and dates carved into them. What do you think they were – love conquests from years ago?' She grins.

Gabriel rises. Expression falls from his face. 'You saw them?'

'Yes,' she stutters, feeling like she might have overstepped the mark. 'When I came to get the footstool. But I know you didn't make them. The dates were years ago, long before you came. I was just making conversation…'

He looks at her, as though he struggles with something. 'I've got some work to do,' he says, finally.

She doesn't need to be told twice.

The house looms large, flowers in their first bloom across the patio and the sun bright on the white paint. Daffodils lift their faces upwards. Willow sees a figure by the door.

'Sunny?' He's dressed in jeans and a hooded top.

'Willow – I was going to call, but I just had to come and see you. I can't bear it. I'm really worried about her.' He holds his phone, glancing down at it, but it's silent. 'No word anywhere.'

Willow's jaw tightens. 'Can we tell Maarten? Can we report her as missing?'

He frowns, biting his nails. 'I'm going to speak to him. What if it wasn't just the rows? We fought over nothing – she wanted to leave early and I wanted to stay to hear your speech.'

Willow thinks of Fliss last night. 'She was pretty upset'

– *selfish, self-centred*, her words fly back to taunt her – 'it was a stressful night...' She doesn't want to say anything out loud, tempt fate.

'Willow, what if something's happened to her? What if while we're hoping she'll forgive us and call, she's somewhere in trouble? What if she needs us?'

'I heard voices?' Willow's mum opens the front door. 'Oh, Sunny! I was wondering where you and Fliss were. I've just heard about that boy from last night. In critical care. One paper said he's not expected to survive. His poor parents.'

Willow closes her eyes, the ground reeling.

'Willow!' Her mum cries out but Sunny has his hand on her arm. 'Come in,' her mum says. 'Lizzie has left tea and cake on the table.'

The room is still spinning as Willow sinks into the sofa; the pressure of not worrying her mum about Fliss is too much. She looks at Sunny, nods a little.

'Elspeth, we can't find Fliss. Not since last night. We think she may have gone to a hotel.'

'Fliss?'

Willow nods. 'We're looking for her, Mum.'

'She's done it before,' her mum says, clearly thinking, her eyebrows lifting and falling. 'I tried calling her this morning, but no answer.'

'Sunny is going to tell Maarten,' Willow says, taking her hand.

'The police!' Her mum's eyebrows lift higher. 'You think you need to involve the police?' She turns to Sunny, but it is Willow who replies.

'We don't know where she is, Mum. And last night was...'

What had it been? 'Well, two falls from the cathedral – it's worth checking in with them.'

Her mum's face is white. Her hands, holding the china cup, are shaking.

'Mum, are you OK? I'm sure Fliss is OK.'

'The idea of falling... from a tower. You know I hate heights! That poor boy – and now you say Fliss is missing!'

'Mum.' Her mum has tears on her face and Willow grabs a tissue from the flowery box and leans forward, wiping them away.

'We'll find her,' Willow says. But for all her promises, when she reaches out for Fliss, feels for her, there is nothing. Except a sensation of falling. And the echo of a scream.

34

MAARTEN

Adrika knocks on the door of the flat for a second time.

'This definitely the right one?' Maarten says, looking down the corridor.

'Should be.' She knocks again.

A click sounds behind the door and it pulls open a crack. 'Yeah?'

'We're looking for Jaz Braxton. Police.' Adrika's words disappear through the gap of air between them.

'Police?' The door opens further. A man stands before them in tracksuit bottoms and hair standing up on end. 'Excuse the state of me. I was in bed. I work shifts. I'm a paramedic.'

'I'm sorry to have disturbed you. We have this as Jaz Braxton's address. Is he at home?'

The man shakes his head, yawning. 'No. Haven't seen him. But then he knows to be quiet when I'm asleep. Wouldn't he be at work?'

'The cathedral is closed today.'

'Oh, shit, yeah. The fall. I spoke to the crew who brought him in.'

'Do you know where he might be, if he's not at home?' Adrika is polite.

'Erm… Have you tried his uncle's? Oh, and he had a date last week – but I don't know her details. He might be with her? Sorry. I'm shattered.' He yawns again. 'I haven't seen him much in the last few days. He was out last night. At that party.'

'And when you have spoken to him, would you say he's seemed like himself?' Maarten asks. 'Nothing unusual?'

'Well, you know his grandad's just died? He's been upset. Obviously. Poor bloke. He was round here the morning he died. Can't believe it. I see it a lot with work, but you never get used to it. Here one minute, gone the next.'

'Joel Braxton was here?'

'Yeah.' He yawns again. 'Yeah, he came round. I was getting ready for work. They had a cup of tea. Had a bit of a row about something – a lot of swearing. He was gone by the time I was dressed.' He shakes his head. 'Not the last words you'd want to say to your grandad. If you'd known. Hindsight and all that.'

'Do you know what their argument was about?' Adrika asks, as Maarten's mind spins.

'Nah. Something and nothing probably. But there was shouting. Look, I really need to head back to bed for a bit. I can give you Jaz's number? You probably want to speak to him.'

Outside, Adrika shakes her head. 'Still no answer.' She lowers her phone.

Maarten looks up at the sky, blue with sun falling through the clouds like fingers. He had thought when he was young it was the kind of light that collected souls. Took them up to heaven. He has no idea what he thinks now.

'So, Joel Braxton visited Jaz. That's the first we've heard of it. I wonder if his dad knows? Or Michael Braxton.'

Adrika taps the back of her phone with two fingers. 'Doesn't sound like it.'

'Yes,' he says. 'And Jaz has been missing all morning.'

'What's our next move?'

35

WILLOW

The cathedral feels different tonight, Willow thinks. She thinks of Joel Braxton in the empty aisles at night, and of the champagne then blood last night. Right now, it's filled. People wander the aisles for seats. Someone has put coats on a row of chairs up ahead and some discussion has broken out about whether they can reserve so many seats.

Willow ducks behind a pillar. She wants to be here for the service – she feels a responsibility to Joel Braxton that she can't shake. But she doesn't need a front-row seat. She's promised her mum she'll join them for dinner in town afterwards and she wants to be able to slip away unnoticed.

She checks her phone. Sunny had called earlier to say he was heading to the station to talk to Maarten then he'd meet her here.

The chill in Willow's stomach has been there since late morning. What if Fliss *has* fallen? What if she was mugged on the way home and is lying in a ditch?

Willow thinks back to coming round on the stairs, with fresh blood on her head. She'd been so insistent it had been nothing, but shadows have appeared in the grey of her memory, moving quickly. What if she had been attacked, and the same person then attacked Fliss?

She'd walked the whole park that afternoon looking for any trace of Fliss. It was like she'd vanished.

'Abide With Me' begins on the organ; there's shuffling, people stand to sing. The notes fill the room, and Willow closes her eyes. She had been there, and she could have helped. She'll always remember it.

'Hello, Eliot.' Theo squeezes in next to her, and he winks, picking up a hymn sheet and holding it out.

'You came!' she whispers, more pleased than she can say.

'Course I came. You haven't seen Fliss yet, no? Any news?'

She shakes her head. 'Nothing. Sunny's worried. I am too. Should I even be here?'

'Let's stay for this.' The music is swelling now. 'I'm right here, Eliot.'

Willow sings, *Help of the helpless*, and the hymn sheet blurs with the tears she can't shake.

There is a hand at her elbow.

Heart racing with shock, she jumps, jolted, but it's Sunny, and she begins to calm until she sees his face. He is anything but calm.

'Follow me,' he whispers, stepping backwards.

Theo lets her pass first, then squeezes out. His face shows little, but his lips are pressed together, thin and white.

Sunny is moving quickly, and they almost jog after him.

Feeling on display, the last thing she had wanted, Willow follows him. Their footsteps are drowned in the final verse, and they leave the nave as the congregation sits for a reading. *Come to me, all you who are weary and burdened, and I will give you rest...*

Willow races to catch Sunny.

'What is it?' she whispers. It's twilight in the cathedral – the bright of the fading sun outside has faded first in here. The light is soft and coloured with glass.

'Come here.' Sunny leads her outside and into the graveyard that sits at the east end of the cathedral. Headstones from centuries ago lie, and they pass these, moving up to the top corner of the graveyard, and Sunny leads her fast over the grass, crossing the path, to the small cobbled car park, through which the path to the city winds uphill.

'Here – I found this. Don't try to touch,' he says. 'It's down the gap in the drain, which is why I think it's stayed here so long and hasn't been handed in, or stolen. The police are on their way. Adrika's here.'

Willow sees Adrika now, standing quietly. She's dressed in a white T-shirt, jeans and a leather jacket. She looks younger. Willow can barely breathe.

'What?' Willow steps forward.

'Don't touch,' Sunny says again.

And as she peers round a tree, down a gap next to the cobbles, she sees it. It's Fliss's bag. The shiny one with the fancy label from last night, from the cocktail party. And half out, smashed, the screen shattered, is her phone. It lies at the bottom of a drain dip – a thin gap between the path and the flower beds.

'What?' Willow hears herself say again. 'Why?' But she looks at herself from a distance, like she watches the scene in a playback. She is cold. Fliss.

Fliss.

Sunny shakes his head. 'She'd never leave her phone.' The last rays are thin as they pick out the pale brown of his eyes, his skin – whiter than normal. 'Something has happened to her, Willow.'

Willow is dizzy. Fliss – in trouble? She reaches out, clutches at the tree for support.

She finds Theo, who takes her other arm. The graveyard behind them is dark and cold, and the surroundings tilt.

'I've phoned it in,' Sunny is repeating. 'This is evidence, so don't touch. One death, one in hospital, and Fliss missing. It's too much to ignore. It's too much of a coincidence.'

Willow opens her mouth, but nothing comes out. She has no words of hope, nothing to offer. Her fingers tremble, the bark of the tree hard under her nails.

Sunny's phone rings and he answers. His words swim around her, and she hears only a few of them, *no blood, smashed phone, possibly taken.*

Fliss.

It is her fault. Whatever has happened to Fliss will always be her fault.

36

MAARTEN

A drone flies low over his head. Dogs bark as they run from the van, and the area around the cathedral is awash with vans, bodies, torches, huge lights. The air is fresh and cold; night is rushing in and the hollow feeling in his stomach feels emptier with each shout, each flash of light, each glimpse of Sunny's face.

'Sir, we'll start up here, then sweep around the lake. Divers are on standby.' He nods as his officer leaves to group the additional volunteers, lead them out to cover the park carefully, thoroughly.

Two falls – both of which are under investigation – and Willow being found unconscious last night have bumped the missing status of Fliss Eliot to serious risk. Sunny had been in to talk to him that afternoon – already worried, Sunny had covered the first steps of a search. Doors had been knocked on, hospitals checked, and CCTV of the cathedral had been thoroughly examined after the party. There was no sign of her anywhere after 10.23 p.m. last night.

Now, a smashed phone and an abandoned handbag,

found outside the area of a crime scene where Fliss Eliot was last seen, has stirred the investigation.

Word had got out that it was Sunny's fiancée they were looking for. Officers off duty had come in, some retired officers, volunteer officers. St Albans may be a small city, with a smaller station than many in Hertfordshire, but they were loyal.

'Maarten, I'm joining this one.' The super nods as she walks towards him, zipping up her coat, lifting a hand to wave goodbye to a car driving away. 'I had Mick drop me. We didn't have anything on this evening. Thought I could lend a hand.'

'Ma'am,' Maarten nods, smiling despite the tension that rises like steam around him. 'Thanks for coming.'

'You'll need all the help you can get. The park is over a hundred acres. We think she could be injured?'

'Yes. Her sister was found unconscious in the cathedral after Noah Lewis's fall. Fliss's disappearance is the third of three suspicious acts within the space of an hour, and they mark a path. Noah is pushed, Willow knocked out – possibly knocked unconscious – then, leading out of the cathedral, Fliss's phone and bag have been found.' He shakes his head. 'If she's out here somewhere, under a tree, or fallen in water... Well, it's warming up, so we're lucky it's not winter, but the nights are still cold. It's been almost twenty-four hours.'

The super glances at the officers, standing in their search teams, ready to start. 'Sunny is here?'

'Yes.' Maarten hadn't even suggested he go home.

'OK. Good luck, Maarten. I'll see you when we're done.

Can we take statements tonight from those who saw her at the party? I'd like to have something ready for the morning.'

'Of course. When we're done here. I'd better head up front. Catch you at the end.' He steps out towards the top of the park, a chill on the air and in his throat.

'What's the Dutch for gut instinct, Maarten?' the super shouts after him.

He turns, surprised. '*Voorgevoel*!' he calls, the dogs even louder now.

'Well, mine is good. It's telling me we'll find her. Not too long now – a good outcome. I can feel it!'

He manages a smile as he nods, turns, and the flagstones of the cathedral grounds become the grass of the park beneath his boots.

Why is it he expects this night to drag long? *Kak*.

He cannot shake the emptiness in his stomach, the ever deepening pit. He needs to ignore his instinct on this one. Procedure, a careful search, and they *will* find her.

Yet he cannot shake his brain free of the questions that line up ready to ask later, about where she could have gone, who might have taken her, whether they… Fliss is so young. So full of life. And Sunny will never get over it if anything happens to her.

Maarten could weep. Looking out into the dark, he thinks of her broken phone, her twisted handbag. He thinks of her out there. Alone in the dark.

Kak.

37

WILLOW

'You want to head back?' Sunny whispers, and Willow can barely hear, but she takes his hand and squeezes it.

'No. Not too long now, until we find her,' she manages. Her throat is tight and she feels empty. She's closed her eyes out here in the dark, to see if she could feel Fliss anywhere, but nothing. It's fanciful, this idea that you can feel your loved ones, that twins can sense each other's presence. But there have been moments she's thought of Fliss a minute before Fliss has called her. There was that time in London, Fliss had leapt into her head for no reason, and then she'd walked into a restaurant and there she'd been, having lunch with a friend.

But it's not like she has an internal telephone. It's just thoughts that she makes sense of afterwards.

Willow is in a team with Sunny. They've trudged the park slowly, and now stand behind a line of trees that edge some woods up past the building housing the Roman mosaic floor. The grass is slippery underfoot.

'What's up here?' she asks, thinking the trees are sinister

in the dark. She'd never venture somewhere like this on her own at night. If Fliss had come all the way up here last night, it would not have been a choice.

The spirals and stories that build in her head are too much – the pressure behind her eyes is tight and her jaw is clamped hard. Her head aches, her neck aches.

'We just need to walk through. The dogs have already been this way and found nothing, but we're going to look with torches, check trees. It's unlikely we'll find anything – if the dogs haven't. But I asked if we could just go over this area one more time. Most of the park is open – and there are so many people here during the day, she would have been found if she'd fallen or been knocked out. But up here is different. Small paths, dips, the woods. I'll feel better if we check again. One more time before heading back to the station.'

Willow thinks of Fliss curled at the bottom of a ditch, fallen from one of the narrow paths that wind through the trees. The ground hasn't dried out in here; the April sun hasn't yet reached the earth.

Sliding as she climbs a path, Willow grabs a branch to steady herself.

The moon hasn't found a way through the tightly knit trees, and an owl hoots somewhere, making Willow start.

The dream: fingertips brushing stone, fingernails biting; the night opening up in a black void, a pit. Then she'd fallen? A scream.

Dreams are nothing.

'Watch out here – it's muddy.' Sunny shines his torch on the path in front of her as they climb a steep bank. They're high up at the top end of the park now, but they could be deep in a forest for all Willow can see. If Fliss has made her way here for any reason, and fallen, then it would be almost impossible to spot her.

And she can't feel her.

Her chest is tight as she thinks of Fliss, twisted and broken, waiting in the dark for someone to find her.

At the bottom of the fall. Her scream unheard.

38

WILLOW

'Can you remember what time it was you last saw Fliss?' Adrika sits with Willow, whose mind races.

She can't get the image of the smashed phone out of her mind, the screen shattered into tiny pieces. She banishes the idea that Fliss is somewhere broken, body twisted. The idea Fliss is in danger paralyses her. Had there been something menacing at the cocktail party? Something she'd missed?

The search had produced nothing and they were going back over the last time Fliss had been seen. There's little time to waste. The golden first twenty-four hours of a missing person investigation had passed now.

Willow needs to concentrate.

Think. Think.

'It was before the speeches. It must have been about 9 p.m.' She cries, and she's angry with herself. Angry she had fought with Fliss. Angry that she's crying again, when she needs to stay calm, to focus and help find her.

'Willow, I know, it's awful. But we're going to get her back.' Adrika is calm, and she nods at Willow to go on.

'Well, you know we had a row. And Sunny must have caught her on the tail end of the row with me, because she was already angry. She must have left the cathedral then.' Willow's hands shake. She's on the edge of panic and it's hard to breathe. A weight presses on her chest. She can only take shallow breaths and they're getting shorter.

'Willow, I need you to focus. Think clearly. Did you see anyone else there who gave you cause for alarm? Did Fliss say anything you can think of that might tell us something? Did she mention going to meet anyone?'

Shaking her head, Willow's cold. Fliss. *Please let her come back*.

Willow's phone buzzes and a text message flashes up from Mum:

I'm outside with Dad. I haven't told Nonie yet. Are you still here?

'Mum's here,' Willow says, shivering.

Adrika leans forward, her voice insistent. 'We *will* find her, Willow. Think about that evening. *Anything* that occurs to you, you phone me. No matter what the time. We will find her. I promise you.'

Finished, Willow runs from the room, and her mum's face is tear-streaked. 'Oh, Willow! Sunny phoned us. I said we had to come straight here.'

'Oh, Mum! Where can she be?'

'Well, you know Fliss. Ever resourceful,' her dad says, but his face is white. His hands grip her mum's arm, like he's holding her up, or she him.

'I've spoken to Maarten Jansen. He says they're looking wider than the park. The search is so thorough, I'm sure we'll...' Beginning strong, her mum's voice cracks and Willow tightens her arms around her.

'This was supposed to be such a happy week!' Her mum sobs on to her shoulder, hot tears leaking on Willow's T-shirt.

'They'll find her,' Willow says, sure of no such thing. She channels Adrika's words, Adrika's certainty. 'They will find her.'

'I hope there's news soon.' Willow sits down needing the firm plastic of the seat beneath her.

Adrika appears. 'Can I get you a coffee? Mrs Eliot? I'm Adrika, I work with Sunny.'

'Elspeth.' She grips Adrika's forearm. 'Please, tell me, do you think she's safe?'

'We have to think so. We have to stay focused, believe in a good outcome.' Adrika sits down. 'We'll do our best. Now, coffee or tea? Please, have a drink, Elspeth. It does help.'

'I...' Unsure of what her mum had been going to say, Willow looks over, catches her eye. Her mum takes her hand.

'Can you feel her?'

Willow shakes her head.

'I wish I could.' Her mother's voice falters, then carries on. 'I feel like half of myself. Half in this room, half elsewhere. I've always felt this way. With Fliss missing, it's worse, but it's this feeling exactly. I've felt part of me is missing, all of my life. This sense of there being a voice in the background, a gap. I'd thought for years it was your grandfather – that he'd left a gap when he died. He was so firm, strict, such a presence. He used to grip my hand – tell me to walk tall, not to cry. It is my first memory of him: I was walking down a church aisle and his grip was so tight on my hand.' She flexes her hand and stares at it. 'He was hissing at me, *Do not cry!* She lets her hand fall. 'I was terrified of him – always was. I thought he must be the cause... But it's not him. It's bigger. There's a gap – like Fliss missing – like part of me has been ripped away. I can't bear it!'

'Mum?' Willow hugs her. 'Oh Mum, they'll find her. We have to believe it. Sunny says he'll drive us back. Come on, let's go. We can't do anything else.'

Her mum rises, tears streaming, and she staggers as she takes a step forward. Sunny takes her other arm.

'Oh, where is she? My baby girl!'

39

MAARTEN

'*Kak!*' Maarten swears, banging his hand down hard on the desk. It's late. Must be past eleven now and it's rare that a case touches him as personally as this one. Rare he feels so raw. Liv has just phoned, and she'd kept the tears out of her voice, but she'd sounded strained. They've all got to know Fliss over the last few months.

Maarten can't even imagine how Sunny must be feeling. He's holding it together – barely. But Fliss's mum this evening, just looking at her face...

'Sir?' Adrika steps into the doorway, pauses.

'You're still here? Your shift doesn't start yet. You should go, Adrika. There'll be enough to do tomorrow.'

She slides out a chair and sits opposite him. 'I can't go. I've been over and over it – and I've found something. Theo Durand's statement has a line in it – he spoke to Fliss on her way out, but then he said he saw her talking to another man.'

'You're right.' Maarten thinks back. He'd been irritated with Theo for his flippancy. 'Is he here? I saw him earlier.'

'I've sent him to draw up a sketch – he's with the police artist now.'

He pauses. 'Do we think it could be Jaz?'

'I have no idea. I'm hoping forensics will bring something back soon. Fingerprints from her bag, or maybe there's something on her phone – a number to follow.' She taps the desk with her fingers, looks at the wall.

'I can't make it work. One death Tuesday, a fall from the tower. Two witnesses to the fall. One witness to say he was alone. Nothing to suggest it's not suicide. Then Wednesday, Noah Lewis falls from the tower, inside this time. Again, no witnesses to how he ended up hanging on to a pillar so high up. Willow Eliot one of the last to see him before the fall.' He shakes his head. 'And allegedly he attacked her – or made a clumsy attempt to kiss her. Either way, he falls and bangs his head. Willow Eliot has his blood on her arm, and her shoe has his blood on the heel – with a corresponding mark on his head.' Maarten shakes his head again. 'She was at the cathedral around the time of Joel Braxton's death, and then her sister goes missing.' The frustration builds like a pressure behind his eyes. They're doing everything right, but they're nowhere.

'You think it has something to do with Willow Eliot?' Adrika asks. Her face reflects his own disbelief.

'It's not that I think she's behind any of this – but she's woven in so tight we have to consider her involvement. Can it really be a coincidence? Maybe it isn't *her*, so much as *to do* with her.'

'*Could* she have pushed Noah?' Adrika's fingers still drum on the desk.

He nods. 'I think so.' He's been going over the times for hours.

'She arrived with Noah at 7 p.m., or just after,' she says, writing on the board.

'Yes. You and Liv chatted to both of them,' Maarten says.

'Then she disappeared off with one of the wedding guests – Theo Durand. They went outside, had a glass of champagne.'

'…then she argued with Fliss.' Maarten rises, stretching, walking to the board. 'The two men, Noah and Jaz, fought. And that fight is interesting. Jaz is a possible suspect. He's given nothing away, but we have no alibi for him at the time of Noah's fall. And the fact that they argued…'

They both stand in silence, looking at the notes. Adrika circles the fight, draws an arrow off. 'Let's come back to him.'

'As for Willow, after the argument with Fliss, she went up the tower. What – 9.45 p.m.?'

Adrika nods, scribbling. 'And then back down to kick off the speeches at 10.30 p.m. Noah fell afterwards – we have 11.04 p.m. as the official time, based on footage someone took on a mobile phone. And no one else was up there. The door to the balcony nearest him was locked, but the other door to the tower was left unlocked, and Willow knew about that. But Theo Durand saw Noah after Willow.'

Maarten nods, thinking of Noah, hanging: his knuckles had been white, his voice strained with effort. 'How long do you reckon he could have hung on for – five minutes max?'

Adrika stands back, pen in hand. 'The attention of the audience was focused on the speeches. Is it possible he was pushed earlier and managed to cling or balance for a while? Maybe his foot caught a ledge? He could have been pushed earlier. There's no CCTV up there.'

'What if it isn't just Willow who is at the centre of this, but the family?' Maarten says.

'You mean Willow and Fliss are involved in some way?'

'I don't know. But Willow was there, and now we think Fliss was – taken? Or certainly left in a hurry.'

'Could be. Maybe Fliss saw something, saw someone.'

Maarten lifts his coffee. 'Let's go deeper into the history. Let's start with the fall Sunny was looking into, the 60s tower death. Joel Braxton was a witness. Let's start at the beginning.'

It's time for the past to speak.

40

ALICE

The blanket covers both their heads and the air underneath is hot. They sit on the floor in between their beds in their secret camp. No one can find them here. Right now, Alice's tummy is tight and Betty's hand hovers over the bruise on Alice's upper arm.

'Does it hurt?' Betty asks. 'It's very big.'

Alice thinks. 'It hurts if I touch it.' She presses it now and the pain is sharp. 'Ow!'

'Don't touch it, Alice!' Betty grabs her hand. 'You mustn't!'

Alice can't remember exactly what she had said. It had gone so badly wrong. They had been dressed to go to something in the cathedral. Her hair had been tied back tightly and it had made her head itchy. She had scratched it. Then scratched it again.

Daddy had been pleased with both her and Betty. They had waited by the front door, as he went back upstairs to get something.

She was scratching when he had been on the stairs.

'Stop that, Alice,' he had said, as he'd come down. 'You need to look smart for the service.'

They had left the house and Betty had held her hand. They had giggled when Betty started doing impressions of their teacher at school. Alice had laughed as they climbed the hill behind Mummy and Daddy, and by the time they reached the huge doors of the cathedral she was laughing so loudly that tears were streaming down her cheeks.

'Quiet, Alice!' Daddy had hissed as they had joined the stream of people heading inside.

But the more she tried to make the laughter stop, the worse it became. Betty had her mouth clamped shut and only her eyes were laughing, but Alice couldn't stop it coming down her nose in snorts, and escaping through her teeth and lips.

'Alice!' he had hissed again, as the cathedral had fallen silent, and heads bent in prayer. But this had been even worse. A big bubble of laughter had taken hold of all the muscles in her tummy. She had thought of Betty, striding up the hill doing her funny walk, and saying, 'Be quiet, children!' exactly like their teacher.

But as well as the laughter, she could also feel the terror. She knew if she laughed, Daddy would be very angry. Her itchy head suddenly felt now as though ants crawled all over it, and she scratched it so hard it had hurt. But still the laughter came.

Alice had counted all the feet she could see in the pew with her head bent.

The laughter rose. Higher and higher.

'Be quiet, children!'

It had burst out.

Betty whispers now, quiet under the blanket. 'Were you scared, Alice? Were you scared when Daddy took you out of the service?'

Tears prickle at Alice's eyes. She's always scared when Daddy gets angry. It's getting worse. He's never like that with Betty, and recently she's started to feel cross about that. Once she even felt cross with Betty. Why did Betty get it right all the time?

There just must be something wrong with her.

'Are you allowed to go today?' Betty asks.

Alice touches the bruise again, very gently this time. She thinks about the birthday party for Maeve Roberts, who lives in a big house. 'I don't think so. Daddy said Mummy would take me out instead, and you're allowed to go to the party.'

Really, Alice didn't mind missing the party. She loves spending time with Mummy. Mummy is always kind. Mummy is never cross.

'I won't go, if you're not going,' Betty says, but Alice knows that this would make Daddy cross too. She knows that Betty going is a prize, and that watching Betty go is supposed to Teach Her A Lesson.

'Try to be good, Alice. Can you try? I don't like it when Daddy gets angry.' Betty looks so sad that Alice tries to smile.

'Of course,' she says. 'I'll do it for you.'

41

WILLOW

The sky is clear as they follow the bobbing path of Sunny's torch down to the lake.

'Fliss?' Sunny calls. 'Fliss?'

Willow shivers, her hands pushed deep into her pockets. Unable to do nothing, she and Sunny had decided to search again. She couldn't bear the thought of Fliss being out here, possibly hurt.

The air is crisp and it helps with the burn in her cheeks. Her face is on fire – all the tears and wiping them away.

'Fliss!' Sunny calls again.

Willow's mind is racing to all the dark corners of grisly stories, the worst of every horror film she has ever seen. The scream in the night, the feeling of falling.

'Who's that?' She can see a figure up ahead. It's by the side of the lake. They're almost past the old pub, about to cross the bridge that leads to the lake.

There is no one else around. The figure ahead sticks out. Like a clue. Like a suspect.

'Who?' Sunny looks around. 'Fliss?' he shouts again.

'No – over there, by the edge of the lake. Look, whoever it is has just thrown something in the water!' Willow runs. Her feet move before she tells them to. The figure ahead has a hoodie pulled down over their face. They slouch. And at the sound of her shout, she sees their head whip round quickly. Take a step back.

It's gone 2 a.m. and there is no one around. Who is throwing something into a lake at 2 a.m.?

'Hello!' Willow runs faster. With her second shout and her footsteps, loud in the dark, the figure up ahead looks at her again quickly, then turns and runs.

'Stop! Please, stop!' Willow's chest is tight, breath restricted.

From behind her, Willow feels Sunny power past. The night is lit with the pale moon, and the arms of the trees wave in the dark. There is rustling, shadows, secrets of the night. Willow chases Sunny.

'Stop! Police!' This time it's Sunny shouting.

The figure has made their way up a grassy bank, up into the wider section of the park, away from the lake. The park is filled with traces of its Roman history. Remains, patches of history in murals and walls. And the figure sails past the stone of hundreds of years.

But Sunny is faster. Willow sees him fell the figure with a flying tackle and she gasps, catching her breath, bending over her knees and resting her head, as he roars.

'If an officer tells you to stop, you stop!' Sunny is like a lion. Fierce. But she can hear the strain in his voice, it's cracking. 'What are you doing out here?'

Willow looks at Sunny as he pulls back the hood of the

cloth jacket the figure is wearing. He's moaning; he must have hurt himself when he fell.

'Jaz!' Willow takes a step forward. 'It's Jaz! Jaz from the cathedral! What are you doing out here?'

Saying nothing, he squirms on the ground, clutching his ankle.

'Sunny, he threw something in the lake. I'll go.' Willow races back to the lake.

Sunny shouts after. 'I'll get the team down here.' He turns back to Jaz. 'Are you going to tell us what you're doing here?'

But Jaz still says nothing. He shakes his head, writhes and squirms, but is silent.

Sunny is on the phone. Willow can hear him speaking to Adrika when she returns.

'What are you doing, Jaz? Fliss is missing! What are you doing out here?' Willow, shaking, kneels in the dirt, looks at him, pleading. 'Jaz, is this something to do with Fliss?'

But Jaz says nothing. Mute. Defiant. He stares at Willow, then looks at the ground.

Willow shivers; the pale light of the moon seems to fade, as if the night were clouding over. Fliss is out there somewhere. On her own, needing them all.

Hold on, Fliss, she whispers. *We're coming.*

42

MAARTEN

'He's ready, sir.'

Maarten rises. He'd sent Sunny home, but it was hard. He knows how he'd feel in his situation.

'Did we get an ID on the person last seen speaking to Fliss, before she left the cathedral?'

Adrika nods. 'The drawing threw up a likeness of Jaz. I've got Theo in another room. He's confirming with photos.'

It's not a surprise. Jaz is there at every turn.

'Do you want me in there, sir?' Adrika falls in beside him as they step down the concrete stairs towards the interview room.

'Yes. But you know you should just go home?' Maarten looks at Adrika. Her face is pale and her hair is tied back. She looks ten years younger; looks exhausted, but he understands how she feels. The loyalty to Sunny. The force breeds loyalty. Cultivates it. 'Have we got the results of what Jaz threw in the lake?'

'In a fashion. The team aren't done with them yet, but so far it looks like letters. There are only a few words on them we can make out at the moment, but they might come up with something better soon.'

Adrika hands Maarten a page.

'There was a bunch of them, but the water had got to them. And the ink on there is pretty indecipherable. Here, sir, this is the clearest page we have.'

Maarten stops outside of the interview room. He looks down at the photocopy. There's very little to make out. The address at the top corner has 'London' written on in, with 'W9' as part of the postcode.

There are a few words further down the page. One mentions 'money', and then a reminder of something. Part of the date is clear: 1980s.

'That's interesting,' he says. 'That's very interesting. I have no idea how this ties in but it seems historical again. Let's bluff it out. See what we can get from him.'

The door feels heavier than usual as Maarten enters the room, the lights brighter. Jaz looks even younger than he remembers, as he pulls out the chair and slides in. His face is pale, whitened. His dark hair looks damp, but he had been lying on the grass when they'd arrived in the park. Sunny hadn't allowed Jaz to rise. But he hadn't stepped out of line. He hadn't forgotten who or what he was. And for that, Maarten is grateful.

'For the sake of the tape...' Adrika speaks, and Maarten waits until Jaz has stated his name.

'Jaz.' Maarten keeps his voice soft. 'Jaz, can you just tell us, please. In your own words, what you were doing out tonight? You know a young woman is missing. You know that there have been two falls from the tower in two days.

Time for covering your tracks has long since passed. Please, in your own words.' Maarten sits back, not knowing what he thinks about this young man, connected so closely, but his involvement in the crime is not clear.

He must still be upset? Certainly, his flatmate thought so. Must be grieving. But he had argued with Noah Lewis hours before he fell. And his grandfather had been at the flat on the day of the death, and they had argued.

It would be so much easier if Jaz would just tell them. Maarten needs to take this one slowly.

'Did you find them? Did you find what I threw in the lake?' Jaz stares at the table, hands rigid in fists. His shoulders rounded. Defeated. Defensive.

'Yes.' Maarten says nothing else. He waits.

With a sigh, and a droop, further still, Jaz says quietly, 'Shit.'

Maarten waits out the silence. He's tired. He's angry. He is concerned for Sunny, worried about Fliss. But he waits.

With a voice tiny, tired, Jaz speaks, and Maarten has to lean forward to scoop up the words.

'Then you know.'

'Jaz, I need you to tell us. I need you to be clear. Can you tell us what you were doing, and why you threw the letters in the lake?'

Maarten knows only a piece of this, but can't do the jigsaw.

'How much did you read?'

Maarten shakes his head. 'It doesn't work like that. You tell us now. That's what you do.' He can feel anger in his stomach like acid. It's gone 3 a.m.

Jaz narrows his eyes. He doesn't look furtive, but like he's thinking. Lines appear on his brow, smooth out, appear again. He shakes his head.

Why? Maarten thinks. *Why doesn't he just tell us?*

A firmer shake of the head. Jaz looks up. 'No,' he says. 'I'm not going to say anything. I'm sorry.'

He does look genuinely sorry. Martin can't understand it. It doesn't feel like defiance. It's more measured.

'Don't you want to go home?' he asks. 'Based on what we have, we will hold you. This is stupid, Jaz.'

'No. I can't. Not yet.' Jaz sits up. Resolute. 'No. I'm sorry.'

Adrika looks at Maarten. He nods.

'Let's try another tack,' she says. 'Forget tonight. We know that your grandfather visited your flat the morning of his death. Could you tell us about that, please? Your father seemed to think you had no relationship with him.'

Jaz whitens further. His eyes are wide. 'Who told you that?' His head shakes, like a tremor. 'Was it Sekani? My flatmate?' His shoulders sag.

'Jaz,' Maarten leans forward. 'It's not important who told us. It's more important that you didn't tell us. We spoke to you about your grandfather the other day. You said that you'd seen him at the cathedral and that was it.'

'No,' Jaz shakes his head. 'I said the last time I'd seen him was at the cathedral. I was really careful not to lie. I didn't tell you about the morning, but I didn't lie about it.'

The late-night semantics are too much.

'Look at it from our point of view. You rowed with your grandfather on the morning of his death. You rowed with Noah the evening he fell from the tower. Then the night a young woman is missing, you are seen talking to her as she leaves the cathedral, and then you are found on your own in the park, throwing possible evidence into a lake, that you won't talk about. Jaz, you better start talking. I'm not sure where you got your understanding of the law from, but not telling us about something because we haven't asked directly doesn't mean you're not keeping things from us. This is a potential murder investigation, and a missing person investigation, and we believe the two might be linked. And you're linked to all three incidents. So, if you are in any doubt, then now is the time to start talking. Right now.'

43

WILLOW

Friday morning had come early for Willow. She'd given up in the end and risen at 5 a.m. and gone for a walk. She can't rest. She and Sunny sit at the kitchen table, waiting for her parents to come down.

'Want to go up to the cathedral?' Sunny says, lowering his phone. 'That was Adrika. They're finished with it. It's open again.'

'Why?' Willow can think of nothing worse than going back there.

'Let's take a look around. You never know what we might think of. What might jolt our memories.'

She looks at him. He stares out of the window of Martha's house. Looks back to her. 'I can't just sit here. Not anymore,' he says.

The feel of the cathedral is different today. There are a few people dotted around who are clearly press. Others move slowly, pointing up at the high roofs.

'Do you think they're here because of the falls?' Willow asks, watching one couple, heads bent, fingers pointing.

'I'm sure they are,' he says, shaking his head. 'Nothing like something sensational to draw a crowd.'

They pause by the exhibition. Some are standing there, looking over the pieces. It feels so far away – it had been only three nights ago that she'd arrived here. It feels like weeks.

There's a whimper from the left, and Willow sees Lizzie, standing with a tissue up against her eyes, reading some of the exhibits.

'Lizzie, are you OK?' she says, taking a step forward.

Lizzie's eyes are wet as she looks at Willow. 'I still can't get over it. I saw him the other day, when he was here. Large as life. He's obviously older now, but still, I'd have known him anywhere.'

'Did you know him well?' Sunny asks.

'Oh, I suppose you could say.' She shakes her head. 'I used to think he'd had it hard. I was there when he saw that woman fall from the tower. Years ago. I felt sorry for him back then. What a thing to see!'

'But not when you'd got to know him?' Sunny asks.

She shrugs. 'He was what he was. Rules were different. Times were different. That girl, the one that was sent here' – she gestures to the exhibition – 'to Hill Barnes. I doubt that would be the case now.'

'What do you mean, the girl?' Willow asks.

Wiping her eyes, the tears slowed, Lizzie nods to the picture on the board. It's of an old building, black and white, surrounded by fields. 'She was sent there. The daughter of the woman. Joel saw them. He was working up on the cathedral roof – I don't know what he was doing, but he could see the tower. The mother and daughter had gone up, climbed the steps. The next thing he sees is the girl has climbed up on the parapet, then the mother followed – trying to wrestle her down. And she tumbles, all the way. I was only young at the time. I must have been eight, maybe nine? I heard the screams – a crowd gathered quickly. I was out with the family, on a walk.' She shakes her head.

'Oh, but that's awful!' Willow says.

'Imagine,' Lizzie says, looking at the black-and-white photograph, 'growing up, thinking you'd caused your own mother's death.'

44

MAARTEN

Adrika runs in. 'We've got a witness! Let's go.'

'What?' Maarten scrambles, grabbing his coat.

'A witness to the fall – the 60s tower death! Lizzie – the cleaner at the cathedral. Sunny's just been on the phone. I think we should go there – less intimidating. Come on. He's asked her to wait.'

Lizzie sits at a desk, in the office. Willow had brought coffee and left them to it.

Maarten watches her carefully. There's something there he can't get a hold of about her grief over Joel Braxton – something like regret, and it doesn't sit easily.

'In your own time,' Adrika says. 'If you could just give us an account of that day – when the woman fell. Whatever you remember. I know it was a long time ago.'

Lizzie presses her hands together. 'It was a long time ago, but you don't forget a day like that. It's like a film now, pressed into the back of my mind. I remember details – even the smells. It was this time of year.'

'Just go from where you can remember,' Adrika says gently.

'The first thing I remember, is the shout, *Alice!* It was the sister I heard first, shouting for her. I was at school with them – I vaguely knew them.

'It happened too quickly. I couldn't keep up. There was screaming, and we all ran outside. So much noise – the father was there too, shouting, *Betty! Come back!* The father was angry. I'd seen him before. I didn't like him.

'And there she was, Betty, the girl who'd been shouting for her sister. She was standing, shaking, puppy eyes – she just stood, staring at the woman on the ground.

'That's when I first saw the woman. Just lying there. A heap. No chance she'd survived. I couldn't breathe. My parents pulled at us, tried to take us away. But we couldn't move. No one could move.' Lizzie clutches her chest, closes her eyes.

'And the crowd! Sirens rang through the fog. The girl, Betty, was still screaming, this time for her mother. *Mummy!* It went right through me. They were twins, the two girls. I looked for the other one. And I looked at the father. He just stood there.'

Maarten holds his breath.

'They were seven years old – I found out later. Anyway, the twin called Betty was screaming. Crying for her sister, for her mother. Tears on her face. Her fists were balled.' Lizzie balls her own fists. 'And she was wrestling with her father, who was holding her back.

'*Don't let the child see*, the father said. But he was walking towards the woman on the ground as he said this. He wanted to. His face...

'Flat on the flagstones. Her arms kinked to the side. She must have slid part way down the roof – there had been a moment, one man was saying, where he thought he could catch her. He was quoted in the newspaper the following week: *I ran to catch her. I thought I'd get there...* A young man with a dog on a lead was standing there. He was trembling. We were all in shock. He was in the paper too, saying he ran, that he thought *maybe if she could hold on...* His dog was yapping, straining at the leash. There was a lot of noise. My head hurt. The girl was screaming, *Mummy!* then wrestling with the arms that held her back. *Where's Alice? Alice?*

'And we all looked. She'd appeared from by the cathedral. She walked slowly. Then stood still.

'Her sister screamed again, but she was held back by the father, who looked at his other daughter with an expression I've never shaken. Like he was scared, like he wasn't sure what she was going to say, to do.

'But she just stood. Stood at the edge of the crowd, not moving.

'Even minutes later, she hadn't moved. She stood, still trembling. Right at the side. Staring at her mother. Not really moving, not crying. Nothing.

'The police arrived then, and one took hold of her coat. He starting shouting at her, *What happened? What happened?*

'Still, the girl said nothing. Nothing at all. Her whole body shaking like she'd been pulled out of ice. White, her mouth parting, as though she would speak – but nothing.

'It was Joel who saw the whole thing. He walked slowly, we were all in shock.

'*It was an accident.*

'His voice cut through the crowd, and they parted for him, we all stepped aside. He was well known, well liked, Joel. He'd been the verger at the cathedral for a couple of years. Young, good-looking.

'*An accident – so sad*, he said again. He raised an arm, and a finger, like he was pointing at someone in a line-up, but there was only the child. Just the shaking child. He looked shocked. There were tears on his face.

'*Poor girl*, I thought. I wanted to run to her, but I didn't dare.

'Joel told us all, *Just an accident. She was kicking, flailing, and the mother was trying to hold on to her, but she was unbalanced. I was too far away – I was on the side roof. I watched her – the mother was trying to protect her, but the girl had climbed up on the wall, I wondered if she was trying to jump off. I heard her shout, "Fly!" And the mother was trying to hold her back, to help her down. She climbed up too. I tried to get to them, to help them. But then... It happened so fast.*

'The crowd turned their eyes, all of us, all at once. We all turned our eyes and stared at the girl.

'*Is this what happened?* The police officer knelt down then, like he was being kind, but his voice was soft with shock, not compassion. *Did you do this?*

'But she didn't speak. Not then. She didn't speak again. In fact, she didn't speak at all. Through questioning, through the court hearing. Even when her sister was crying for her. That girl never said another word.

'She was a child, too young for any responsibility, they said she needed to go away for her own good. We talked about it at school. And they took her to the hospital. She went to Hill Barnes, a threat of harm to herself and to others.

'I never saw the father again. He moved away. And her sister, her twin, I never heard of her again.

'They left the house for her. It was rented out, to pay for her fees, and put in her name. I don't know where. I don't think the father or the sister ever visited. I don't think they ever came back.

'But I'll never forget the screams of the twin. She screamed loud enough for the both of them. *She didn't do it! She didn't do it! She wouldn't do it! Alice! Alice!*

'There was no one else to speak for her, and who would listen to a seven-year-old? And they said she killed their goldfish and their hamster on purpose, she set their house on fire. She was a danger to herself and the community. What else could be done?

'I'll never forget them taking her away. She was already a ghost.'

PART THREE

PART THREE

45

ALICE

1962

There is so much happening and so much she doesn't understand. She hasn't seen Father for such a long time, or Betty. She can't ask for them, can't ask for anything. Her mouth won't make words. It's like there's something in her throat. Something too big. She can't swallow it, can't cough it up. It just sits there.

'Over here, Alice!' A camera flashes so brightly she turns her head, blinks. Black spots dance in front of her eyes.

'Here! Look this way!' Another shout, another flash. Crowds gather. Lots of men, lots of suits.

'Out of my way. Just a child.' The officer who takes her through the crowd had been kind that morning. 'Brush your hair. You want to look nice for the judge.'

Alice closes her eyes, but then trips on a step. The concrete edge of the hard step bangs her knee, and her mouth opens to yelp, but still, no sound. She can't tell anyone. The officer up ahead tugs on her hand, not realising she's fallen. For the rest of the day her knee will bleed beneath her grey tights, and no one will know.

Once inside, it's quieter. Feet tap on floors and sounds echo but there is no shouting, no jostling. No one really looks at her. Not for long. They look at her, through her, talk about her.

'Shouldn't she have a WPC?' says a woman on the desk they pass, giving them something to hang round their necks. She speaks to Alice, 'You want a woman with you. Little duck like you.'

Alice looks at her. Her blouse is tucked into her blue skirt band, and it pulls as she leans forward. Gaps appear between buttons and her flesh presses through, looking for a way out.

Mummy had been slim. She had silver lines below her belly button, which she told Alice were Mummy Badges that you were given when you had children as clever and beautiful as Alice and Betty. There was a photo in the album of them both in Mummy's tummy. She'd been wearing a long summer dress that had curved and fallen over the bump, which looked too big to be real. The thin yellow material of the dress had blown loose, and Mummy had been smiling,

'You wriggled,' Mummy had said. 'You both wriggled at bedtime, and if I ate anything cold. Sometimes if I didn't feel you wriggle for a while, I'd put an ice cube on my tongue and suck it until I could feel you fidget again. You were my special gifts.'

When the girls had asked how they'd got there, she'd laughed. 'I was given a very special seed. It was planted in my tummy, and it grew you both. You held hands in my tummy until you came out. The both of you. I knew you were holding hands. I held you both, and you both held each other.' She would say this after bedtime stories, which she'd read after they were in their nighties. When it was cold, she'd bring up hot stones to put at the bottom of their bed, and she'd get up early to make the dark brown rye bread that didn't hurt Betty's tummy, and when Alice had a sore throat she'd dip a spoon of butter in sugar and let her suck it. When planes started to get busy in the sky, she'd stop in the park and point at the aeroplanes and say, 'Imagine if all those planes landed right now, do you think there'd be room for all the people down here on earth?' And they'd all stare at the sky and Alice would think how big it was, and wonder about going up in a plane one day, and how it would feel. Someone had told her that when you flew up you left your tummy behind, and it had to chase you to catch up, and she'd thought how lucky she'd been that Mummy hadn't got on a plane when she and Betty had been in her tummy. How would a tummy that big have managed to catch up with a plane?

The woman in front of her sits back. The buttons on her blouse loosen, and Alice thinks she doesn't need a WPC. She just needs Mummy. When will Mummy come back? When will she get better and come and get her?

'Come on,' the officer says. 'We're in court one. We'll be needed soon.'

46

ALICE

1962

Adults talk over her head. She catches snatches of it:
Alice,
threat to herself,
grave risk to others,
criminal age of responsibility,
eight years old,
she's only seven,
terrible ordeal,
poor mother.

There is so much to see, to look at. And the noises. People make noises in all directions. A group of children are playing and they're shouting, just outside. She's led through a big room, with beds, children, older girls, some smaller than her. Some are crying; an adult calls to another.

She hears only half of what she is told: *Ward, thirty of you, locked at night.* The sounds come from so many directions her head spins.

Your bed...

The railings on the bed are iron, grey. Once in, the sides are lifted. It's a bit like a large cot. The floor is bare, the walls are bare.

Drink this...

Water, with some kind of syrup.

Swallow these...

Green pills, blue pills.

She watches a girl in a bed nearby. A nurse has a needle in her hand, and the girl looks the other way.

The nurses' uniforms are stiff, their hats sit firm. There's one they all nod to. When she walks past, they all stand quiet.

The sheet is hard, and in parts the thread is rubbed bare. Cold. She pulls the sheet up, and buries her head as the sounds swing all around. Someone is crying. Someone is chatting.

The smell is a bit like the toilets after Mummy has cleaned them, a bit like the cabbage they eat on Sunday.

The smaller children, smaller than her, are not quiet.

She would go to them; the sounds make her sad. They sound like she feels, but she can't make any noise. Nothing will come from her.

It makes her freeze, makes it difficult to move. Difficult to think. So many of them.

The nurses are kind. They smile at her. But she wants to be home.

They all sit in lines. Food comes in trays. She doesn't know what it is and she can't swallow.

Lights out, comes the call.

A click. The ward is in darkness. There is nowhere to go.

Scared, alone, everything grinds to a halt. Everything. Appetite, thinking, feeling. It grinds to a complete stop. She grinds to a complete stop.

Alice is as cold as the sheet, and she can't sleep. Her heart races as she squeezes her eyes tight. It beats so loudly and quickly, it might fly out of her chest.

Come for me, she thinks. *Betty, come for me.*

Lying flat, looking up at the ceiling, a spider crawls above her, but she can feel its feet on her skin. Everything crawls, creeps.

She counts the tiles on the ceiling, starting again once she finishes the first round.

Betty, she thinks, and squeezes her eyes shut. Tight and hard. Tears come anyway. Beads of tears run hot and fierce down her cheeks, and never in her life has she felt so entirely alone.

She doesn't think of Mummy. When darkness finally comes, Mummy only comes in her dreams.

47

MAARTEN

'Adrika, I'm going to Michael Braxton's. Being Jaz's uncle, and knowing the cathedral so well, he might have some clue where Jaz might have taken Fliss.' Maarten speaks too loudly on the car phone. He's exhausted. The search for Fliss last night had produced nothing and the interview with Lizzie had started early. It's 9.30 a.m. now. 'I'll call you when I'm done here.'

The car turns up their road and he knows it's early to arrive unannounced. The sun is already warm, and were Fliss not missing, it would be a perfect morning. How such horror can run in tandem with the world still spinning will never cease to amaze him.

He turns on to the Braxtons' drive, and the garage door is wide open. A huge 4x4 pokes out, the front corner of which is crushed.

Heather and Michael lean over the car, and visibly jump when Maarten's wheels hit the gravel. He turns the engine off, watching them. They look to each other, before applying smiles to their faces.

The girls' faces peer from the lounge window. Again, he marvels at the house. It's not just the size, it's all the extras, the expensive sofas, the car. Michael Braxton must be doing well.

Heather straightens, her smile slipping quickly as Michael steps forward. Maarten watches her as he climbs out of the car, swinging the door closed. *She looks*, he thinks, *like the rug is slipping from beneath her*.

'Maarten, morning!' Michael's voice is jolly. Overly jolly.

'Michael. Sorry for disturbing you so early.' Maarten says it anyway, though it's clear whatever he's disturbing isn't a relaxing morning. 'Everything OK?' He says this looking at Michael's face. There's a pale bruise on his left cheek, near his eye.

'Yes. We've had a bump.' Michael gestures to the car, glancing at Heather.

'An accident? Did you report it?' Maarten says.

'I drove into our wall – just a parking thing. Not a road accident.' Michael smiles again, but it's tight, too bright.

Maarten scans the driveway for signs of a crash or broken wall, but then shakes it off. He can return to this. Fliss missing is the matter at hand.

'We're holding Jaz,' he says.

'What?' Heather steps forward. 'Jaz? In jail?'

'We're holding him, for questioning. And I want to know if there's anywhere you know of where he might detain a person. Any place you know of, which he owns, or goes to. Anything at all.'

'Jaz?' Michael shakes his head. 'But Jaz hasn't done

anything. Missing? Is he supposed to have abducted someone? Or are you talking about murder?'

'His grandfather has just died; we're investigating two tower falls,' Maarten says, looking at Michael, finding his sympathy for him thinning, his patience like pulled string.

'But Jaz didn't kill Dad,' Michael says.

'And now there's a woman missing,' Maarten says.

'Michael,' Heather says, stepping forward. 'Michael—'

'Heather, I've got this.' Michael doesn't take his eyes off Maarten. 'Jaz wouldn't kill anyone. Wouldn't kill his grandfather. And as for a missing girl, I don't even know—'

'Missing *woman*. And he was found during a search for her, throwing papers into the lake in the middle of the night. Moreover, he omitted to tell us of a row he had with his grandfather the day he died and of a conversation with Fliss Eliot before she went missing. He fought with Noah Lewis hours before he was pushed from the cathedral tower. The evidence that Jaz is involved in this is strong enough for me to detain him, even to charge him. But my main priority right now is to find the missing woman. Do you know of anywhere we should search for a woman, were Jaz to have abducted someone?'

Michael and Heather stare at him. Heather looks to Michael, and Michael simply shakes his head. He opens his mouth, but nothing comes out.

'I'm very serious, Mr Braxton. More serious than I can convey.'

'I really don't think Jaz could do any of this,' Heather says softly. 'You said she's called Fliss. Who is she?'

'Fliss Eliot,' Maarten says. 'She's the sister of Willow

Eliot, who was at the cathedral the night your father-in-law died. She was at the cathedral cocktail party, wearing a silver dress, and she left around 10 p.m. Her phone and bag have been found, but she has been missing for over thirty-six hours now.'

'Oh my God.' Heather's hand rises to her mouth.

'We can't help you,' Michael says. His hands twist. 'Please, believe me. I don't think Jaz did what you think he did. I really don't.'

Heather, whose hand has been pressed against her mouth like a dam stop, rears back. A cry explodes out, and she half steps back, half runs, turning, and disappears into the garage; and Maarten watches her vanish into the black.

48

ALICE

1967

The sun is warm, and Alice picks up a trowel. The gardens and farm at Hill Barnes are extensive. It's the best thing about being here. The farm is being closed down slowly, and Alice will miss it when it's all gone. Outside, with the plants and the flowers is her favourite place. Away from the ward.

Spring has arrived again and the sun is opening all the flowers, lifting the buds in the earth.

Alice turns her face upwards, closing her eyes. At certain moments, she could be anywhere.

Opening them, she turns to the earth. Kneeling, she digs her fingers into the soil. She likes to work further away from the hospital, close to the large building where some of the equipment is stored.

This place is quiet. She explores sometimes when no one is around. There are stairs up to the top floor, where spare buckets are stored. There's a basement too. There was flooding earlier in the year, when the snow melted. The whole lower part of this garden flooded, and a few men have arrived today to clear out the basement. Piles of equipment stack up on the lawn. The men shout to each other; some laugh.

Gazing up, she sees most of them heading back up to the house. One remains. She knows a new floor is being laid today; one of the gardeners had told her. They've taken on a few more part-time labourers and the patients aren't allowed to do things like lay floors and use concrete.

The one man who remains has a familiar gait. Alice stops what she's doing and watches him.

She's can't place him, but she can't breathe. She stares.

He's pushing a wheelbarrow, with a large sack in it, and when he drops it and turns, she sees his face.

Her trowel slides from her hand.

Sounds recede.

She knows this man.

49

MAARTEN

Sunny's wedding is planned for tomorrow. There's been no word about cancelling. But Maarten throws his coat over the back of his chair and wonders at what point someone will say… Will he wait by the west door of the cathedral, hoping she's been in hiding until the big moment? Sympathy sticks like a blade in his throat. Fliss has been missing for over thirty-six hours and they are no closer to finding her.

'Adrika.' He speaks into his phone. 'Pop in, would you?'

As she sits, he briefs her on the car dent he'd seen at the Braxtons'. 'Get someone to follow up on it? They were behaving strangely. Anything from you?'

She looks as exhausted as he feels, as she pulls out her notes. They'd all got to know Fliss recently, and everyone likes Sunny. The whole station is taking this personally. No one is resting.

'Well, Jaz is still not saying a word, but I've got his bank statements, and he had a large deposit from Joel Braxton in the last two weeks.'

'A large sum? How large?'

'Two hundred thousand. Large enough?'

'Two hundred thousand?' Maarten shakes his head. 'Where did that come from? That's too much for him to be silent anymore. Let's go and speak to him again. Ask someone to take him into the interview room.' He picks up his iPad. 'Oh, and Heather Braxton – I think she might know something. Something to do with the car, but she was very upset about Jaz. Can you call her and ask her to come in?' Maarten thinks of her scream, of her running away. 'Get her to come in on her own. In an hour? Let's speak to Jaz first.'

50

ALICE

1967

There's a girl missing. She'd heard someone mention it in the corridor. Maybe not a girl, maybe a woman.

Alice halts, her hand holding the wall, her fingertips cold as her nails dig into the white of the plaster. It's early; she's not long out of bed. They start rounds soon.

The police are here. She can see them in their uniforms. She'd seen the car arriving, making a slow ride up the drive.

She edges closer down the corridor, trying to listen.

Are they here to see her? She wonders if Betty is missing. She's been waiting for her to come for such a long time. She feels the loss of her like a sting; she carries it around, a wound.

She writes down a plea sometimes for the staff. *Please ask Betty to come. Where is my sister?* Maybe they've decided to listen to her and have gone looking for Betty? Maybe they'd discovered that she is missing?

'Excuse me.' It's one of the nurses. She's pushing a wheelchair and the angry eyes of Peter stare up at her. His hands are restrained. She hasn't seen him for a few days.

Peter had arrived recently and is a few years younger than her. He'd cried non-stop for the first few days. He has looked as lonely as she feels. She'd stood next to him, to try to comfort him. His tears hadn't stopped.

Today he is pushed out into the garden, and she follows. There is something about him.

The nurse leaves him parked in his wheelchair and goes back inside. The gardens are beautiful here. The daffodils are opening again, and the sun is warm on Alice's skin.

She picks a flower, and walks over to Peter. Holding it out to him, she smiles.

He looks so small. He has dark rings around his eyes, and she wonders if he cannot walk. But no, he stands, and takes the flower from her.

'Hello,' he says. 'I'm Peter.'

She nods.

'I know you can't talk, they told me. They've said I can sit out here for a bit, now the sun is here. My mother is coming for me, you know. I'm not going to be here long.'

Alice thinks of her mother. She thinks of Betty. Why does no one come?

Peter is doing something funny. His eyes have rolled white, and his arms have gone floppy. He falls to the ground, and he starts to shake.

It doesn't last long, but Alice is scared, and wants to call for help. But she still can't cry out. Can't speak.

She kneels on the grass, where Peter now lies. His eyes open slowly, and he looks very tired.

Taking his hand, she sits and picks up the flower she had given him, smelling it, and passing it to him, placing it near his face.

Birds are singing, and the sun cranks up its heat. Peter's face is damp, and she wipes tears from his cheek with the sleeve of her cardigan.

'I want Mummy,' he says, as his tears flow faster. He turns on his side, curling up into a ball. 'Why won't she come?'

For some reason, Alice finds her voice cracking open, like a rusty tin – sharp at the edges. 'I'll look after you,' she says.

He looks at her quickly, and he is as shocked as she is.

'You spoke,' he says, sitting up. 'You said something!'

'I did,' she says, touching her lips, holding her fingers there.

'Peter!' A shout flies across the lawns. 'Peter, did you have another episode?'

Frightened, Alice stands up and steps away.

'Lift him in.' There are a few nurses now, and they bundle him up into his chair, strapping his hands down again, and they push him away.

Alice opens her mouth to call after him, but the stiff uniforms of the nurses are like a wall. With Peter, her voice had opened up in a rush. The words had slipped out. Now he has gone, now all the nurses have arrived, her voice has vanished again. And whether it's habit now, or something else, she can't spit out the words that shape themselves in her mind.

*

Days later, the police come again.

'They're here about a missing girl,' Alice hisses at Peter, as the nurse pauses to talk to someone else in uniform.

'Do you think it's her? Betty? Do you think they've come to speak to you?' Peter says.

Alice can hear the tremor in his voice, which is matched in his hands. She wants to reach out and hold his hand, but you have to be careful about touch in here.

'I don't know. I hope so.' She looks back at the officers who are up ahead in the corridor, with a notepad and pen. 'I don't know why she doesn't come. I worry something bad has happened to her. Something worse than this.' Alice has tried hard with her voice, but it seems it's reserved for Peter. Only for him. It's their secret. She's testing it. She doesn't trust it not to disappear.

'I don't think there's anything worse than this,' Peter says. He sneezes, but as his hands are tied he can't catch it, and he looks defeated. 'Do you ever think that maybe she just doesn't want to come?'

'What?' Alice takes a quick breath, feels as though she has been stabbed. To be ignored, to be forgotten would be like being killed. Worse than being killed. The only thought that sustains her, throughout all of this, is that one day Betty will come. And she will take her away. She will stop this. As soon as she is able. As soon as she can. 'No!' she says, more loudly than she intends, and the nurse looks up, suspicious – you have to be careful about voices in here, too. Alice must hide her voice from everyone now. Until it's safe to speak.

Collecting herself, she squeezes her eyes shut, turning off

any leaks, opens them again, smiles at Peter. 'No, of course not. She would never do that. She will come for me, when she can. Unless…' She looks back at the officers. 'Unless she can't. Unless she really is missing.'

51

WILLOW

Sunny sits at the table. He wears the same T-shirt he was wearing the day before. His left hand is scabbed over and he has cuts up his arm. It's almost 10.30 a.m. and the house is in stasis.

He sees Willow looking and shrugs. 'From chasing that bloke,' he says, barely looking.

Willow thinks she has never seen someone look so broken.

Theo is cooking. He is making scrambled eggs, and the smell makes her stomach turn.

Luckily, they don't seem to have woken Martha. Or Nonie. Willow feels bad she hasn't seen more of Nonie. With Fliss missing, Willow has felt uneasy sitting down with her in case she let Fliss's disappearance slip. The last thing Nonie needs is more worry.

'I hope he's talking,' Sunny says, spitting words at the table. He scratches at one of the scabs.

'What are the next steps?' Willow asks, not needing to ask who Sunny is talking about. Time pulls slowly.

'Usually, the first twenty-four hours are the most important,' Sunny says. 'We're still close enough. We have a suspect. No sign of blood. We just need to make him tell us where she is. I could. Give me five minutes and...' His fists curl. He closes his eyes.

'Are you sure it's him?' Theo says. He puts plates out on the table. Salt and pepper sit in the centre, and they all have mugs of cold tea. He's been with them the whole time. 'If it isn't him, will we lose time?'

'They won't stop looking,' Sunny says. 'They'll be following up on all the leads. They'll find her. They *will*.' He shrugs. 'They have to.'

Theo nods.

'What are you thinking?' Willow says. Theo is quiet, but his fingers tap on the table.

He shakes his head. 'Nothing. Pick your fork up, Eliot. You think you can't eat, but you won't last long without food.'

His mouth smiles, but his eyes don't quite get there. Tiredness has sketched its way over his face too. His picks up his fork, leading by example, but she sees he doesn't get much past a mouthful before the silver tines rest back on the table.

'Well, I was just thinking, we were all there. I know we've all gone over our statements again, about when we saw her. But would it help if we did it again? Could we retrace our steps? It might – well, it might give us something to do.'

Willow glances at Sunny, who looks out of the window. Then he inclines his head. 'Can't hurt,' he says. 'And other things – anything that didn't seem like much? Not necessarily to do with Fliss.'

Theo begins, 'Well, I did tell the police this, but I saw Fliss talking to Jaz on the way out. I've identified him. I didn't think anything of it at the time – I didn't even know she'd had the arguments.'

Sunny nods, and Willow writes it down.

'Willow?'

'I can't think…' She closes her eyes. She thinks of the tower. Of Noah's touch. Of pulling back, and the blood appearing on his forehead. She rewinds, thinks of arriving, worrying about her dress. There was something in the middle. There'd been something.

'I did see – well, it wasn't anything.' She stops, thinks of exactly what she had seen. 'I saw Michael Braxton there, at the party, talking to Jaz.'

'The son? The son of the dead verger?' Sunny asks, surprised.

She nods. 'Yes, I know. I thought it was a bit odd. I would have thought it was the last place they would have wanted to be. He didn't look like he was having a good time.'

'What were they doing?' Theo asks.

'They were talking to Jaz. Noah went over to speak to them – mainly to Jaz. I think he was trying to show off. But they all looked – tense. I mean, it's not surprising, after the day they'd had. When Noah went over, Jaz kind of moved away to talk to him, and the Braxtons left. I was nearby, and when they walked past, they were – well – disagreeing.'

'Arguing?' Sunny says. 'Like how? Like having a row?'

'No, not really. More like – well, like he hadn't done

something that she thought he should have done. I think she said, *We should say something*. I think that's what it was. I hadn't really thought about it until now. But now that I do think about it – it was odd. It was odd that they were there in the first place. But how could they be involved?'

52

MAARTEN

Heather's black hair is piled up. She wears a plain white T-shirt under a denim jacket, and she stares at Maarten as he enters.

He glances at the clock. It's 11 a.m.

He can't read her expression. She waits for something, composed. But like for surgery, for the dentist, for an exam. Whatever she is waiting to say, he wants to hear it. She doesn't look like she's going to enjoy saying it.

'Heather,' he nods.

Adrika follows him in, beginning the interview admin.

'Your turn,' Maarten says to Heather when Adrika has finished. 'Please. Go ahead. We'd like you to tell us what you know about the evening of the cocktail party. Could you please take us through it, from your point of view?'

He can tell, when she begins to speak, that she's used to presentations of some kind. Maybe she's a teacher, or does some kind of job where she pitches, but she's clear, she looks them in the eye and she obviously expects to be listened to.

He doesn't doubt for a second she's telling the truth. She has come willing to share something, and it's not easy for her to say, but he believes every word that lands in the room.

'Fliss Eliot – the girl in the silver dress.' She takes a breath. 'Jaz wasn't the last person to see her. It was us.'

'Us?' Maarten repeats. 'You?'

'Michael and me. You know we were at the exhibition opening? We went—' She shrugs. 'I don't even know why we went. We went out of some misguided sense of duty on Michael's part. He said we should go. I didn't want to. Joel wasn't dead twenty-four hours, and we still hadn't told the girls. We thought we'd tell them the day after. They weren't asking questions. They don't see much of him, and Michael said he'd gone home to get something. There wasn't any urgency. I don't think they necessarily understand death.' She looks down. 'Maybe they do, and that's an easy lie for us to tell ourselves, but either way, we already had the babysitter booked for the party and they love her, so it would have been more upsetting for them to miss out on her visit. And Michael said we should go.'

'For work?' Adrika asks.

'Probably. I don't know, he just said we should go, and he was the one grieving the most, so I thought I'd just go along with it. I was exhausted. He must have been too. Grief is *exhausting*. It just drains everything from you. And the admin – bloody hell. Michael had already started talking about the funeral and the sheer list that it involves.' She drops her eyes.

Maarten knows he should let her tell it at her own pace,

but she had mentioned Fliss and the urgency of finding her is fierce. 'Fliss?' he prompts.

Heather nods. 'Sorry, yes. Well, we left early. Michael has a parking space at the cathedral. With work. We'd driven to the party. We were tired – we'd had a row. Anyway, we were driving away, and then this girl in a silver dress appeared on the road, out of nowhere.'

Maarten's stomach turns to ice. He thinks of the crushed car and looks at Adrika, whose fingers grip the edge of the table. 'Fliss – is she?' he begins.

Heather shakes her head quickly. 'No, I don't think we hit her. Michael swerved, he was fast. He swerved straight into a brick wall – the front of the car is crunched. It's a mess.' She purses her lips. 'You might have seen it this morning. He shouldn't have been driving. He didn't drink any alcohol, but the day had left him drained. But I'm moving off the point. I don't think we hit her, but she must have seen us last second, because she leapt to the side. I got out, once we'd stopped. The airbags opened; it was all messy. Michael got a black eye.'

Maarten thinks of his face that morning.

'I ran out – I was pretty hysterical by then. She'd disappeared out of view, and I thought maybe...' She runs her hands up and down her face. 'She'd fallen. She said her bag had fallen down some gap, and she couldn't see it. She was crying. I helped her up – asked her if she'd been hit. I wasn't sure we hadn't hit her. I dialled 999 as I was talking; I was going to call an ambulance. I was crying, she was crying – it was dark and it all happened so fast.'

'Oh, Fliss,' Adrika breathes out.

'She said she'd jumped out of the way. She screamed at me – called me a bunch of names, or rather Michael. All the names you might call a driver who comes out of nowhere in the dark. I couldn't even swear he'd remembered to turn on the lights. It's a new car. He's wanted one for years, and I've always said no – we don't need a huge car, and we can't afford it...'

'What happened to her?' Maarten asks urgently. 'What happened to her?'

'She ran off. She was upset, so I ran after her. I hadn't got through to the ambulance and I told Michael to report the accident and that I'd see him at home. But I got to Holywell Hill and I couldn't see her.'

'You should *absolutely* have phoned us.' Adrika is incredulous.

'I told Michael to report it!' She shakes her head, looks at Maarten, Adrika. 'I didn't know he hadn't until this morning. We were arguing about it when you arrived.' Her hands push and pull their way up and down her face again. 'It's an expensive car and the premiums are high – he said we can't afford to lose the no-claims. And he said if no one is hurt you don't need to report an accident.'

'Fliss is still missing,' Maarten says. 'When you say she wasn't injured, are you sure? If she's banged her head, run off...' He thinks of the park at night. If she'd tried to walk back to the bed-and-breakfast house her parents were staying in, she'd need to cross the park. If she'd passed out, wearing only a thin dress, then she's been out for a dangerous amount of time. She could be lying somewhere still. The searches had found nothing, but that doesn't mean they haven't missed her. Or if she'd run into the road, and been hit by someone else, and they hadn't reported it...

Adrika stands up. She says to Maarten, 'I'll go and speak to the search team.'

He rises too. 'Yes, and check the hospitals again. Heather, we have more questions, and we'll want you to look at a photo to confirm it was Fliss, but we need to update the team. Can you stay, please? Can I just ask, what time did Michael come back? Did he say he'd seen Fliss at all when he was bringing the car back?'

Heather shakes her head. 'The car was a nightmare apparently. I don't think he saw anyone. He had to drive it back in first gear. I was so exhausted by the time I walked home – it was midnight, and I paid the babysitter and went straight to bed. I didn't see Michael again until the morning. I have no idea what time he got in.'

'He didn't come back?' Adrika asks.

'Yes, he did. But I was out like a light. I just don't know what time he got back.'

'So, he could have been out all night?' Maarten asks.

'Well, no. He came straight back. But with the car...'

'That's what he told you,' Maarten says. Anger boils. 'He almost hit a woman with his car, didn't report it, then you didn't see him, and he stayed at the scene of the accident?'

'Well, yes, but it's not—'

'Where is he now?' Maarten asks.

'At home, with the girls.'

Maarten looks at Adrika. 'Send a car. Bring him in. Get him here now.'

53

MAARTEN

'Michael Braxton. Failed to tell us about almost hitting Fliss Eliot with the car. No alibi for six hours after she went missing.'

'Any link to Noah Lewis?' The super's voice is clipped. Maarten knows she'd hoped for further progress. She's on her way to a meeting now. While the evidence against Jaz is mounting, it mounts also against Michael. 'With Michael possibly being the last to see Fliss alive, we need to look closely at him. But Jaz has no alibi for the evening, and I've heard he's still not telling us everything.'

'We're looking into it all. Sunny's called. He's left a message. I need to call him back. He mentioned the Braxtons in the call.' Maarten checks his watch. It's almost noon.

'Sunny did?'

'Yes, Willow Eliot has remembered something. Adrika's gone over to speak to her. A car has gone to collect Michael Braxton now. I've got their financial history here – I wanted to go over it before I spoke to him. Heather Braxton has mentioned lack of money a few times. And Joel Braxton gave Jaz a large sum of money. The day he died. And the brother – Ferdie Braxton – he said that Michael gets all of the inheritance. It seems it's quite substantial.'

'Keep me updated. But keep Sunny out of it – you know any evidence that comes from him we'll have problems with.' The line goes dead.

Maarten picks up the financial records. Heather Braxton had not been lying. The monthly repayments on that large car of theirs were huge. And they'd booked a holiday to Disney World in the summer, and they must have been staying in some top-end hotels. Why this sudden expenditure?

He leafs through the previous few years – steady. Then this year, a holiday costing over £10,000; a car worth over £60,000. Why take on two large sums? What was he expecting to change?

He picks up his phone. 'Adrika, are you busy?'

'Just pulling up now. I'll be back soon – is Michael Braxton there yet?'

'No. Hopefully within the hour. Any word on the inheritance? Ferdie Braxton implied it was all going to his brother. Do we know the sum yet?'

'Give me a minute. I had an email in, but I haven't looked at it yet.'

He waits. The sound of a car horn comes through on the speaker. The cathedral bells sound.

'Here we go – yes, it seems it all goes to Michael Braxton. Whoa…' She whistles down the line, long and low. 'Roughly two million. Two million! Where does a verger get that from?'

Maarten writes the figure down and circles it. That's enough to bet on with a car and holiday.

If you *thought* you might come into that figure soon.

If you *knew* you were coming into that figure soon…

54

WILLOW

Willow helps her mum unfold the clothes in the suitcase and hang each item carefully.

'I just need something to do,' she says to Willow.

Adrika is coming soon, but Willow is worried about her mum. She's crying all the time.

Willow thinks of where Fliss could be – she searches in the dark for her when she closes her eyes. There is nothing. Is she bleeding somewhere?

'I think the worst – every now and again. And I know I shouldn't. I just...' Her mum cries again, and Willow hugs her.

Telling Nonie had been hard. They'd discussed just not saying anything, but Nonie deserves to be part of this. She had gripped the table like she was going to fall from the chair.

Her mum hangs the dress she'd brought to wear to the wedding. 'I sent a photo to Fliss once I picked it,' she says, touching the silk.

'Do you both want tea?' Jack slips his head round the door. He is ashen.

'Yes please,' her mum says, watching him disappear. 'I can't drink any more tea,' she tells Willow. 'I can't swallow. But he needs to keep busy as much as I do. We'll both go mad if we just sit here. The pressure of sitting still!'

'Oh, Mum,' Willow says.

'You know, sometimes I can't catch my breath. My chest is like a balloon and there's no space for all the inhaling and exhaling.' She sits next to Willow, and stares round the room. 'And this house!'

Another dress is tight in her hands.

'This house is unnerving. Firstly, there's the view of the cathedral. It should be a selling point: a park, a cathedral complete with tower. But my chest tightens every time I see it. With its stone steps that curl up and high: make you breathless, and the walls, getting closer and closer the higher you get.'

She shakes her head. 'And it's more than the view. This room. It's squareness, which looks exactly right. *Too* right. The bed in the centre. It looks like a picture I've drawn.'

Willow takes her hand. Her mum is rambling now, and Willow feels tears prickle in her eyes. Everything is falling apart.

'The antique iron bed frame – I hate it! When I first saw it, in this square – too perfectly square – room, I felt cold. I just feel constantly like there's something I've forgotten to do, like a stove left on that will cause a fire… You know, the first night we got here I actually went down to the kitchen to check the kettle wasn't sitting on the Aga, burning dry?' Her mum drops her head into her hands.

Willow rubs her back. She knows that these feelings are

all just a manifestation of unease. Her mum has pinned this house with concern about Nonie travelling, about how Fliss was coping with the wedding, Willow being dumped. And now Fliss missing.

She pushes away the thought that this might be a sign of something else, that maybe her mum is starting to forget things.

No. It's just that all these worries have pinned themselves to this house, and it's easier for her mum to dislike the house, to feel so intensely uneasy in the house, than to carry the worry with her. She has unpacked it here, like the dropped suitcases.

But still.

They need to stay here, no matter how anyone feels about it.

Now Fliss is missing. They cannot move from this spot.

Her mum looks out of the window at the cathedral tower, the park.

'If I stay here a minute longer,' she says softly, 'I will scream.'

55

MAARTEN

'Sir, Michael Braxton's not at home. There was a babysitter with the girls when the PC went round to pick him up. She said she's not sure where he went. Said something about needing to go into work. The car's still there. He must have gone on foot.' Adrika sounds like she's already moving. 'I'm heading to the cathedral now. Meet you there? I'll bring a PC with us. We might need an extra body and Timberman's around. He's big.'

Maarten lifts his jacket, checking the time. It's gone noon. Why would Michael Braxton go to the cathedral today? What is it about the cathedral?

It all seems to lead back there. What is Michael Braxton hiding?

His anger boils. He thinks of Sunny's voice when he had called – broken. Fliss is missing and Maarten is certain that Michael Braxton is involved somehow.

'Sir!' Adrika calls. She's standing over by the tapestry on the walls. 'I waited for you. I've asked Timberman to watch his office, make sure he doesn't leave.'

Walking across the flagstones, Maarten thinks of the party the other night. The chatter, the drinks, the poetry.

He pauses next to the exhibition. The old hospital displayed in the black-and-white photos. Hill Barnes. Why does that name ring a bell?

His brain flicks through the last few days: it was the name of the hospital they'd taken the young girl to – the one who caused the 60s tower death.

Passing the greenery laid out for the Palm Sunday procession, he heads down the steps to the offices and pauses outside Michael Braxton's. There are raised voices.

Maarten lifts his hand to Adrika, to listen, but she is already still, and they both hold their breath as the voices rally back and forth. It doesn't sound like anyone's won yet, and Maarten lets the muffled words fly past him, trying to catch them as they twist through the wooden door.

'*can't ignore…*'

'*compensated…*'

'*police must be told!*'

'*dead now, isn't that enough?*'

The argument seems to finish, as a bang sounds, like a book slamming on a desk. The door pushes open and Maarten takes a step back, wondering who he will see.

It's the verger – Gabriel.

Maarten catches his eye, and Gabriel slows. Colour in his cheeks – heightened – pales.

'I wonder,' Maarten says, 'if we could have a word.'

56

WILLOW

Willow knocks on Nonie's door. There's a faint answer, and she pushes it open. She carries a slice of Victoria sponge. Lizzie had cut them all slices. They lay uneaten on patterned plates on the table downstairs. Willow still hasn't seen Martha. With all the worry about Fliss, she hasn't really thought of it until now. She resolves to check on Martha after she's spoken to Nonie. There's no word on Fliss. Nothing at all.

'Nonie, how are you?' The curtains are open, but there's a thin net hanging down, filtering the glare of the sun through the glass. The light coming in from the park is soft and Nonie is propped up on pillows, looking at the window. She turns her head slowly to Willow as she enters.

'Willow, my darling. How are you?'

'I'm OK. How are you? Did you sleep?'

Nonie nods. 'Yes. But this news.' She raises a tissue to her face. 'Poor Fliss. I just can't stop thinking about her. Where can she be?'

Willow forces a smile on her face, trying not to think of her twin at the bottom of some fall, twisted, alone. 'You know Fliss. If anyone can be the subject of a drama and emerge unscathed, it's her.'

'This place.' Nonie's voice is quiet, almost a whisper. She lifts the tissue, lowers the tissue. Her hands tremble.

Willow sits on the edge of the bed. She places the cake on the bedside table, and passes Nonie the tea. Nonie likes her tea so hot it can scald the tongue. Willow knows if she doesn't drink it now it will just sit there, cooling.

'You don't like St Albans?' Willow helps with the cup, turning it so Nonie can reach the handle. 'You don't think it's pretty?'

'Pretty?' Nonie looks at her as though she's speaking in tongues. 'Pretty? It's got nothing to do with pretty. The moment I heard she was moving here, then *marrying* here!' Nonie's eyes close. 'That was the first afternoon I had a turn. My blood pressure has been all to pot since. This place – why here? Why did it have to be here?'

'Don't worry. It's not so far away. Fliss will come home to visit. It's an easy train ride.' Willow mentally crosses her fingers that Fliss does not make a liar of her. That she's found.

'Oh, it's got nothing to do with that.' Nonie sounds cross, upset. Her voice cracks. 'I should have just stopped it! I could have stopped all of this!'

'All of what, Nonie?' Willow takes her hand, with its creases and its lines. She can remember holding this hand in church when she was young. She'd never known her grandfather. Nonie had seen them at least once a week since they were small. She lives nearby in a flat in Edinburgh, and her front room was always open to them. There was always cake – Battenberg, French fancies, homemade shortbread. Nonie's was a flat of treats. They'd often had Sunday tea there, after church and Sunday School. *Choosing Tea*, they'd called it. You could start with cake, eat the sandwiches without their crusts, then return to cake if you wanted. Any of the food, in any order. Egg mayonnaise with cress had always been Willow's favourite. Fliss liked the tinned salmon, red with bones. Fliss had always liked the more expensive choices. She had once demanded sparkling mineral water. Nonie hadn't even known what it was.

'Can't you just drink water from the tap?' Nonie had said, her pencilled-in eyebrows disappearing in their arch up into her hairline.

'Remember when Fliss brought home her first pot of caviar?' Willow says to Nonie, to make her smile.

'Ha!' Nonie manages a laugh. 'Yes. I've always relied on Fliss for bringing home the best of the best. She's always enjoyed trying to broaden my horizons.'

'Dad was cross. He said caviar from the local supermarket wasn't really caviar. Remember? He brought us some home from a work trip. Fliss hated it, I could tell. Her eyes were watering when she ate it, but she said it was delicious.'

'That girl will go places. I've never known anyone to reach so far, to pin her hopes so high.' Nonie's eyes are green and watery. 'Willow, I'm so scared.'

Holding her hand, the skin paper thin, Willow squeezes it

gently. She can't speak. Her throat is tight, and words won't rise. And she can't promise anything.

She's as scared as Nonie.

57

MAARTEN

'They're all in, sir: Michael Braxton, Jaz Braxton, Gabriel Davis. Three rooms. Which one do we start with?'

Maarten picks up his coffee from his desk. 'Michael Braxton. He and Heather were the last to see Fliss. And it's highly possible he saw her after Heather had left. I'd say he's our number one person of interest right now. Ready, Adrika? Fliss has been missing for thirty-eight hours. It's critical. Let's throw it all at him: he didn't tell us about his debt; he hasn't come forward with whatever is going on at the cathedral with Gabriel Davis; there is something going on between him, Heather and Jaz; and, most importantly, he didn't tell us about the accident with Fliss and was the last person to see her alive. If we're going to find Fliss, then I think Michael Braxton is our best chance.'

Maarten pulls the chair up to the table as Adrika opens the interview, 3 p.m., Friday, and he studies Michael Braxton's face. He met this man two days ago, when his father's body was found. He would have sworn when he met him that he was as he seemed: a hard-working clergyman and dedicated family man, and his father's death a cause of grief and sadness. Jaz is the same.

He is still pale. Maybe it's a family trait, but Maarten's only known him since a death in the family, so it's likely just tiredness and stress. But there is a tension on his brow that could have sat there before this week; his bank statements certainly give him reason to worry.

He is unassuming. His wife, Heather, is more striking. She's seemed the one in control, the more attractive, the more self-possessed. Michael Braxton has brown hair that is greying at the sides, he hunches slightly at the table, his voice is soft when he speaks, almost apologetic. It's a comforting voice – Maarten imagines it sits well with a congregation who have not come for any surprises, who want a gentle reminder about a faith they hold dear. Michael is nodding, looking earnest and miserable as he confirms his details, and Adrika glances at Maarten.

'We need to talk to you about a number of things,' Maarten says. 'But I'll start with the most pressing issue. We had a visit from your wife this morning, and she explained the details behind the damage to your car.' He leaves it for Michael to digest. He obviously had no idea Heather had been in, which was Maarten's guess. The argument they'd had this morning indicated a complete breakdown of communication.

'I...' he stutters, but his eyes close. He bites his lip. 'I...'

'Michael, I'm going to keep this brief, as a woman has been missing now for thirty-eight hours, and you were one of the last people to see her alive. Not only that, but you almost knocked her down and failed to report it to the police. We don't know for sure she wasn't injured. Moreover, you failed to share this information when I spoke to you at your home. I hope you realise how serious this is?'

Michael Braxton melts before Maarten. His entire frame loses its hold. His words spill out of him, in a flood.

'I didn't see her again! Honestly! You have to believe me. Whatever Heather has said – when Heather ran after her, I didn't see her again!'

'You mean to tell me that she left her bag behind? It fell, when you almost ran her down. We found it yesterday. You mean to tell me she didn't come back for it?'

'I didn't see her! Honestly! I swear! I crashed the car; I just didn't see her. I was driving out and we were arguing. I wasn't going fast, but she flashed in front of me. She must have been going quickly. She was wearing something silver, so I saw her in a blink of light and I swung the car. It's completely crushed at the front. Bloody crumple zones. It will cost a fortune to repair.'

'What did you say to her?'

'Nothing! I got out and looked at the car, and Heather went to speak to her. She was upset. I could hear her shouting. I didn't have strength, to be honest. I was exhausted. I just needed to go home. We should never have gone.'

'Why did you go?' Adrika asks. 'Your father was found dead that morning. Why would you go to an event like that in the evening?'

'For work...' Michael starts, but he wavers, and the lie is so weak Maarten wants to spit it back at him.

'Mr Braxton,' Maarten says, injecting as much of a

warning into his tone as he can. 'Michael. Why did you go to the party?'

Michael hangs his head. Hangdog. 'To speak to Gabriel and to try to find the letters. I assumed he had more of them and he certainly had the originals. Gabriel had only given Jaz copies. And I thought if I could take them, then maybe it would all go away. That's why I went. I needed to find him. To ask him to stop.'

58

MAARTEN

'It's just such bullshit!' Adrika stamps down the corridor. She throws the door open and it rebounds with a clang. 'Such bullshit! Two deaths, Fliss missing, and he's trying to keep some dirty little secrets!'

'Let's speak to Jaz. What if Fliss saw something? Heard something? Who knows what Michael Braxton is capable of when pushed to the limit?' He pauses. 'Are you OK?'

She nods. Her hands tighten into fists then she opens them, drops her shoulders. 'It's hard. It's hard staying calm when Fliss is out there somewhere – I can't watch Sunny lose her, sir. I can't. If it was reversed, if he was looking for someone I loved, Sunny wouldn't rest until they were found.'

'I know.' He nods. 'But we're her best shot. Ready?'

Jaz looks as though he hasn't slept, hasn't eaten. Maarten had checked his details and knows he's twenty-four, but he looks about twelve today. As they enter the room, Jaz is rubbing at his eyes with his long thin fingers. His black hair hangs bedraggled around his face. He's only been in custody for approximately twelve hours, but it's taken its toll on him. He looks up as they enter, and Maarten can almost see through him. He's fading away.

'We have your uncle here,' Maarten says, sitting down. 'And Gabriel. And we know about the letters. We need to hear it from you. We need to hear, from your point of view, what all of this is about. I need you to start from the first letter.'

'You've got Uncle Michael here?' Jaz says. He looks at the table. 'I was hoping...'

'What, you were hoping we wouldn't find out?' Adrika speaks sharply. 'You were hoping you'd all just get away with this?'

'We're not getting away with anything. Really. It's not like that. It's not about...' Jaz looks at them, and Michael can see tears in his eyes. 'It wasn't like that. Not at the start.'

'Go from the start,' Maarten says. 'Now.'

Jaz nods slowly. 'Well, the first I knew of it was last week. It was Gabriel who spoke to me.' He shrugs. 'I didn't want to know any of it. It's not my bag. It's not me at all.'

'Go on,' Maarten prompts.

'Well, they've been redecorating. Downstairs. There was a pipe leak or something, we had a bit of a flood – walls wet, rugs ruined. So, they've been doing each room one by one. Gabriel's been in Grandad's old office for years – it's more of a cupboard really – so he had to move out while they took the plaster off the walls to let everything dry out. And when he moved back in, he found them.'

'The letters?' Adrika asks.

Jaz nods. He looks miserable.

'They'd been tucked behind old stones, loose in the wall. Then plastered over and painted.'

'What are they, Jaz?' Maarten asks. 'Whose letters?'

'They're Grandad's – Joel Braxton's. They're copies of letters he's sent. I have no idea why he kept them. Part of me thinks it's because he thought they would never be found. Not for years. But the other part of me thinks it's because he was hoping they *would* be found. Like some kind of twisted legacy. To show how clever he's been. To show how cruel he's been.'

'What did they say?' Adrika asks.

'I haven't read all of them. I read two. Then I told Gabriel I didn't want any part in them, but maybe he should go to the police. He said he felt that was our job. The family's job. So he showed them to Uncle Michael, who said he was going to decide what to do.'

'What did they say, Jaz?'

Jaz wraps his arms around his body, his thin frame more pronounced. He looks even younger. 'They were letters of blackmail. Extortion. Really simple. He's written to people who were in Hill Barnes as children, and he's requested money for silence.'

'But how did he know? How did he have access to these names?' Adrika is making notes.

'He worked at Hill Barnes part-time. Gardening. He saw the kids, knew who they were. He must have kept notes. He kept his ears open. This was back in the 60s and 70s. All he had to do was follow their progress. The ones who were successful, then it just took a letter, ten, fifteen, twenty years later. They're framed as a hard times letter but it's all bullshit: he asks them for a "confidential" deposit in exchange for his own confidentiality about their mental history.'

'But' – Maarten shakes his head – 'the sheer magnitude of it, the planning!'

Jaz looks at him, bites his lip. 'He's a monster. My dad always said so. But I don't think I really understood. Not until now. He was one of those rare people who are absolutely unable to feel anything for others. They only see themselves. They only see their situation.'

The clock ticks in the room as Jaz rubs his eyes again, and Maarten thinks of how this changes things. There were a lot of people who might want to hurt Joel Braxton, and if Noah had found this out, there was reason to silence him.

'So, what did you do?'

'I went to see Uncle Michael. It's been a bit of a mystery over the years – Grandad's money. He gave Uncle Michael a large deposit, years ago, for his first house up north. It wasn't a secret – he made sure my dad knew about it. My dad – Ferdie Braxton – he's a pilot, but he fell out with Grandad years ago. Always managed to rub Dad's face in his money. It's not millions and millions, but it's more than you'd expect, for a verger. I thought he must have won the lottery but didn't want anyone to know in case they insisted on Christian charity. He even bought a few houses over the years, and the rent has paid off the mortgages. With the boom in property since the 90s, the money he had has at least doubled, in some cases tripled. He bought one of those pretty three-bed terraces years ago, for less than £100,000. They go for six, seven times that now. It's crazy.'

Maarten thinks of the pretty terrace he lives in. It *is* crazy. But that would make sense. If he'd bought a few of those houses years ago, then it would add up to a couple of million.

Jaz continues. 'Well, the letters seemed to explain it. If he managed to coerce some significant sums back then, and invest it wisely... It's dirty money. It's not money I want any part of.'

'But surely you can't ignore this?' Adrika says.

'I didn't! I went to Uncle Michael, said we needed to expose him. That this had gone on for long enough. That people were owed payback, that he couldn't be allowed to get away with it.' He looks down again.

'What did he say?' Maarten asks, as gently as he can. He looks no more than a boy now.

'He said to leave it with him. That we had to tread carefully – that people wouldn't necessarily want their secrets exposed. But...' He trails off.

'What? But what?' Adrika leans forward.

'Well, I'm not sure he knew I'd read the letters. These secrets, they're not really secrets at all, are they? That exhibition they've had here brought it all home, you know? People sent to those old mental health hospitals, for all sorts – for babies out of wedlock, for depression. And the treatment! Fuck. Lobotomies in the early part of the last century, locked in isolated cells. The mental health hospital in St Albans took children. For all sorts of reasons. Somehow Grandad knew who these children were, grown up. He was clever with who he threatened: an MP, a high-profile journalist, a senior police officer – people with something to lose. In the 80s, there was such shame about problems with mental health. People were suspicious... They still are to some extent. Even now. You have a broken leg, people can see it. Six weeks in a cast is something people understand. But six weeks off because you can't get out of bed, because the news makes you too sad to move, because the world looks dark. Even now people don't understand it. But back then, there was real shame. If you'd spent a few years in Hill Barnes, you wouldn't shout about it, would you?'

The room is silent. Maarten looks at Adrika, and she shakes her head. The enormity of it. This was not what they had been expecting. What he thought? That maybe he had killed his father in order to inherit the money. But this was a different game altogether.

Maarten looks at his questions. 'So, just going back to Braxton's death. You received a large sum of money into your account a few days ago, and this money was received after you had talked to Michael Braxton about the letters?'

Jaz nods. 'It was a bribe for silence. I think Uncle Michael must have spoken to Grandad and asked him to give me money. Grandad pretended it was a conciliatory gift. But I'm sure the timing was to do with the letters. I think if my uncle had been the only one to know about them, he would have stayed quiet. He has a lot to lose. Don't get me wrong, he's a good guy – he's a great dad to the girls. He's looked after me. But these last few years he's changed. He likes to keep up appearances now: the new car, a fancy new kitchen he'd paid for – the girls both have ponies, did you know?

And both in private school. I know Heather worries about it. She tries to rein him in.'

Adrika scribbles quickly, nodding. 'So, Michael Braxton would have preferred to stay silent?'

'Yes. But when Gabriel showed them to me, I told him we needed to speak up. And Gabriel must have told Uncle Michael who must have told Grandad, because all of a sudden, I have this money in my bank. And he came to see me, that day. He came to the flat and was all smooth and slick. Said he knew we'd never got on, but he'd sent a little something my way, maybe to buy a flat.' Jaz shrugs.

'And you weren't tempted?' Adrika asks.

'No. I said what he'd done made me sick, and I was going to return the money. We had a row. He called me a load of names, said I didn't understand anything. He slagged off my dad – said I had his genes, I was a good-for-nothing...'

Jaz looks down at the table again, and Maarten feels a surge of sympathy. He had come in here so certain Jaz was behind the murder of an older man, the disappearance of a woman. And Noah. Maarten glances down at his notes. 'Noah' is circled with red pen. He believes firmly that what happened to Joel Braxton holds the key to uncovering what happened to Noah Lewis. Possibly even to finding Fliss. If they can make headway with the first fall, from Tuesday night then they will be closer to working out what happened with Noah.

'What about Noah? What was the fight between you and Noah?'

'He'd been through my desk. He'd found some of the photocopied letters Gabriel had given me. Gabriel kept the originals as he didn't want Uncle Michael and me to just get rid of the evidence. He was pushing us to do something. Said it was our responsibility.'

'And what did Noah say?'

'He didn't really know what he had. He skimmed one, didn't realise who they were from. I think he assumed I had sent them. He was trying to make trouble for me; we've never really got on. He thinks I only got the job because of Uncle Michael. We didn't get very far into it, when you came in. It was stressful. Grandad had just died. I didn't know...'

'What?' Maarten looks at him. He gets there must be a multitude of feelings tied up with his grandfather dying, and not finding any resolution. But there was something more there.

'Well, when I saw Uncle Michael there, with Heather, and with Grandad only dying that day... I worried. I kind of leapt to conclusions. I was talking to them after the fight with Noah, and I asked if Uncle Michael was planning to go to the police. Heather had no idea what I was talking about. My uncle wanted it buried – he said if Grandad was dead, then there was no point in opening a can of worms. But I said it needed to be put right. If they were children in the 70s, then they're still alive – they need an apology and their money back. They paid him to keep quiet out of a shame that should never have existed in the first place. But Uncle Michael said he was going to go to Gabriel's office and see if the letters were there. That's why we were arguing. And Heather lost it. Made him leave, said he needed to go home and tell her what we were talking about. She was livid.'

'And because they were arguing, he almost hit Fliss Eliot in the car park,' Adrika says.

'He must have done. But he had no reason to harm Fliss. Honestly! That wasn't why I was quiet last night. I didn't say anything because…' He grinds to a halt. Wraps his arms tighter.

'Then why, Jaz?' Maarten asks gently.

Speaking to the table, his voice so soft it barely reaches them, Jaz says, 'Because I was worried Uncle Michael had killed Grandad. Pushed him off the tower. That it would bring an end to it, avoid the embarrassment of it getting out, get him the inheritance. All the problems solved, in one fell swoop. And I wouldn't blame him. I'm glad he's dead.'

Jaz lifts his gaze, looks Maarten in the eye, defiantly. 'I am. I'm glad.'

59

MAARTEN

'Christ!' Adrika leans her head back against the wall. They stand outside the interview room, reeling.

'No. Wasn't expecting that,' Maarten says. 'That's some story.'

'Where does it leave us?' Adrika says. 'I believe him; I believe Jaz. I can't see him pushing either Joel or Noah from the tower, or having anything to do with Fliss.'

Maarten shakes his head, checks his phone. 'No news from the search. Still no sign of Fliss. I think we're back to Michael Braxton. He could have killed his father, then pushed Noah when he realised Noah knew about the letters, and if he was arguing with Heather in the car, when Fliss was outside, she could have heard what they were talking about. Who knows what he did?'

Adrika nods. 'Even if she didn't hear anything, his paranoia by then could have been off the scale.'

'Yes. Let's leave him to stew for a bit longer, then go in all guns blazing.' He looks at Adrika. She's still refusing to go home. He hasn't really slept much since Wednesday night.

It's gone Friday lunchtime, and they've not eaten. 'Want a sandwich first?' he asks, his stomach tight; he can't face any food, not while Sunny is in knots, not while Fliss is still missing.

Adrika shakes her head. 'Let's do the last one. Let's get all the pieces. We'll interview Gabriel, hear his side of things, then go back to Michael Braxton.' She takes a deep breath. 'I won't be able to look Sunny in the eye if we don't.'

60

ALICE

1967

The ward is silent as Alice creeps out. It's early in the morning. Most are still asleep. The nurses are huddled round their station, which is unusual. They'd usually be doing breakfast now, bringing food and pills. They all hold mugs in their hands. They look serious and Alice listens quietly. She's become good at being part of the background.

'The police are coming back today,' one says. Alice is sure she's called Maureen.

'Do you think she's dead?' The red-haired one says this, and they all gasp, but only one replies, 'No.'

'I just wonder, if they found her cardigan, what else could have happened?' This is another nurse. 'Her coat was still here. And her husband said none of her things have gone. And there's no way Gill would have left her daughter. She's been so proud of young Lizzie.'

'I can't believe she goes to work at all! With children at home – I've never heard the like of it.' This is Maureen. She sucks air between her teeth.

'Lizzie is ten – she's not a baby anymore. And Gill had to come back, you know that. What with her husband being laid off. I know it's not done. But they have no choice.'

'In my day, they didn't even let married women continue in the job.' Maureen takes a drink of her tea. 'I've heard she was seen chatting to that driver again. I wouldn't be surprised if she's gone off with him. A woman who leaves her kiddies at home to go to work is capable of anything.'

'Gill would never have left her child. The rumours about her running off with someone are nonsense.' This is someone else, but Maureen has been here a long time, and they are wary of arguing with her.

Alice flattens herself against the wall. The doors at the end of the corridor open and some police officers enter. There's a young female, one she's seen before.

They stride towards the nurses, who scatter and stand straighter. The WPC sees Alice and smiles. She's the only one.

'Any chance of a cup of tea?' A tall officer says this loudly. He wears a hat and a long coat. He rubs his nose after he speaks, his face twitching. 'We need to speak to some patients, to see if they know anything. We'd like to get this done as soon as possible. Sorry for the inconvenience.'

He doesn't really sound sorry, and his officers speak to the nurses.

The WPC comes over to Alice. 'Hello, love,' she says. 'I've seen you watching before. I bet you see all sorts of things.'

Alice stares at her.

One of the nurses notices. 'Alice, what are you doing here? You shouldn't be here.'

'No, it's fine. Can I talk to her?' the WPC says. She smiles at Alice. 'I'm Rosy.'

'You'll not have any luck with that one – she's dumb. Has been since she was brought here,' Maureen calls, walking briskly past and adjusting her hat.

'Is that right?' Rosy says. 'You can nod.'

Alice nods. There's something about Rosy. And she does want to tell them about the gardener. Alice takes her hand and tugs gently.

Rosy looks over her shoulder at the tall man in the hat. He is reading a list and he rubs his nose again, then sneezes.

'Sir, I'll just head out to talk to some children if you don't mind.' He doesn't look up.

'Bad news about Saturday's results. Looks like we'll miss the play-offs,' he says, but not to Rosy, to a male officer who is writing notes.

Rosy smiles at her. 'Let's go.'

Alice leads Rosy through the door to the garden. The children are slowly getting up, being sent out, while breakfast is being made. The sun is bright. She points over towards a tall tree.

'Come on then,' Rosy says, and follows Alice.

Peter is sitting on the grass by the tree. He has a wooden cup on a stick in his hand, with a piece of string looping out of the bottom, wrapped around a wooden ball. He swings the ball in the air and catches it. He drops it every now and again. He concentrates hard.

Alice touches him on the shoulder and he jumps.

She gestures to Rosy and Peter looks up.

'Hello,' Rosy says. She smooths out her skirt and sits on

the grass next to Peter. Alice knows it's damp and it makes her like Rosy even more.

'I'm Rosy. I wonder if I could ask you a few questions. What's your name?'

'I'm Peter Gabriel Michael Davis,' Peter says.

'Ah, that's a nice name.'

Peter looks to Alice for reassurance, and she nods.

Rosy smiles. 'We're here about the nurse who's missing. I wondered if you had anything you want to tell me? Have you got any ideas about her?'

Alice pushes Peter on the arm and nods. He looks scared.

'You think I should tell?' he says quietly, and Alice nods again. She holds his hand.

'We've seen the gardener looking at all the nurses,' he starts. 'The one who comes here a few mornings a week.'

Rosy smiles again.

Taking a deep breath, Peters says, 'We saw him having an argument with the pretty nurse with the black hair who disappeared a few hours before she went down there.' He points down by the vegetable patch, near the big shed where they store the gardening things. 'They didn't look very happy. That's it. That's all we know.'

Rosy follows his finger, then she gives them both a big smile. 'You've been very brave telling me. Thank you.' She stands, smooths out her skirt. 'Happy Easter.'

61

MAARTEN

Gabriel Davis has only been here a few hours, and Maarten is grateful for that. It sounds as though he was the only one acting sensibly. As long as he's up front, then this shouldn't take too long. Hopefully there are no more surprises. The morning has been a revelation.

Gabriel must be in his early sixties. He looks pretty healthy. He's short but looks strong. His hair is entirely white, cropped close to his head, but his skin is dark, weathered, as though he's spent a good chunk of time in the sun at some point. He has grey eyes, which give nothing away when he looks up as they enter. He doesn't fiddle with anything, doesn't glance around. He sits still, calm. Almost serene.

'Sorry to keep you,' Maarten says, pulling out a chair and sliding into it. Adrika introduces herself, the room, the tape, and Maarten skims his notes.

'We've spoken to Michael Braxton and Jaz. We understand you found the letters, that you presented them to both men, and you asked them to make them public, and inform the police.'

Gabriel nods. 'Yes. I've always liked Michael. He's kind to people. That counts for a lot in my book. I didn't want to expose his family. I wanted him to do it in his own time.'

'And do you think he would have done?' Maarten asks. 'In time?'

'I'd like to think so,' Gabriel says. He looks at both of them. 'But being kind isn't the same thing as being brave, so I kept the originals in case he didn't manage to come clean on his own terms.'

'Did you speak to Michael Braxton that night?' Adrika asks.

Gabriel shakes his head. 'I didn't want to. I'd told him just enough about what that wicked man had done to people to persuade him to go to the police, and I didn't want to tell him any more. No one wants to ruin a father in the eyes of his son. No, at the exhibition opening I spent most of my time talking to that young journalist, with the French surname – Theo? We only stopped talking when the speeches started. His dad came from the same town I lived in for a while.'

'That explains your accent,' Maarten says. 'Are you originally from St Albans?'

Nodding, Gabriel half smiles. His voice is dry. 'Yes. But my mother was a great admirer of the French, and I had lessons when I was young.'

'Was there more to the letters than Jaz and Michael Braxton know about?' Adrika asks.

'Well, yes. I think you know that I found the letters hidden in the wall? But only because when I moved back into my office after the flood, I saw some scratches on a few of the old stones. Like initials and dates. I had a closer look. Some of the stones were loose, and when I pulled them out, the letters were all stashed behind. And if it hadn't been for that leak, well, we'd still be none the wiser.'

'What were the initials?' Maarten asks.

'I don't know. I don't think they were to do with the letters. The letters were all in one place. The initials are scratched on the stones in the wall. At least ten. Most of the dates on there are in the 1960s and 70s. You can see for yourself.'

Adrika is making notes again.

'And did you know about Hill Barnes? When you saw the letters? I have to say, I've read one of them, and it's not clear. It's quite oblique as a reference. If someone were to skim that letter, it comes across more as a plea for money, less as a threatening blackmail letter,' Maarten says.

Gabriel nods. 'Oh aye, he was clever alright. They all start with a plea for help, a play on his position as verger at the cathedral, gardener at the hospital. Makes him almost sound respectable. But when he mentions remembering them from Hill Barnes, it stands out immediately. There's no mistaking that. If someone has tried to keep that part of their history quiet, then those lines read as though spoken through a megaphone.'

Maarten lifts one of the letters and skims it:

... I see that life has treated you well. I follow your progress with interest. Having been a gardener at Hill Barnes, so many years ago, I remember you well. I remember your

stay. And to see how far you have come brings me such joy. Sadly, life has not treated me as well. I have found myself in a tight situation, financially speaking. I was wondering, given how well I remember your generous nature that I saw at Hill Barnes, if you could find it in your heart to offer a small donation to help ease me out of this current situation? It would be an entirely confidential donation, of course. And in return, I will also ensure full confidentiality about your time in hospital. It would remain just between us...

'And you spotted it? Was it because of the exhibition? Is that how you understood the reference?' Adrika asks.

'Oh no.' Gabriel smiles, glances at his fingers. 'Oh no. I knew about Hill Barnes before that. You see, I remember Joel Braxton from years ago. He never would've bothered me – not worth it, you see. I'm not worth anything to him. But I know Hill Barnes, because I lived there.'

Adrika pauses, then says, 'You were a patient?'

'Yes, I had epilepsy. Have epilepsy.'

He sighs, opens his palms out, looks down at them. 'My mother couldn't cope, was embarrassed. And at the start of the 1960s, when she had me at the doctors', they didn't know what to do except send me away. It's what they did back then. You went into one of those institutions for a few years. I was someone to hide. Someone to fix.' He shakes his head. 'I was there when that nurse went missing. She had a kid – probably be about my age now. At the time, we wondered if Joel Braxton had something to do with it.'

Maarten shakes his head. 'Sorry, a nurse went missing?' The super is likely to know about an older case. She had thought she remembered Joel Braxton's name when it first came up.

'Yes.' Gabriel nods. 'A nurse went missing when we were there. We saw the gardener arguing with her before she disappeared. Joel Braxton – he was the gardener.'

Adrika catches Maarten's eye and writes something down. This is one to come back to later. He will speak to the super.

'Sorry, Gabriel,' he says. 'Please continue. You say your mother decided it was best to send you to hospital?'

'Best for everyone. Best for her. It was the shame, you see. My mother was so ashamed of me,' Gabriel says, 'so ashamed of me it made her skin burn. I would come round after a fit and she would be flushed, hot. She'd be crying, telling me to stop. Not to do it again.' He shrugs. 'I was in there for years. I heard later they'd produced a report in '63 saying we should be living in the community, not in asylums. It took a bit longer for me to get out. Mother was so terrified people might find out. When I left, she told everyone I'd been in a special school in France.' He laughs, dry and rasping. 'As if! I think she thought it had more glamour. She told everyone they'd sent me to an expensive school to be educated abroad. She even got someone to give me French lessons, changed my name, and told me to drop French words into my sentences. Told them I'd gotten used to being called Gabriel, now.

'That's why I couldn't hide this. I understand the people who got those letters. As kind as the staff were, and nice as they tried to make it – well, the loony bins, they used to call them. You don't talk too much about it once you leave. Not if someone's decided you're mad.'

62

MAARTEN

'What if it's two separate crimes?' Maarten says, looking at the board they're updating. The day has stretched long, and is still not done. His head is reeling.

'What do you mean?' Adrika asks.

'Well, we're trying to link Joel's death with Noah's fall. What if it's entirely separate? We know why Noah went up the tower – to show it to Willow. We know, or we think we know, what happened up there – he tried to kiss her, she pulled back, he banged his head. We still don't know why Joel went up the tower – it sounds more and more as though someone lured him up there. Noah's situation might be entirely separate.' He taps his pen on the desk.

Adrika stares at the board. 'Well, Theo Durand heard Noah speak to someone else. It could easily be the same person Joel Braxton met.'

Maarten nods. 'But what did Gabriel just say about Theo? Check your notes, but I'm pretty sure he said he talked to him for about an hour. He said they only stopped talking when the speeches started.'

Adrika, holding the pen, pauses mid-air. 'And Theo said he followed Willow up the tower, but she'd already left. And we know she came down the tower to get to the speeches. So, if what Theo's saying is correct, then they must have stopped talking a fair bit before the speeches. So, either Gabriel is mistaken...'

'Or Theo is lying. He didn't go up the tower at all. In which case...' Maarten looks at her.

'Willow Eliot was the last person to see Noah on the tower.' Adrika lifts the pen to the board, scribbles furiously.

Maarten nods. 'What does that mean?' He knows, but it will be easier to hear it aloud. He looks at the board.

Adrika, adding question marks to the points she's just written up, stands back. 'If Willow was the last person to speak to Noah, and she has his blood on her, and her shoe has his blood on it, his head her heel mark...' She looks at Maarten. 'You think Theo was covering? You think Willow...?'

'Maybe. If there was an altercation, and she left him, he could have been staggering around up there. That bang to the head could have been more serious than we realised. Maybe there's more to it than she told us. I suppose we need to ask ourselves if she *knew* that Theo was covering for her? That would change things. It's possible Gabriel was lying about talking to Theo, but I don't see any motive there to kill Noah. Is it more plausible that Willow killed him, and Theo covered for her? Or Theo did it, and she knew? Either way, they could be in this together.'

63

WILLOW

The large white house is still. The wooden floors have nothing to echo: few speak, few walk anywhere. The flowers in the wide front hall have drooped, and the daffodils that sit in each bedroom, on clean wooden units, varnish sparse in places, have dried up – and no one has refilled them. Willow doesn't have the energy. Mugs sit on surfaces, forgotten. They've stopped talking. Jack asks every now and again if someone wants tea. They try to eat. Willow has been writing lists. Theo has moved in – he's been back to his hotel for a shower and a change of clothes, but other than that he sits with Willow.

Lizzie has been a rock. She'd dropped some biscuits round earlier, telling them, 'I spoke to the cathedral and Fliss has been added to the daily prayer list. We're all thinking of her.' Then she'd cleaned the house, chatting. 'I love this house,' she'd said. 'It means a lot to me. I've been cleaning here for years.' She'd touched the wooden kitchen table as she'd cleaned the floors. She'd looked long and hard at Willow's mum. 'I can't imagine what you must be going through,' she'd said. 'I have two at home, about the same age. You never stop worrying about them, do you?' Then all done, she'd left them to their waiting.

They all sit round the kitchen table going through the motions of an evening tea break. The phone rings.

Everyone jumps.

Willow grabs her phone as all hands reach for theirs – *the police?*

It's Theo's. He disappears out of the kitchen. An unknown number – Willow had looked when it flashed up. They had all looked, once they'd stared at their own blank screen. Any sound of a phone is all they wait for.

Sunny has been in and out. No one has mentioned the wedding. Any suggestion that it won't go ahead tomorrow is an admission that they believe Fliss won't be back. Willow can't even see the way to tomorrow. It's years away.

'Willow?' Her mum's voice is tired, but there's a spark in there. She looks at the space where Theo had been.

'I'll go. I'll see.' Willow leaves the room, and it's a relief to step outside of the heavy silence.

She stands outside the door to the lounge and listens. Only hearing Theo's side is difficult, but she can hear him agreeing to something, hears him mention the station and saying he'll be there in about twenty minutes.

He steps outside, and the colour has drained from his face.

'What is it?' she says, feeling sick.

'I have something to tell you,' he says. 'You're not going to like it.'

*

'Why did you lie?' Willow walks to the station with Theo. Any movement is better than nothing. Her blood races. 'I mean – lying to the police! Who does that?'

'Well, you were in a state the other night. You'd seen that other bloke kill himself. Then Noah – and you kept saying you were the last person to see him before he fell. That it was terrifying you. It didn't seem like much. I was supposed to be up there with you. I *should* have been up there with you, Eliot!'

'But you weren't. And that's not your fault, but lying about it won't make it better. It doesn't help!'

'I thought I was making it easier for you!'

Willow shakes her head; her feet pound up the hill, across the park to town. The station lies down one of the old roads leading off from the centre, down from the white museum. She's angry. Some part of her had sparked a little when she'd heard him say he'd lied for her – did it mean…? But mostly she's just angry. As much as Theo means to her, has always meant to her, this is no way to behave. It's the first time she's ever been really angry with him. Even when he was with Fliss, she was mostly sad. Now all she can think about is getting Fliss back, safe. This is no way to do it.

'But Theo, what if it hasn't helped?'

'What do you mean?'

'Don't be stupid. What if it's sent the police in the wrong direction? What if they've missed something because they weren't looking for it? What if Fliss…' She stops on a choke.

'Look, Eliot, I'm sorry. I did it quickly – it was late, I'd had champagne. I didn't know Fliss was missing – we didn't know. You were upset, and I just wanted to help. I don't—'

She looks at him. 'I'm going back to the house. Call me when you're done.'

Theo shouts after her, the words sailing through the crisp air. 'I didn't know what to do. I did it to protect you. I did it *for* you.'

64

ALICE

1967

'Have they found her?' Peter speaks quietly. 'Have they found the nurse?'

Alice shakes her head. She looks out of the window of the ward. They'd usually be allowed outside now. The sun is shining.

'Where is she? I heard the police.'

Still quietly, her voice cracking open like a nut each time she uses it, she says, 'They've got dogs. I don't think they found her, Peter.' Tears run down her face.

'What?' He puts his hand on the glass and begins to cry too. 'What did they find?'

'They found her dress. I heard the nurses talking. They found it buried. The nurses said. They were running outside earlier. They all started shouting. One of them screamed. They were digging, planting seeds.'

'But what does that mean?' His voice is small. High-pitched.

'They found blood on it. I think it means she's dead.

That's what the screaming was about. One of the nurses kept screaming, *She must be dead!*'

Peter's fingers wind into Alice's and she grips them hard.

Alice thinks of the nurse's daughter, growing up without her mummy. What would she think? Would she think that she had left them? There's a funny feeling in Alice's tummy again. The same one she'd had when she had first arrived. It's back again, and she tries to ignore it, but she can't face eating. Her chest is tight.

Betty's not coming. She still hopes, she still dreams of her. But she's not coming. Most of the time Alice knows. But she still wishes. She closes her eyes to the police, the dogs, the huddle of nurses at the side, clutching each other like they're drowning.

Betty, she thinks. *Please, come now.*

She sees the gardener looking on. He pauses at the side of the green grass. He simply looks on and doesn't say a word.

65

WILLOW

'I don't understand why they want to speak to you?' Her mum shakes her head. 'You've already told them about Wednesday night?'

Willow waits for Theo to call – waits for the police to call. They will want to find out if she knew Theo had lied. If they had lied together.

'Yes, but Theo had told them he'd seen Noah up on the tower after I'd left. And he lied. He'd been talking to the verger for the hour before, and the police know that. It means they know he lied, and they think I knew too.' Willow buries her head in her hands. 'Oh my God! It's such a mess! And it will distract them from finding Fliss.'

'But sweetheart, they won't be distracted for long! What on earth can they think?'

'That I pushed Noah! I was the last one to see him before he fell! And even worse…' She sobs now. Shame courses through her veins. Floods through her like acid. It burns.

'What? What else can they think?' Her mum shakes her head again. 'What, darling?'

'I think he will tell them about...'

'What? Go on, Willow. Tell me.'

'That Fliss found out. That Fliss had guessed about Theo. Theo and me. I think he'll tell them. And I was found unconscious, but they might not believe that. What they know is that I wasn't around when Noah fell, and I was out of everyone's sight for a while.'

'But what about Theo? What will they find out?'

'Oh, Mum! Theo and I...' She cries afresh. 'Theo and I had a night together! We haven't even spoken of it – not since. We're chatting, like everything is normal. But it's not – that's why I don't care so much about Otis. I've been in love with Theo ever since I met him, and last year – well. We met for drinks when we were both in Brussels. We got drunk – really drunk. It was hot, and it just kind of happened. We had breakfast the next day, but I bottled talking to him about the next step. I was still with Otis and I'd been obsessed with Theo for so long... And he almost talked of it, but then nothing. And then I went to Rome for the placement and then the exhibition. But if Fliss knew, she'd never speak to me! It's girl code, sister code, twin code. It's a betrayal, Mum. I don't think she knows, but that night she suspected, when we rowed. She brought up Theo and me, and if people heard, and Maarten jumps to conclusions, then... I let her down, Mum. I really let her down, and I threw it all in her face. I chased her away!'

Her mum's hand is soft on her arm. 'Oh Willow, Fliss is getting married – and not to Theo. She's marrying the man she loves. You haven't got in the way of anything. You can put that behind you. When she gets back.'

'It's more than that, though – don't you see? They think our row was worse! That I might have done something to her! In the heat of the moment! I went off on my own. I honestly can't remember what happened – just that I came round; it's a blank. But I can't remember, and they will wonder if I found Fliss outside. If the row continued. I was the last person to see Noah Lewis, and he said someone pushed him from the tower. And I argued with Fliss, and now she's nowhere. Oh Mum, they'll think I hurt them both!'

'Oh, Willow.'

Lizzie knocks on the door. 'I'm sorry to bother you.'

Willow swallows hard. She will need to go to the station soon.

Her mum says, 'Yes, Lizzie? What is it?'

'Well, I don't know… I don't want to cause trouble. But it's Martha. I haven't seen her around all day. And when I think about it, she wasn't here yesterday. I don't know what to do – but, well, I went to her room. I thought she must be asleep.' Lizzie bites her lip. 'She's not there. And well, her bed is freshly made, and the curtains are drawn. And there's no sign of her. I think it's strange. Too strange. What if Martha's missing as well?'

66

MAARTEN

It's so late. The dark creeps in at the corners of the day, and no one has slept for such a long time. Fliss is still missing. Maarten had sent a search team to Michael Braxton's and Gabriel Davis's houses. They'd both complied. He feels like he's rushing at a brick wall.

The super sticks her head round the door. 'All OK, Maarten?'

He nods. 'We're doing a search on the houses. Still no word on Fliss. We're getting closer. Looks like there's a lot of history to this one. We're going back to the 1960s and 70s. Seems Joel Braxton, the first death, has some history related to the old mental health hospital, Hill Barnes.'

The super nods. 'Yes, I read your report. Interesting. You know, one of the first cases for my mentor was at Hill Barnes. A missing nurse. Gill Coombes. They found some clothing but never found her. I called her this morning after seeing your report. She told me she'd interviewed some children, who said they'd seen a part-time gardener rowing with her. The officer in charge spoke to the gardener, who gave them an alibi for later in the day, so it never went anywhere. But Rosy never believed they followed it up. Her boss was a sexist prick, apparently. No time for the testimony of women or children. Keep me updated. I still see Rosy. She'll be interested if Hill Barnes ends up part of this. That case was never resolved, and she was always convinced by the children.'

His phone rings. Adrika.

'We found CCTV in the bin outside. It's been ruined, sir. But it's there. Gabriel told us the system was broken all week, but someone must have taken the footage from Tuesday night, and then broken it. It implies Gabriel is more closely involved. He was in the pub on the hill the night Joel Braxton fell – he was there until Willow called him. His alibi stacks up, so why lie about the CCTV? What is he hiding? I'll be there in fifteen minutes.'

'You told us Joel Braxton was on his own the night he came to the cathedral. You said there was no CCTV for the evening in question. We found the CCTV in your bin. So you either know who killed Joel Braxton and you're covering, or it was you – somehow. The CCTV is useless to us. But I'm sure you've watched it. What's the story?' Adrika stops, managing to stay calm despite her exhaustion and frustration. Maarten waits.

Gabriel looks to the floor. His voice cracks and creaks. 'I had to throw the CCTV away. It was corrupted. I took it home to see if there was anything I could do. But I had to throw it away. It wasn't just that night, it's been down for about a week now. I didn't have a choice.' His shoulders drop and he rounds forward, a heaviness pressing him down.

'You had no choice?' Maarten says.

'You broke the law,' Adrika says, her voice rising, her professional tone cracking slightly. 'You can't throw away evidence. We know you confronted the family about the letters, threatening to expose Joel. This isn't looking good, Gabriel. This doesn't look good at all. You argued, you were at the scene around the right time. You threw away CCTV.'

'I threw it away before he died. I just hadn't got round to replacing it.'

'Did you report this to anyone?'

He shakes his head. Looks at the table.

Maarten watches him. 'Gabriel, is there something you want to say to us?' he asks.

Gabriel looks at him, eyes blue-grey, clear. A tiny shake of the head. 'He wasn't a good man.'

67

ALICE

1967

The sun is out as Alice and Peter sit on the lawn. The police still haven't found the nurse. Just her cardigan and the dress. The husband has been here again with the little girl. He was crying last week. Some of the other nurses were crying with him. Nothing. There's no sign anywhere.

Alice is almost a teenager now. Peter is still the only one she speaks to. He's been here just over a year.

'That gardener over there, he's still watching the police,' Peter says.

Alice's head is a jumble. There are so many stories in there. The court case, the papers, what the police had said, what the nurses had said. She's heard her story from so many different mouths.

That verger, though. The gardener. He works part-time here, and there's a story in her brain that cycles round and round. One version of her history.

She's never said it aloud. She's never heard anyone else

say it. She doesn't even know if it's true. But she's sure he's part of her story.

'He's a bad man,' she says to Peter. 'You keep out of his way.'

'Why do you think he's so interested in the police?' he asks. 'We told Rosy. She must have spoken to him. The police would have taken him away if he was really bad.'

Alice doesn't know. But she remembers her last day in the cathedral. *The police don't catch all the bad men*, she thinks. Even though everyone talks of it differently, she remembers every second of that day.

'I think he lies. I think he tells huge lies. I think he's a bad man.'

What had happened that day? She sits and allows it to rest in her brain. To unfold. It had come after she had heard Daddy and Mummy talking about her. Daddy had been angry. *What would they do?* he had said. *What would they do about her?*

Three weeks later, Mummy had taken Alice up the cathedral tower. 'Just you and me,' she'd said, smiling, and Alice had held her hand. She can smell that day. She can smell the air. Spring had arrived. The daffodils were still in bloom. Her minds drifts, takes her back there. To Mummy, who still comes to her in her dreams.

It's almost Easter. The cathedral is busy with activities all week. There are people everywhere and flowers burst from all directions. The daffodils are still blooming, and Alice feels a flush of excitement.

She is seven years old.

'Look!' she says, pointing at a huge figure leaning against

a wall. The effigies are to be carried through the centre of St Albans on a pilgrimage. And the foot-washing is in a few days' time. Alice loves Easter. It's when she knows the park will start to warm up, when she knows the sun will be in her bedroom when she opens her eyes. She has so much energy, and winter is cold. In the summer she can run and run.

'Shall we go up the tower?' Mummy says. 'Look, it's open.'

They start the winding climb, and Alice loves the feeling of her legs getting stronger, the excitement of rising. The walls become narrower the higher they rise. They pass the belfry, glimpse the town spread out below them in tiny parcels through the narrow windows in the thick stone walls.

She runs ahead, tripping up the steps.

'Wait!' Mummy laughs.

And at the top, the whole of the park opens out, the lake, the twisty lanes.

'There's our house!' says Alice, pointing at the top of the huge white cottage.

'And over there, where we had a picnic last week,' Mummy says.

'Do you think we could fly from here?' Alice asks.

'No, darling.' Her mummy frowns quickly, but looks kind. 'Remember what happened to Hector? We'd fall. And it's such a long way down.'

They both look at the roofs below them, slanting outwards. If you fell from here, then you'd bounce and slide, and hit the ground.

'It would hurt, wouldn't it?' Alice says, thinking of Hector, their hamster. Her eyes fill with tears. 'Do you think it hurt Hector?'

'No, not very much. But don't do something like that again – not without coming and asking me?'

Alice shakes her head. Mummy bends and kisses her. Her lips are warm, and she produces chocolate from a pocket. 'Here, Alice. If you have big ideas again, can you come and tell me? You're so clever, and you can do so many things. But can you tell me first? Just so I can make sure it all goes well? You're still only seven. There's a lot to learn.'

Alice nods, seriously, taking the chocolate. 'Yes,' she says.

'Hello.' A man appears behind them and her mummy frowns.

'Hello,' she says, her hand tightening on Alice's.

Alice knows she's seen him before. In the cathedral. She chews the chocolate, her head tilting to the side.

He's been trying to talk to Mummy a lot recently. That's what it is, how she knows him. And Mummy has taken to rolling her eyes a bit when he leaves, like she does when the cat used to knock over the milk bottles on the step, and they'd smash; or when the hamster would get out of his cage when they were cleaning it.

Alice feels sad for a second, at the thought of Hector again. She's trying not to think about him. She feels a tight clutch in her belly – the same clutch she'd felt as he'd fallen, and there was a quick flash of knowing that he wasn't going to fly after all. It feels like something's pressing in her tummy, and it makes it hard to breathe, hard to speak.

'Now, Lisbeth, you've been avoiding me.'

There's something funny in the man's voice, Alice thinks.

He sounds like he's telling her off, but also as though he's praising her. Her mummy pulls on her hand.

'Let's go,' she whispers.

Alice nods.

They step towards the door that takes them back down the stairs, but this man steps between them and the door.

'Now, now, Lisbeth,' he says again. This time he sounds much more like he's telling her off. 'Come on. I know. I've seen it in your eyes. You're thinking it too.'

Thinking what? Alice wonders.

'Joel, please. I've got the girl here. We're just going to go down the stairs.'

'You thought you'd bring your girl up here, to tease me? You think that would put me off?'

'Joel, I'm serious. Let us go back down the stairs.'

There's something in the man's expression that makes Alice feel frightened. The wind up here feels colder, and she thinks of the fire at home. She turns to look at the top of their cottage, and longs for toast and warmed milk.

'Lisbeth. How about just one kiss?' he says, and he steps forward, taking her mummy's arm.

'Let go of me, Joel! I'll scream!'

'We're up here alone,' he says.

Alice hates the way he smiles as he says this. His mouth curls up, in the same way her headmaster's does, just as he picks up the cane.

'Leave her alone!' Alice says. She can feel the frustration back. With this man. Whose hand is on her mummy's arm, and his other hand is holding her by the chin now. Her mummy is struggling, pulling away, stepping backwards.

'Get off me, Joel!' her mummy shouts. 'Get off me!'

'One little kiss,' he says.

The man's voice is different now. He sounds like he's been running, his breath is coming faster. Alice is very scared.

'Mummy!' Alice shouts, and her mummy catches her eye.

'Run, Alice,' her mummy says. 'Run away.'

But Alice's feet are stuck to the tower roof. When she manages to unpeel them, she doesn't run towards the stairs, but towards the man, and bangs her fists into his back. He doesn't even turn around.

He's leaning over Mummy now, and they bend back over the edge of the tower.

'I know you feel the same, Lisbeth, the way you say hello to me, the way you smile at me. I know you want to kiss me too.'

The man is almost panting now, like dogs do in the park.

'Mummy!' Alice screams. She has never felt so helpless. She runs at the man, and pummels him, over and over.

She can't get to him. Not from here.

Looking at the parapet, if she can just reach up...

She jumps up, and climbs to the top. The cathedral roof lies below her, but she can reach him here. She grabs hold of the top of the parapet with one hand, and with the other, she reaches for the man's hair. Grasping it tight in her fingers, she kicks at him, feeling her toes connect with his skin, and she hears him yelp.

'Alice! Get down!' Mummy screams.

'You bitch!' shouts the man.

Alice clings on, and kicks again.

He reaches for her, and his hand grabs her foot. Kicking it

wildly, trying to free it, she wobbles and tips further towards the roof, but her grip on the wall holds her tight.

'Alice!' Mummy screams again, and now she climbs, pulling herself up on the wall, reaching for Alice.

And they are both reaching for her. Alice stops kicking, but her blood is racing. Her mind is swarming with thoughts, none of which are clear in her head. Her hands tremble and she starts to scream loudly, over and over, 'Mummy! Mummy!'

'Alice, I'm here.' Mummy is beside her up on the parapet, reaching for her, when it happens.

And it happens quickly. The man is pushing forward, grabbing Alice, grabbing Mummy. Her mummy leans backwards, and as he tries to hold her arm, Mummy lashes out at him, and he punches her hard, once, on the cheek.

They all seem to scream at the same time. Mummy has slipped over the edge of the parapet, and her hands now cling to the edge of the tower. She screams loudly.

'Please! Help me!'

But now the man is backing away, and Alice can't move. He still has hold of her leg, although he's staring at Mummy, not her. He takes another step back, and she falls from the parapet to the roof of the tower.

'Please!' her mummy cries. 'Please help me!'

But now his breathing has changed again – it's almost stopped. He stands very still.

'Mummy!' Alice screams.

But slowly, so slowly, her mummy's fingers slide out of view, and the scream as she falls is as loud as anything Alice has heard.

Alice closes her eyes, praying as hard as she can. 'Please fly, please fly,' she prays, her eyes tight, and the feeling is back in her tummy, like someone's pressing a foot on it. Her throat is tight, and she can't swallow.

'You did this!' The man circles and points down at her. 'You! If you hadn't been here, then this would never have happened! It was your fault! Why did you climb up there? You killed her!' He runs for the steps, running so fast that the door bangs hard on the building. Before he goes through it, he turns and shouts, staring at her hard. 'You killed your mother! And if you tell anyone, anyone, I was here, I will come for you. You had better not say a single word!'

Alice is frozen. The last few minutes unreal. Like something in a dream. Or a nightmare.

'Mummy,' she whispers. But she mouths the word, as something clicks in her neck, and the word buries itself in her throat, in her guilt. She has killed Mummy.

68

MAARTEN

'What now?' Adrika looks exhausted. Her skin is pale and her eyes are red.

'We leave Gabriel for five minutes and then we go again. Why would he remove the CCTV if he wasn't him? Our assumption has always been that the person who pushed Joel Braxton off the roof is the same person who pushed Noah, and the same person who knows where Fliss is. But perhaps we've been off-track.'

'Five minutes?'

He nods.

'I'll get us a coffee.'

'Sir!' a PC shouts from down the corridor. 'We have Willow Eliot on the phone. Someone else is missing. I'll head out now to take a statement.'

'Who is it? We'll follow you there in half an hour.'

'It's the owner of the house Willow is staying in. Martha Adams.'

*

'How did the confrontation with Joel Braxton go, Gabriel? Why did you pick that moment?'

'Aye, well.' He shrugs. 'He saw me at the cathedral that day. I think Michael must have told him what I'd seen. The letters.' He sighs. 'He'd recognised me years ago, when I took over the job. That afternoon, that's what we were rowing about. He said he recognised me. Told me I needed to repay his silence with my silence.'

'And did you kill him?' Adrika asks quietly.

'Kill him?' Gabriel looks down. 'Oh, I didn't kill him. I destroyed the CCTV, but I didn't kill him. I could have, I think, if it had come to it, in the moment. But killing isn't like that. You do it to defend someone, to protect a life. I couldn't just kill him. Just like that.'

'So, who did kill him?' Maarten asks.

'I don't know. The CCTV was destroyed. Accidentally.'

'But you must know who this person is?' Maarten asks. 'You wouldn't have gone to such lengths?'

'It makes no matter if I have a few guesses.' Gabriel sits back. 'None of it's proof.'

'Look,' Maarten says, as calmly as he can muster. 'Forget Braxton for a second. We now have two missing people, and I need you to tell me anything you suspect. Anything at all.'

'Two?' Gabriel asks. 'You said there was a young woman, but now there are two?'

'Martha Adams – who runs the B&B by the cathedral. She's been missing from Wednesday night too – as far as we know.' Adrika sits back, exhausted. 'Both of them. Neither have been seen for days.'

'Martha's missing?' Gabriel sits bolt upright. 'But you need to find her!'

'Yes, Gabriel,' Adrika shouts. Maarten has rarely heard her shout. She slices the air with her hand to emphasise her point. 'That's what we're trying to do!'

'But you know where she'll be?'

'Gabriel, we have no idea. Please. Do you know?'

'Of course! There's only one place she'd go. You need to leave now! It's old. She could be injured! Please!'

69

ALICE

1987

'That's it, another deep breath. I'll put the music on. Just hum along.'

It had begun with humming. With this new counsellor, who is younger than her, and is kind. And has a look of Betty at times – the same smile when Alice was scared, the same way of reassuring her. Of laughing gently when she felt tight – of talking her through the feeling of the pressure building, of fizzing, of popping.

She had slowly hummed. Almost inaudibly to start with.

The counsellor had picked songs from when Alice was small, music that had been on the radio – that Mummy played. She would bring in a selection of records and let Alice choose.

When her mother had started to feel closer to her, it had hurt so much to begin with. Alice would cry for hours, and she was worried they would think she was going backwards, that tears meant she was losing control.

But instead, the counsellor had smiled at her, and hummed

along too. She had pushed tissues at her, and made her cups of tea. The sessions became easier. Easier and harder.

Then the humming became louder.

They practised breathing, counted breaths in and out. Alice counted in her head, counted with a drum, with a xylophone.

And so slowly, she had made sounds, then notes, and then...

'Alice! You did it! You spoke!'

'Alice? Did you understand? You'll be released. There is much more care in the community now, and Hill Barnes will be closed down in the next few years. But your progress has been remarkable. The fact that you're talking again, well, it's quite frankly astonishing.' The doctor's head is shaking as she speaks. 'The results we've had with this new counsellor are beyond my expectations. At thirty-two, you've really come a long way. I feel confident you'll do well. How are you feeling about it?'

Alice looks at her hands, the lines that have formed there. The fingernails that she picks at, pulls at if she feels upset. She counts the lines – she knows how many there are, but the counting is calming. The idea of there being a life outside of Hill Barnes is impossible to imagine. It's like thinking you could step inside the television. You could live all the lives you see others living. So many choices. Too many choices. Her cheeks are damp, her mouth salty, as she speaks. 'I can leave? But where do I go?'

The doctor smiles. She's worked here for five years and

Alice has always liked her. Slowly, the staff have changed, the hospital has changed. The drugs that she was given each day have disappeared. The needles for when she was upset. The long ward beds have thinned out. There haven't been any new patients for years.

The fact that she was mute meant she'd been written off as unable to look after herself, having been in for so long. But with her confidence to speak to others, with her ability now to see that she was only a child when her mother had died, that she wasn't really to blame – that it had been just a horrible accident – then her treatment had changed considerably.

The counsellor had talked with her about her father, the way he spoke to her, the way he would make her pray, the way he hit her. 'There are different ways children respond to such rigid behaviour expectations,' she'd said. 'Some of the reactions you've described, which worry you, we might see now as something like Oppositional Defiant Disorder, or Hyperkinetic Disorder. I'm not saying this was the case with you, but I want you to understand that children can have problems. It's not just about "good" or "bad" behaviour. You've talked about some compulsive traits, and there are ways we can help you to manage these. Remember, you experienced severe trauma, Alice. You were a victim. As well as the beating, you lost your mother and witnessed her death.'

She was viewed very differently. *There was no reason*, they said, she wouldn't be able to look after herself, *even after all this time*.

'Well, it's up to you. Your house in St Albans is still here.

It's rented out, and you could either move back into it, or you could leave it as rented, and move to somewhere else entirely new. Would you like to think about it?'

Looking out of the window, Alice thinks of St Albans, of the parts of it she remembers. She remembers the park, she remembers the cathedral. She remembers *that day*. The new counsellor has helped her talk of that day. She has finally been able to say out loud what happened *that day*. It is so long ago, so fixed in her past, that it doesn't really matter anymore which version is real. There's the version that came from the court case, there's the version in her head. But either way, she has lived her life in this hospital. No words will undo that.

'If you want, you could speak to the police about what really happened. It's not too late,' the counsellor had said, once Alice had finally spoken. Finally, been able to speak.

But she had shaken her head. She knows the authorities are not to be trusted. All those men. They had believed the verger. Not just once, but about Gill Coombes as well. The courts had put her here – taken her away from Betty. The police had ignored what she and Peter had told Rosy. She will never tell the authorities about that day. They could just as easily send her back – say she's relapsed. Telling the authorities does no good. Even thinking about it makes her throat close up.

It has taken so long to get here. To be able to look at herself in the mirror, to find a voice. And it had been an accident after all. He had set things in motion, but she recognises he hadn't set out to kill her mother. His attack hadn't got very far. And it was twenty-five years ago. Had what happened to her given him a taste for violence? Had it been something that led to whatever happened to Gill Coombes?

There will be some kind of reckoning, she feels. At some point. She's not sure she believes in God anymore, not after watching her mother pushed from a tower in one of His cathedrals. She's not sure she could wait for a Day of Reckoning. But there must be some sort of reckoning. Life is about balances. It's about halves. She is one half of something, and she always has been. The way she looks at it now is that she is here so that Betty has lived. Has she lived through Betty?

Sometimes, she has pangs. She's had toothache for no reason. Pain with no clear cause. And it's a specific type of pain. It's a pain she's aware of, but it touches her like a ghost.

Occasionally, she is crying before she realises it.

And the other way. There are moments of happiness, from nowhere. Moments of warmth.

Life is about balance and halves. Betty has spoken for her. Betty has lived for her.

It's her time now.

And Joel Braxton will face a reckoning one day. She has served his time. She is owed.

'I can't stay here,' she tells the doctor. 'They know my name.'

'But not your face,' the doctor says. 'You were seven years old when you came here. No one will recognise you. I would suggest a name change. We can help you with that.'

Alice nods slowly. 'I think I'll start somewhere else. I'd

like to try somewhere near the sea. I've seen the sea a lot on the television. Can I move there?'

Smiling, the doctor leans forward. Her brown hair swings as she nods, and she reaches out, tapping the tissues, pushing them towards Alice.

She's so young, Alice thinks. *How much can she really know?*

'Yes, I think that sounds like a good plan.'

'I'd like to come back here at some point. I'd like to move home. But first I need to learn how to live – I'll do that by the sea.'

'Do you have any ideas what you'd like to change your name to?' the doctor asks. 'I have some name books if you'd like?'

Looking back at her fingernails, Alice thinks briefly that she will need to let them grow a little, if she is to meet new people. Real people. Have a Real Life.

'My mother's middle name.' Alice's voice cracks. 'I'd like to be called Martha, please.'

70

WILLOW

The officer sits quietly taking the statement.

Willow pours a glass of water from the jug, passing it to Lizzie, whose hands are shaking.

'He's to blame for all of this. All of it.'

'Who?' Willow says.

'She's talking about Joel Braxton,' her husband says, taking off his coat and sitting down. He puts his arm around Lizzie. 'We'd decided not to say anything, to let sleeping dogs lie. We've seen how some women are pulled apart on the stand. Almost more on trial than the men. So Lizzie had decided not to say anything.'

He takes her hand. 'I think it's time to tell the police. I think, now that he's gone, he can't hurt you anymore.'

'He...' Lizzie closes her eyes. 'Well, out of wedlock... I was young; it was different then. My father...' Lizzie shakes her head. 'Sometimes things happen. Sometimes things happen *to* us.' At this, her eyes fill with tears and Willow is cold. 'Something happened to me when I was seventeen. I said no, but I didn't really understand what it was until later. We didn't really learn about it at school, and my stepmother never said. It was the 70s. Afterwards, she said it was something she was going to tell me before my wedding night. So he'd started before I realised it would hurt. He'd finished before I realised I was bleeding. I ran home, and told her. She was…'

Lizzie freezes. She looks out of the window into the dark. 'She didn't speak to me for at least a week. She said we had to wait. *Wait and see.* But six weeks later, I still hadn't got the curse, and she said, *Well then*, and that we would have to *tell father*. She said it would *kill him*. She said, *what were you thinking?*'

Willow's fingers knit together and she tilts forward, just an inch. 'Did you get to keep the baby?'

'Baby?' Lizzie's eyes find hers; they're clear and empty. 'They said I had to put it up for adoption, and that it would be best if I didn't look at it or hold it after it was born.'

Willow feels sick.

'I remember the birth, and afterwards. I could swear I heard it cry. I was out of it. I was exhausted. There was a sheet, and it was taken away. I was so tired. And I was crying. There was blood…' She looks down and her hand, raised throughout the telling, falls to her side. 'They said not to speak of it. It wasn't until years later, after I'd had my Maeve, and after I gave birth to her, I just couldn't stop crying. Finally, years after I was married, Jim—'

Lizzie's husband holds her hand.

'—Well, I just couldn't bear it anymore, and Jim made me see a doctor. He said now there were people you could talk to about things like this. The doctor sent me to a woman and I told her everything. And she said it was OK to feel sad. I couldn't say what I'd felt up to then. I'm not sure I'd felt anything at all. I thought I was faulty – defective. Guilty. But actually, I was just sad.'

Willow says quietly, 'And the man who did this?'

'Joel Braxton,' Lizzie says. 'I told Martha. We talked a lot. I don't know exactly what happened in her childhood, but I know where she grew up. Gabriel knows too. She was at Hill Barnes, the hospital. They used to send unmarried mothers there too, you know. If what happened to me had happened twenty years earlier, I would have gone to one of those hospitals. And I know Martha blames Joel Braxton for her being sent to Hill Barnes; that was something we had in common. We saw him that morning. He came to the cathedral with his family. Seeing him after such a long time was such a shock.'

She looks at her husband.

'But if Martha's missing, she might have gone back to where she grew up. There's a building left of the old hospital. She has a theory that Joel killed my real mother, and now he's dead, she said she would go back to tell her, before the building was torn down. She may have gone at night to avoid the security guard. I was only ten when my mother died. I know Martha thinks of her.'

'What if Fliss is there too?' Willow stands up.

'Why would Fliss be there?' her mum says.

'Martha was at the party. What if she met Fliss on the way out? We've looked everywhere else.'

'Oh, Willow. We should call Sunny!'

71

ALICE

Tuesday evening. Three days ago.

Alice looks out of the window. The cathedral is quiet. The amber lighting soft in the darkness.

The family arrive tomorrow. Her family.

She had seen him that morning. Blinking long and hard hadn't helped. He stood there, large as life. Large as death.

She has waited sixty years to see Betty again, and she will arrive tomorrow. Betty's daughter arrives later today: her niece.

These words are still new in her mind. The idea of it all. But she had seen the other girl – *Fliss*, her name is – she had seen her in the cathedral a month or so ago. There was no mistaking her. She had Betty's face. Betty's eyes.

Like a dream, like a fairy tale, they're coming here. Fliss is getting married here, and they are all coming. She had spoken quietly to Lizzie, who had then suggested to the couple the B&B just across the park: '*If you have any family coming, from out of town, I can recommend a big house. It's a B&B, but you can hire the whole thing. I help out*

*there so could get you a good rate. I know it's hard when
families don't know the area.'*

When the call had come through, Alice had cried and
cried. Betty would be coming home. Would she dare tell her
the truth? She didn't need to decide that now. It would be
enough just to see her. It would be everything.

But Joel Braxton has returned, and Alice is scared. He
is older now, but the idea of him being here, when all her
family are arriving...

She has watched TV. Those crime shows. She doesn't
have a mobile phone, but she bought a cheap one today.
And Lizzie had found his number. She had asked Michael
Braxton if she could borrow his phone to make a quick call.
Dad had been an easy number to spot.

Stealing herself, she dials it now. 'I have some evidence,
from years ago. Meet me at the tower at midnight. The door
will be unlocked. If you don't, or if you tell anyone, I'll go
straight to the police.'

She knows he can hear. His breath becomes short on the
phone: 'Who is this?'

But she doesn't reply. She holds the phone to her ear for
a second, listening to him stumble over what she had said.

So many crimes. He won't know which one to choose.
Lizzie had told her about the rape, and the baby she had
to give up. And Alice remembers Gill Coombes, who had
never been found in Hill Barnes. But Alice remembers Joel
Braxton watching the police, and she had been sure his
had been furtive glances, checking nothing they had found
could lead to him. She remembers the row he'd had with the
young nurse.

There's only one building still standing from that time. And it's due to be demolished in days. It's too late to rake up old truths, but she wants to go there. It's the old building from the end of the garden. It sits on the edge of what is now a park. She remembers the gardener laying a new floor the day Gill went missing. The clothes had been found on another part of the land. The rumour that she had run off with someone had festered. Peter had asked if they should tell anyone about the gardener laying the floor; but the police hadn't listened the first time. Why would they listen to children? So they had said nothing. But Alice had known who he was, what he had done to her. Her eyes had tracked him whether she willed them to or not.

Before the building goes, she wants to say goodbye to her past.

And if there is any sign of Gill Coombes, she wants to tell her, like she will tell her mother, that he is gone.

Just this to do first.

Lizzie had lent her the key for the evening. She will drop it to her on the way home. Lizzie has planned to be with Jim all evening, but she has left her purse at the cathedral so she can say she saw Joel Braxton briefly, and that he entered alone.

Peter has told her how to make her way to the tower so the cameras will not pick her up. There is an easy way through the blind spots, once you know. And he has lifted the tape from the camera over the tower door.

No one will know Joel Braxton was not alone.

*

'Is anyone here?' The black of night allows Alice to hide, and she thinks of sixty years ago. This is not about seeking revenge, but about protection. For her family. He will not come near any of them again.

She is careful not to touch anything. She has worn old gloves that she can burn on the Aga later.

'Hello? Is anyone here?'

He sounds angry, and maybe afraid. But Alice doubts he knows what fear is.

It's easy. He's older now. There's a tape ready to play on the edge of the tower; she'd stuck it down. The button is in her pocket, and she presses it.

'Here, I'm over here.' The recording plays out into the black, and Joel Braxton walks towards it. His breathing is heavy after climbing the stairs, but he is still strong.

'Where are you?' he calls. 'What's this about?'

'Here. You'll need to climb up.'

Alice had left the small collapsible step out. She'd needed it when she positioned the recording device on the stone, on the outer wall of the tower.

Sure enough, he steps up, to lean over the top, to look. When a man has committed the sins he has, he must think anything is possible.

And all she has to do is push, as swiftly as possible. To lift his feet and push up – like a see-saw. She couldn't do it from the ground, he would be too heavy. But gravity will be on her side.

Now, she thinks. *Go now.*

She rushes. She grabs his feet, and before he knows it, before he's had a chance to say anything, but only to expel air in a half-cry, he is lifted into the night, and he tips up and over the tower edge.

Alice trembles. The tears come quickly.

'Rest now,' she whispers. 'He is gone.'

And if her mother has ever returned to this spot, she can leave it forever.

She can hear him cry, from down the sloping roof. But there is no return passage. '*Nor stone, nor earth,*' she whispers, '*nor boundless sea.*' Nothing will bring him back up to here. To solid ground. As cruel as he is, as vicious as his life was, he is bound by mortality like everyone else. In the end, he was due to fall.

72

WILLOW

The night is black as Willow swings the car into Highfield Park. There's no lighting, and she isn't sure where the building is, not in this dark. It's completely disorientating. The car slides to a halt on the grass, on the mud. For a second, she just trembles.

She dials Sunny, but there's still no answer. She leaves a message. 'Sunny, I'm here. I'm going in.' Her mum had said to wait for Maarten to arrive, but she had taken Lizzie's husband's car keys – he'd left them by the door. She just needed to get there. She knew the area from the map at the exhibition and if she had told anyone, they would have stopped her, made her wait. She'd texted Theo, still not back from the station.

But Fliss needs her.

Lighting up the torch on her phone, she finds a path and, picking up pace, runs through the trees. Her heart beats quickly. Either side of her, the branches shift in and out of the periphery and adrenaline hits like a tsunami. She is rocked, out of her depth.

'Fliss!' she screams. 'Fliss!'

Running, breath tight and limbs pounding, she sees a break in the trees, curving to the right, which must be where the path lies. It all looks so different in the dark. It could be years ago.

'Fliss!'

There. The building lies in the shadows up ahead. The moon draws the shape, frames the building. Darkness pools outwards, in shapes that balloon and shift. Willow pauses. She gasps at air like she's drowning.

Is Fliss really in there?

The first step she takes shifts her slowly. One foot, then the next – the trepidation almost paralysing. Worrying about what she could find, worrying that she's already too late, the pull she has felt since the morning is stronger than ever. She wishes Sunny would answer. She wishes she had asked Theo to come. But the pull towards Fliss has been too strong.

She phones Sunny again, but still no answer.

There is only her, and she needs to go in. She is so sure Fliss is here, she can smell her. She hears her voice inside her head.

This time she whispers, like an answer, 'Fliss.'

She steps past the old lawns, an old vegetable patch. The door is open, hanging on its hinge. The building only has a couple of days left, and tape has been erected all the way around. *Disused building. Do not enter.*

The smell of damp arrives on the breeze like a warning: rotten floorboards, unsafe walls. Ducking her head, she enters the building. The floorboards creak their welcome, and she thinks of Alice. She thinks of Lizzie, of Gill Coombes.

What this building has seen.

'Fliss!'

The first couple of steps on the stairs are broken. The boards are cracked in the middle. She climbs up the side, holding on to the old wooden rail, which shudders beneath her fingers. She calls again. But there's nothing. And she climbs the winding stairway up, up, up.

Tears slide down her face now; her fingers tremble, her jaw is clamped hard. Her body fights her. Her senses are slowing her.

'Fliss!'

'Willow?'

The call comes from below. Her first reaction is to freeze, thinking it's Fliss in answer, but she hears her name again, and realises – Theo. He has come.

'Willow?'

Pounding the steps, she flies back down. Another floorboard gives way; she trips and half falls, half leaps the last few steps. As she lands, she buckles and collapses into the dust, landing at Theo's feet. He bends and grabs hold of her arm. Pulling her up.

'You came!' Willow says, flinging her arms around him. 'You came!'

'Of course I came, Eliot. Once I realised where you must have gone. Where she must be. I heard them at the station. They're following, just clearing the red tape, apparently, as it's in disrepair.' Theo's face is pale, grey. The dark is almost absolute in here, and the light comes from behind him, from her phone.

He looks around, gripping her tight. 'You OK?'

'She's here somewhere,' Willow says.

Theo takes her hand. 'Let's find her.'

'I haven't tried through here,' Willow says. 'I think through here, at the back?'

Breaking cobwebs, walking quickly, avoiding spikes from old, unidentifiable metal objects. Bumping up against falling plaster, falling brickwork. They make their way through the centre of the building. Darkness like a solid mass. The blue torch from the phone punching through, dust swirling.

Outside of the bubble of brightness, the shadows press and threaten. Tears are tight in her throat; she feels dizzy. At the back of the building, they enter one large room. It looks like it was a number of rooms once, but the fire has destroyed some of the walls. A collapsed passage is clear through to one side. There are stairs leading downwards. There must be a basement underneath. The scream, falling. If it had been Fliss she heard, then there must be another level.

Willow can feel Fliss.

She runs forward, but Theo reaches out, holds her back, taking her hand.

'Go slowly,' he says. His hand shakes.

Almost crouching, the roof is so low down, Willow leads. She tests each step with her foot, before landing her weight. And they inch down. The smell is like nothing she has smelt before. Pools of water must sit down here, festering, and the air is thick. Theo coughs; Willow feels sick.

Something runs over Willow's hand, and she pulls it back quickly, unsettling the steady descent. She screams, a quick sharp shot out into the night, and then she tumbles into space, crashing hard. Behind her, Theo screams her name. She lands in something damp, and clouds of dust obscure even the light from the phone, which has fallen nearby.

What she can see, in a burst of relief and horror, is Fliss. She lies on the hard floor, on her side. An arm tossed forward, and the dress with sparkles, so bright at the cathedral that night, is ripped and dark with dirt.

Pealing out into the night, sharp and sudden, her phone rings. She sees Sunny's name flash up.

'I've found her,' she says, leaning towards her sister. 'Oh God, Sunny, I've found her. Call an ambulance. I'm at the old Hill Barnes building. Call an ambulance and come and find us.'

Willow can hear Sunny talking as she leans forward. Fliss's face, almost her face, but usually brighter, her more sparkly self. Dulled now. She looks ill. The other half of herself. She leans in and rests her cheek above Fliss's mouth, and the faint rush of air, so light it takes her a second to feel, is nevertheless real. Fliss is breathing. Fliss is alive.

'Oh my God,' she whispers. And this time it's a prayer. 'Oh God, please. Please let her live.'

And from behind, a whisper.

'Willow?'

Her eyes adjust slowly to the darkness, but she sees someone else lying flat. It's hard to hear – the voice is weak, but familiar. Is it...

'Martha, is that you? Oh, Martha, what happened?'

'I found her. I followed her out of the cathedral – was going to talk to her.' Her voice is broken, and she pauses for breath. 'She was crying. Then I saw the car... She ran into the park. I followed, called to her, she thought it was your mum. She thought it was Betty.'

Martha's voice is even fainter now, and what she's saying makes little sense to Willow. Willow tries to reach her, to crawl a little further forward, but her arm is too painful.

Martha lets out a raspy exhale. 'She was confused. Saw, I think, what you'd almost seen, that first night. I told her. What had happened – what I'd done. Said I was coming here. To finish. Before I spoke to Betty. So it was all complete. The nurse. Lizzie's mother. I came to tell her it was over.'

73

MAARTEN

Maarten reaches the park and Sunny is out of the car before it slides to a halt. He's running under the trees in the dark as Maarten slams the door. Sirens grow louder in the night air.

Please let her be alive.

He follows Sunny in long strides, slipping in the mud beneath the trees.

The house looms quickly, flying at him as his pace finds surer footing.

'Be careful! It's not safe!' he shouts after Sunny, but he knows it's pointless. Sunny is hell bent.

'Fliss!' Sunny's shout reaches Maarten in the overgrown garden, and as Maarten enters the creaking old building, he hears a call from down below. There are cracks in the floorboards, and gaps where the wood is rotten.

Sunny's feet pound, and then he cries out.

'Sunny!' Maarten runs faster.

'Are you here?' Adrika's voice comes from behind. 'I've got torches!'

A beam shines at Maarten as he turns around, blinding

him, and he squints, raising a hand on instinct. He takes a torch.

'Where is he?'

'I think he must have gone further in. His call came from below, like a basement or something.' Swinging the torch forward, yellow light floods the room and it's worse than in the dark. Cobwebs, spiders, bits of wood and metal protrude.

'Here, I think this way.' Maarten heads forward, the damp air catching the back of his throat. He heads into the shadowy light.

74

ALICE

Wednesday evening. Two days ago.

Alice had watched Willow's speech, stood with Peter; the cocktail party for the opening of the exhibition in full swing.

'She did well,' he says, and Alice nods, unable to believe she is here – standing looking at her family.

If she's going to tell them the truth, she will have to be brave. When Willow had arrived the first night, and Alice had sat up, wide awake, with bated breath...

She had managed to get through the first conversation, but just looking at her was like a dream. Her chest had hurt.

'I'll be off now,' she says.

'Shall I walk you home?' Peter says.

'No. Not tonight.' She smiles. She and Peter had stayed in contact all this time. When she told him she was thinking of moving back to St Albans, he said he was going to move back from France, and would find her. He'd taken the job as verger a few years before she had finally made the move.

He had offered marriage. His life. But she has never been able to take it. Not while the past still swirls around her.

But this week is her chance. Joel has gone. And Betty has arrived. The ghosts are lying down. Vanishing. She needs to visit Gill Coombes. Lay the last ghost to rest. Tell her that it is taken care of. She could never speak to the police, but justice is finally done.

'See you tomorrow,' she says, and she kisses him on the cheek.

He is surprised, and he takes her hand. 'Sleep well, Alice.'

Outside, the air is colder. It's still only spring. Summer will arrive soon enough.

Should she go tonight? Could she go and say goodbye, to Hill Barnes? To Gill Coombes? To Alice – to accepting Martha, and saying goodbye to the past?

She could drive there. Park in the housing estate and walk there. A last farewell before she speaks to Betty. She had hidden from her for most of the afternoon – saying hello had felt too big.

But tonight. A midnight vigil. A release. It's over.

She walks into the park towards her car, parked down on the lane outside her house, but a flash of silver catches her eye. Someone is crying, walking in the park.

Alice remembers who had been wearing a silver dress earlier, and she speeds up. 'Fliss, is that you?'

'Mum?' The girl spins round.

Alice is speechless for a moment. 'No, I'm Martha. I run the guest house where your mum is staying.' Her throat is tight. 'I'm heading back there now. Are you OK? I saw the car.'

'You sound exactly the same as my mum.' Fliss takes a step towards her. 'Now that I see you, you look similar too...'

Fliss shimmers under the moon. She shakes her head. 'You look, and sound so like her... Is there any chance you are distantly related to Elspeth Eliot? I'm sure you're not! But I once saw a marriage certificate for my grandad – I never knew him, but he got married here in St Albans...' She takes a step closer, peers at Alice, realises she's being rude. 'Sorry, you're obviously nothing to do with my crazy family. I'm rambling. I've drunk too much champagne. I'm tired. I'll walk back with you. Come and see my mum. Your doppelganger!'

Alice opens her mouth to speak. Nothing comes out.

They stand and look at each other.

'I'm your aunt,' Alice says, blurts out. 'I'm your mum's twin. But she doesn't know.'

'Sorry?' Fliss takes a step back. 'My aunt?'

'I was put in a home – taken away. I don't think your mum knows I exist – I think they said...'

'Wait, what?' Fliss says. 'I can't believe it! I was right? And Willow didn't know! Oh my God. They'll go bananas. You do look so...'

Alice can't breathe.

'I'm Fliss.'

'Martha. I used to be called Alice.'

'No way! Sorry, it's a lot to...'

A bat flies past, low, and Fliss jumps. 'Where did you say you were going? Back to the house? Does Mum know?'

Alice shakes her head. 'No one knows – no one in your family. You're the first.'

'Wow. This is... I mean...' Fliss shakes her head again. 'This is wild! And you're going home? To tell her now?'

'I was actually going to the home. To where I grew up. I was going to see it once more, before it's knocked down. Then I was going to tell your mum.'

'Right, I'm coming. I'm coming now! I'm not missing this. This is the biggest thing! You'll have to come to the wedding.' Fliss takes her hand. 'Martha, welcome to the family! Let's go. I want to see the home too! We do that first then we wake Mum and tell her! Willow will go crazy when she hears all this! I can't believe I got in first!'

75

WILLOW

Everything hurts. Sound ricochets above her, shouting. People must be here soon.

'They'll get us out,' she says, her voice a whisper, a croak. 'They're here. We'll be OK. You'll be OK. I love you, Fliss.' She finds Fliss's hand, and grips it – it's cold.

Looking at her, craning her head up – her neck starts to hurt, has she strained it? She reaches to look at Fliss, and she looks again at the edge of the other woman. Lying still and quiet now. Faint in the dark.

'Martha,' she whispers.

And then it all fades. The feeling of Fliss's hand, which she grips hard, in the dark. This hand, the very first thing her hand had ever found. It is the last thing that hangs in her consciousness.

76

MAARTEN

'Really? Noah Lewis will be OK?'

Maarten shakes the hand of the doctor. 'I can't believe it!'

'We're so pleased – we weren't sure he'd pull through, but he's been getting steadily stronger. He's awake, with his family. Talking. Even eating. He doesn't remember anything from the evening or about his accident yet, but if you send someone in tomorrow, he's likely to remember slowly.'

Phoning Adrika, who is still with the Eliot family at the other end of the hospital, Maarten thinks of how this changes things – so much has happened. 'Noah Lewis is awake. No – stay there, I'll come over to A&E now.'

'Have you seen them? They're OK. Oh, thank God, thank you, Maarten! Willow has a bad sprain, and her iron levels are dangerously low. It's why she's been so light-headed, so dizzy. They're giving her an infusion, and Fliss is fine. She's awake, talking. Exposure. A broken leg. Oh, thank you! Thank you for finding them.' Elspeth throws her arms around him and hugs him hard. Maarten thinks how close it had come to being too late – that Fliss and Martha would have been unlikely to survive any longer being so cold, without water. And the building due to be demolished.

'Elspeth, I'm so pleased,' he says. 'The doctors need you, though, if you're ready to come. They need your permission for a surgery.'

'Sorry? I don't understand?' Elspeth says, and Maarten looks to Adrika for support. 'The girls are OK. I've seen them – why do the doctors need my permission? I've just spoken to both their doctors. They don't need any surgery?'

'Yes,' Adrika says, 'the girls are OK.'

Elspeth looks confused. 'Then why do you need to talk to me? I don't understand what you're saying?'

'It's Martha, the woman who they found with Fliss. The woman who owns the guesthouse.' Adrika stalls.

'Martha? I don't understand why you're asking me?'

Maarten takes a breath. 'They need to perform a surgery. And they need to ask the next of kin. And it seems' – he looks at her, realising the enormity of it all – 'that it's you. You're her next of kin. It seems that Martha is your twin.'

'Will they be OK?' Maarten asks the doctor.

She nods. 'Yes. Both fine. The older lady has injured her leg. The younger one has a broken leg, is badly dehydrated, and is suffering from exposure. Too cold down there. But you found them in time. Three days would have been too long. I'm sorry, I'm needed. I'll find you later.'

As the doctor leaves, Adrika hangs up on a call. 'They've

found bones down there.' She raises her eyebrows. 'We'll have to wait for confirmation, but they've called in a crime scene. They're guessing human bones. What Gabriel Davis told us, about the missing nurse. Well – it could be her. It could be Gill Coombes. Looks like they've been buried down there a long time. The old floor in the basement is cracked, probably the stress from the fire a month ago. It's a busy night tonight.'

77

ALICE/MARTHA

They're all here. All of them. Her sister, her nieces.

Some stories are long and twisty. There are chapters that are brighter than others.

This is both the happy ending and the beginning of a new plot. One with family – her family; with a future, with shared secrets.

With Peter.

When Alice had first seen Willow, she could barely breathe. But slowly... Her voice was her own again and talking to Fliss had been easier.

And *Betty*!

Betty is outside the room. She can feel her.

Alice thinks of arriving at the old building, her chest tight with a goodbye.

He's gone, she had whispered, into the dark.

Fliss had darted forward. *This was where you grew up?* And it had spun fast out of control. The floor giving way.

One minute there. The next minute falling.

Fliss had screamed as she had gone through some

floorboards, Alice close behind her. To have found everyone, then to almost have lost them.

She closes her eyes, reminding herself that they are all safe. That the old chapter is finished. No one can hurt them now.

There's a sound at the door.

It's Betty. And Alice can't see any more, through the tears.

78

WILLOW

They sit with Fliss. It's almost 3 a.m.

Willow has finished her infusion, and one of her arms is in a sling. She can walk, and there is a bed in the room for her. They'd managed to find a room for both her and Fliss, and she doesn't feel tired. She'd had a garbled exchange with Fliss – *I'm so sorry, about what I'd said – in the row; I'm so sorry* – she'd told her about her night in Brussels with Theo – but Fliss had been holding tight to Sunny. She'd just shaken her head. Then she'd slept.

Willow watches her now, gripping Nonie's hand.

'Is she really going to be alright?' Nonie asks.

Willow tightens the hold on her hand. 'Yes. She's just sleeping. She was awake about half an hour ago. She says she still wants to get married tomorrow.' Willow laughs, which turns into tears.

'Silly girl,' Nonie says, hanging on to Willow's fingers like they might slip away. 'She'll not be up to a wedding tomorrow.'

'You never know, with Fliss.' Willow's mum enters the

room. She looks about ten years older. She sits next to Nonie, and looks at her. 'All these years. And you never said a word.'

Nonie begins to cry quietly. 'I couldn't, Elspeth. I just couldn't. I met your father almost immediately after the funeral. He moved you up to Edinburgh. Advertised for a nanny. It went from there.'

'You never said a word.'

'What could I say?' Pulling a tissue from her sleeve, Nonie dabs at her eyes. 'He told me the whole story. He had no doubt – he believed Alice had...'

'My mother. He believed my twin had caused my mother to fall from a cathedral tower?'

Nonie nods. 'Yes. It was different back then. Everyone believed what that man said. And she was a difficult child. I've read up on it since. Nowadays they'd give it a name, but back then they didn't know. They hadn't a clue. She was called difficult, and that was it.'

Willow thinks of Martha, of Alice, and all those years on her own. 'And he left her there, for her whole life?'

'That must have been his intention, yes, but I think she left in the 8os. She went to a seaside town. That was the last I heard. He asked me to bring you up as my own, and I did. You remember him. Appearances were everything to him. Having respect from the community. He was a big churchgoer, but didn't go in much for understanding... He wore a tie every day! I didn't know half of it before I married him. But the drink. He suffered, Elspeth. He never made peace with it.'

'But how didn't I know? How could I forget my *twin*? My mum who died?'

'You had no memories before that day. They were wiped clean away. The only memories you had were of your sister, and well, he told you they were of an imaginary friend. Your imaginary friend. She was called Alice, your twin. But you had a bit of a lisp when you lost your front teeth. *Liss,* you used to say. And your dad would say, '*Naughty Liss. She's naughty. We left her behind.*' Nonie shakes her head. 'And when you used to cry for her at night...' Nonie reaches out and touches Elspeth's cheek. 'You used to cry for her, and wake yourself with your tears. He said I had to say it was just your imaginary friend, who hadn't come with us to Edinburgh. And when he held your hand, if you ever got upset, he'd say...'

'*Do not cry,*' Elspeth finishes for her. 'He'd just tell me not to cry. My first memory. Walking down the aisle of a church.'

'It must have been your mother's funeral. You moved to Scotland straightaway after. Elizabeth Adams became Elizabeth Abbott. Then Elspeth Eliot after marrying Jack. Instead of Betty, you became Elspeth. And he asked me to raise you as my own. And I did my very best.'

Willow leans her head back against the corridor wall of the hospital. She imagines it's never quiet here. People are still moving with purpose, or sit in rows of plastic chairs in various rooms. Always waiting.

Theo's name flashes up in her phone. She looks at it, makes no move to answer.

Theo Durand. She had waited for him. She's been waiting for him for so many years. And now...

He has been there for her. He came to the house. He's been by her side these last few days. If she's needed him, he's been there. And surely that counts for a lot?

But he had also lied for her. He had lied to the police, and even now when she thinks of Fliss missing, and Theo possibly complicating the case, and throwing in layers where there needn't be any, she doubts.

Doubt that she hasn't felt before. She's always been so sure. Almost like a faith.

Has her faith in Theo Durand been shaken?

That first time of meeting him. She'd been so young, and it had been her and Fliss's first time away from home. She was ready to stretch her wings, to meet men and to *live*!

When Fliss had claimed him, kept him for herself, had Willow put him up on a pedestal? Had she mounted him on a wall, to be idolised every now and again, safely out of reach, out of grasp of her fingers, her – a mere mortal?

Then that night in Brussels. She might tell herself that she can't remember who made the first move, but she knows it was her. She remembers leaning in, and just thinking, *Now!*

And was it that which swung Theo her way? Did he pin himself on those who laid claim to him?

All those years. If she had stood up and made her move before Fliss, would he have been hers?

A trolley wheels towards her and she steps out of the way, smiling at the nurse who talks to a child lying flat, looking scared.

Willow wanders into the waiting room. She had felt a burst of hunger she hasn't felt for days, and she'd remembered a vending machine in the corridor.

She taps numbers, slots coins. Chocolate falls with a thud in the tray, and she stares at it.

For the first time, in so many years, the thought of Theo does not make her weak. And she realises something, a curtain peels itself back – she has always thought of Fliss as craving everything she had, of spending her life clawing for the halo of the firstborn. But what if it wasn't just Fliss who wanted what the other had? What if the reason she has clung so fiercely to Theo Durand is because, for a while, he belonged to Fliss?

After all this time. What if it had always been true – that Fliss might want what she has, but maybe she is the same. That the reason Theo has shone so brightly is because he once belonged to her twin?

79

MAARTEN

'What do we do with Michael Braxton?' Adrika asks, as they watch Gabriel Davis leave the station. It's almost dawn, on Sunny's wedding day.

Maarten had wanted to go back to the station to release Gabriel. He didn't deserve another minute in the station.

'Have we had the results back from the search on Michael Braxton's home yet?' Maarten asks. 'I think I might have an idea about him. He was so desperate at the end. Let me call the team. See if there is anything interesting there.'

He thought so.

Maarten waves at Adrika. 'Let's go.'

Michael Braxton looks up as they enter.

Maarten waits. He is silent while Adrika speaks, and when she says, 'We found Fliss Eliot,' Michael half nods.

It is clear he had nothing to do with Fliss's disappearance after the near miss. And Maarten sees a ripple of relief on his face. As though this might be the end.

'In other news, Noah has made a good recovery. It's looking much more likely that while the fall may have health implications for him, they will not be life-threatening.'

Michael's eyes swivel to him.

'The search on your property is finished,' Maarten says slowly. 'It was bothering me, why we found a high-heeled shoe with Noah's blood on it, outside in the car park, when Noah fell from inside. I couldn't work it out to begin with.'

Michael holds his breath. Stares at Maarten.

'We found the other one, deep in your car boot, where the spare tyre should be. Did you drop the other one? Running for the car? Worried your fingerprints were all over them? It didn't take you so long to get home because of the crash, did it? It took you so long because when Heather left, and Jaz had told you Noah had seen the letters that night, you went back to look for Noah. You went through the tower door – you had keys, even if it had been locked. You'd heard Noah say to Jaz he was taking Willow up there. What happened, you saw the shoes, and thought that no one would connect them with you?'

Michael continues to stare at him. His lip trembles.

'Tell us what happened, Michael. Did Noah say he wouldn't keep the grubby secrets? Did you offer him money? And even then, he wouldn't do it? What, you hit him with the shoe? You pushed him off the balcony? You must have been terrified. You've never done anything like that before. Did you surprise yourself, with the lengths to which you'd be willing to go?'

Michael bends his head and cries. The words rise slowly and Maarten stares down at him.

'To start with, I just thought, *he's my dad!* But the idea of everyone knowing. And then the money – what if they took it away? If I didn't inherit, I'd be bankrupt. I didn't do anything wrong, I just started out trying to let sleeping dogs lie. There's no good in stirring up the past. And my girls. How do I take their school away from them? All their music lessons? Their ponies? How do I hold up my head?'

Adrika looks at Maarten, her face flushed with disgust.

'When Dad threw himself off the tower, I thought he'd done it for us. I thought he'd done it to keep the silence, to protect us. I told Noah, *he's killed himself, what more do you want?* Noah had seen his name on the letters. I didn't mean to hurt him. He shouted, and I tried to keep him quiet. I hit him once with the shoe. When he fell over the balcony, I panicked. I ran. I ran back to the car, through the welcome centre. I kept my head down. I don't think anyone saw me. I bumped into Willow Eliot, the woman with the exhibition. She was at the top the stairs that lead to the toilets, and she banged her head on the wall and fell. I don't think she saw me. I just ran. When I got to the car, there was only one shoe in my hand.'

He shakes his head. 'I just wanted it all kept quiet. What Dad had done. *Conquests*, he'd called them. That day at the cathedral, he showed me the bricks he'd marked. Once he knew I'd seen the letters, he showed off all the rest of it. I think he was proud of it all. All those bricks with dates, with initials. All those dates – he'd recorded a mark for each one. *Conquests*. Not money this time, but women. He knew

I wouldn't say anything. I've never said anything about our mum. What he did to her. What he did to all those women.'

Secrets don't stay buried for ever, Maarten thinks.

Even those cast in stone.

80

MAARTEN

'So, do we unofficially think Martha killed Joel Braxton?' Adrika asks, standing at the cathedral doors. The sun is stronger now. Kids on bikes cycle down the hill and Maarten checks his watch – 8 a.m.

After charging Michael Braxton, they'd come back to the cathedral to do a final sweep of details. They'd had to find Lizzie, now there was a possible development in the case of her mother.

'There's no proof of anything. We think Gabriel ruined the CCTV, or it was corrupted, as he says. There's no way of knowing, but he has an alibi. Lizzie, the cleaner, saw Joel enter alone. And the CCTV from the rest of the cathedral doesn't pick up anyone else.' Maarten looks out at the dog walkers, the buggies and parents up early.

'We know someone called Joel Braxton late that evening. But the number on his phone can't be traced, and who knows what it was regarding?' He shrugs. 'We should get some rest before the wedding later.'

Adrika nods. 'Well, unofficially, I wouldn't blame Martha,

if she'd found a way. What a life. Her own father sent her to a mental health hospital – had her imprisoned there, and then just left her?'

Maarten shakes his head. 'He couldn't bear to look at her, it seems. He wasn't free after it. He died early from liver damage – he just drank and drank. He never came back here, but the house was in Martha's name. He left her with an income. The rent has given her a good living.' He looks up at the sun. 'The family said he told his new wife all about it. And they even passed her off as Elspeth's mother. It wasn't until she came here...' He drifts off, thinking of a seven-year-old girl being wrongly blamed for causing the death of her mother, and growing up in a place like that. He shudders for the past, for what used to be. From asylums to mental health hospitals full of wards, where people were put and forgotten about.

'But the new wife, she recognised the house?'

Maarten nods. 'Yes, she'd seen photos. And I think she came here, after his death. Martha was released just before the hospital closed down in the 80s, when care in the community was advocated. And this house was in her name. It had been rented out for years. So she came here, as though moving for the first time. She opened it up as a B&B. I suppose she would have carried on, and it would all have stayed silent. But for Sunny meeting Fliss. And for that last building being knocked down. I can't imagine Willow's exhibition was easy to see either.'

Adrika's voice is soft. 'All those children. The women. The men. Chunks of their lives, dispensed into wards, boxes. Stolen away. When people talk of the good old days...'

The chimes of the cathedral bells ring across the park, and Maarten smiles sadly at Adrika. 'Come on, let's get going. I don't know about you, but I need breakfast and a shower before we turn up for this wedding. I can't believe they're going ahead. If everyone stays awake, it will be a miracle. And a few of them will be in wheelchairs for most of it – barely able to stand with all the injuries. Good job they've managed to push the ceremony to the end of the day. Everyone can have a good rest first.'

'Do you think...' Adrika starts, drifts off. Looks at Maarten.

'I think he fell. I think he couldn't go to his grave, without feeling he had been punished. I think the prospect of the exhibition did the same for him. It brought out a reckoning – a levelling. *If* there was anyone else who summoned him to the top of that tower, to where he attacked a young mother sixty years ago... Well. There's no evidence for that. Robyn's finished the post-mortem; in her opinion it looks like suicide. I think it will stand with the coroner. Plain and simple. And now that the body has been found, possibly of Lizzie's mother, Gill Coombes – well, with Gabriel and Martha's evidence and Lizzie's testimony, he would have been facing a murder charge and at least one rape charge. It's reason enough to wish to die.'

Adrika looks out at the park. 'It looks the same, I bet. The same now as sixty years ago. It's just us. People. What people do to people.'

'I think,' Maarten says, swinging his arms forward and clapping his hands together, then rubbing them. 'I think we need a party.'

81

ALICE

Now

Alice sits at the front of the nave with Betty on one side and Willow on the other. Fliss had been insistent.

Things will adjust.

Betty.

She can't take her eyes from her.

Her twin is returned to her. How it will unfold now, she doesn't know. It won't be easy, but she's prepared to work at it. She won't let Betty go again.

Alice lets the tears flow. Times have changed. She is allowed to cry now. Women can do whatever they want. She stands as the music begins. It's difficult – she's still exhausted, but Willow holds her upright.

If she wants to cry, she will. Both her nieces, here.

No ghosts hanging over them anymore. No imaginary friends. They are all together again. Finally.

Peter has come, and he'd taken her hand outside the cathedral. 'Well then,' he'd said, and he'd kissed her cheek, touched her chin with his finger, outlining a graze there.

She can find peace with him now. There's a future for all of them.

She catches his eye as she looks for Fliss, coming down the aisle – wheeled by Jack, but radiant. She'd insisted she would marry, despite the broken leg. No party after – just back to the hospital. But Sunny looks at her as though she floats in on a silver cloud.

What was the line from the exhibition that had caught her eye and stuck with her? *The world was all before them*, and that was them. All of them, together. A future.

Alice thinks of her mother, of a young woman standing at the top of the tower of this cathedral, and she sends up a prayer.

She hopes that if she's watching, she's smiling.

May she rest in peace.

Always and forever.

ACKNOWLEDGEMENTS

A huge thank you to my agent, Eve White, and also Ludo Cinelli and Steven Evans. I'd be nowhere without them.

Thanks to the incredible team at Head of Zeus for all that they do. My editor Laura Palmer is one in a million.

I am indebted to the staff at St Albans Cathedral for their time and their expertise. It is a stunning building and I have thoroughly enjoyed my time spent there. I have rearranged the layout of a few offices, locks and doors for the sake of the novel, but hopefully remained true to the beauty and the history of the building. Particular thanks to Laura Bloom, Lindsay Wong and Diana Harrington.

There were two mental health hospitals in St Albans for most of the twentieth century: Cell Barnes and Hill End. For the sake of the novel, I have bundled them together into Hill Barnes, and all stories here are entirely fictional. The basis of the stories, however, is rooted in research into many other mental health hospitals of the last century, their treatments and many stories told in diaries, books and from word of mouth.

For other research aspects of the novel, I must thank Charlotte Pascal, Shelagh O'Connell, Victoria Quinney, Richard Johnson and Christine Hood.

I'm indebted to those who read the novel and offered advice: Ella Berman, Erin Kelly, Angela Clarke, Kate Simants and Dominic Nolan. Thanks to my CBC writing group and to my criminally minded author friends.

As always, love to my endlessly supportive family, who listen to all versions of all the stories I write, without complaint.

ABOUT THE AUTHOR

RACHAEL BLOK grew up in Durham and studied Literature at Warwick University. She taught English at a London comprehensive and is now a full-time writer living in Hertfordshire with her husband and children. Her thrillers *Under the Ice*, *The Scorched Earth* and *Into the Fire* have been widely acclaimed.